CRITICAL ACCLA
DIANE JOHN

"Diane Johnson has a high regard for the dignity,
the quirkiness, and the complexity of people. She is
respectful of and affectionate toward their simple humanity.
Of how many writers can that truly be said? These are
qualities that mark her as a writer
of the finest order."
—Alice Adams

"Like Jane Austen she steps out of the frame to
anatomize her characters with sudden insight; like
Virginia Woolf she creeps back in to record
their inappropriate thoughts—and their
consternation at having them."
—*Newsweek*

"Diane Johnson's style is entirely her own. She is a born
storyteller, with a marvelous ear for dialogue, and
a gift for the common phrase that breaks into
metaphor, the sudden illuminating perception."
—Judith Chernaik, *London Magazine*

"A master storyteller . . . her sparkling prose is
combined with an intense moral seriousness . . .
each character perfectly drawn."
—Susan Cheever

DIANE JOHNSON is the author of twelve books, including
Le Divorce, a 1997 National Book Award Finalist, *Persian
Nights, Lying Low, Health and Happiness*, and *Burning* (all
available in Plume editions). She divides her time between
San Francisco and Paris.

Lying Low

"A nearly flawless performance. A beautifully constructed, elegantly written book, delicate in its perceptions, powerful in its impact. A remarkable novel."
—Robert Towers, *New York Times Book Review*

"Diane Johnson has a perfect sense of menace. She is impeccable at naming monsters; she approaches her nightmare subject with a solitary rigor, assuring us that everything we thought we saw is there, and turning on the lights."
—Mary Gordon

Burning

"A comic jewel."
—*The Guardian*

"*Burning* may well be the song the sirens sang, so fresh it is, so beguiling that you'll never be able to resist it. This is a swinging novel."
—*Book World*

THE
SHADOW
KNOWS

Diane Johnson

A WILLIAM ABRAHAMS BOOK

PLUME

PLUME
Published by the Penguin Group
Penguin Putnam Inc., 375 Hudson Street, New York, New York 10014, U.S.A.
Penguin Books Ltd, 27 Wrights Lane, London W8 5TZ, England
Penguin Books Australia Ltd, Ringwood, Victoria, Australia
Penguin Books Canada Ltd, 10 Alcorn Avenue,
Toronto, Ontario, Canada M4V 3B2
Penguin Books (N.Z.) Ltd, 182–190 Wairau Road, Auckland 10, New Zealand

Penguin Books Ltd, Registered Offices: Harmondsworth, Middlesex, England

Published by Plume, an imprint of Dutton NAL,
a member of Penguin Putnam Inc.
Previously published by Alfred A. Knopf.

First Plume Printing, March, 1998
10 9 8 7 6 5 4 3 2

 REGISTERED TRADEMARK—MARCA REGISTRADA

LIBRARY OF CONGRESS CATALOGING-IN-PUBLICATION DATA
Johnson, Diane.
The shadow knows / Diane Johnson.
p.   cm.
ISBN: 0-452-27736-1
1. Divorced women—California—Sacramento—Psychology—Fiction.
2. Women—Crimes against—California—Sacramento—Fiction.   I. Title.
PS3560.O3746S5   1998
813'.54—dc21   97–40719
                                                  CIP

Printed in the United States of America

PUBLISHER'S NOTE
This is a work of fiction. Names, characters, places, and incidents either are
the products of the author's imagination or are used fictitiously, and any
resemblance to actual persons, living or dead, events, or locales
is entirely coincidental.

For John

THE **SHADOW** KNOWS

Wednesday, January 1

1 You never know, that's all, there's no way of knowing. There was that man in Carmichael who walked into the beauty shop and murdered all the women by tying them to the dryers and pulling plastic bags over their heads. The wife of my old neighbor Mr. Probst slashed her wrists the week before Christmas, and I saw her the week before that, and her life was all right with her then. People get sudden notions.

Last week our lives were all right here. Things haven't been going exactly well for me lately—not well at all, really—but we were safe, and we try to keep believing in love and harmony. But now I think we are going to be murdered. Just like that. It's not what you'd expect living quietly in North Sacramento.

"Don't ask why people does what they do," Ev says. "They hears they own piece. You stay outta the way is all." She is not even afraid. She is humming and scuffing her shoes around the kitchen, meaning she is comfortable at home. She has a polka-dotted rag tied around her hair; her hair is going back, that's her big worry. The children have no thought of danger and are safely asleep.

They are all I have, the children and Ev, but I am separated from them by this chasm of belief, what I believe may happen and what they believe won't. I hide my panic behind the blank deceptive pages of the book I'm reading. I try to think of other things. I think perhaps I should buy Polly some new pajamas, she's about grown out of those; I was hoping someone would send her some for Christmas. But the murder idea steals in between my thoughts. Almost as frightening as the idea of death—oh, just as frightening—is the realization that life can change on you, can darken like a rainy sky; wretchedness and dread can overtake the lightest heart, can take over the life ruled by love and harmony, an unknown person can suddenly be trying to kill you; you know not why, you are just you.

There have been signs for several weeks, little wrong things, but the day I began to be sure, and the knowledge came over me like a sickness, was yesterday, the day of New Year's Eve, when the murderer in a savage rage slashed and battered our front door. That is an attack you cannot ignore, upon your citadel and upon your imagination. I cannot imagine that we can keep him out next time. It is all too clear to me. I can even imagine a famous police inspector coming along after we're dead to look at our corpses and photograph the blood splashed around. This Famous Inspector ought properly to look like my lover, Andrew Mason, handsome and censorious, but probably will just look like the real policeman I talked to, a short man with red hair. The imaginary one, distinguished, gray, has been furnished to my mind from books, I suppose, or old Basil Rathbone movies.

What happened was that when I came home yesterday afternoon I found that someone had attacked our front door, hacked and slashed it with an axe or knife, and smeared it with some disgusting substance like a mixture of blood and vomit and crankcase oil. Thus smeared and stabbed, it resembled a stabbed and dying person, and my first thought, and my thought now, was that it was meant to be me, or else Ev.

"Some drunk mother out lookin for his wife" was Ev's explanation of it. That shows her view of marriage.

"No, I think it means that someone wants to hurt us, but who could it be?"

She said indifferently, "Oh, A. J., or could be Clyde I guess." A. J. is her lover and Clyde is her husband.

That was funny, because asking myself that question, who could it be that wants to hurt you? I answered very promptly: Gavvy or Osella. I suppose if you ask anyone who it is trying to murder them, they will straightway name loved ones without hesitation. Anyway people they know. Gavvy is my former husband and Osella a woman who worked for us. She went crazy; I suppose we drove her crazy.

It is a fact anyway that someone in a frantic rage mutilated our door. Perhaps they lie outside in wait; perhaps they may come again at any time. Yet I cannot actually imagine the real everyday Gavvy, or Osella either, transformed into a murderer lurking outside, planted like a land mine outside. I keep thinking of the ordinary lucid everyday things I have seen them do, or I keep thinking of what you would need, to lurk day in day out — what a lot of sandwiches, maybe a thermos of gin. Thus it is that I both do and do not believe in our murder.

So I can't bring myself to provide against this murder, exactly. I try to explain it away. The door was just a disgusting random act of vandalism, I tell myself, or maybe it has had this unusual upsetting effect on me because I have reason to believe myself a murderer now, in a way, and life has not been going exactly well here lately. The attack on the door is or is not prelude to danger for us, I don't know which. It's hard to have an attitude to murder because it hasn't happened to you before. You tend to think what a shame, what a shame it would be to be murdered; that would spoil everything.

2 Who could hate us that much? We are just us. Of course it may be just a random act of vandalism; there's a lot of that around. If we are not murdered, then I would like to move away from here. It was a mistake moving here. I thought I was being a responsible mother, moving here to live within our income while I study, fitting myself for the future. But a shack would be better than the neat square walls of this unit.

We live in a housing project owned by the city of Sacramento. Our unit has three bedrooms, a living room, a kitchen and a bathroom, with all the walls painted a light gray in all the rooms, not a bad color of gray but very small rooms with thin walls. When the murderer comes, people will hear our shrieks but not pay any attention, that's how full of shrieks the place is. Blacks, and students, and welfare cases and just people who can't seem to manage things live here, the latter being our category. The row of units, of which ours is at the end, faces another row across a broad brown lawn. This far outside town the land is cheap, so the lawns are broad but disregarded. Our back door opens out to garage stalls and an alley with garbage cans. In each garage is a cabinet where you may lock the things that won't fit into your unit. Mine is full because I used to live in a comfortable big house.

I am a divorced woman. I feel chagrin at the certain knowledge that the newspapers will put this in as if it explains why we were murdered. People think a divorced women is someone lacking in judgment and solvency who has to give up her charge accounts and hangs around lonely in bars and gets mixed up with people who kill her. And maybe it's so.

Yesterday, when this happened, was the day of New Year's Eve. I think that has something to do with it. A cold, low day, with the fog everywhere. I always hate the end of a year anyway, and this one how I hated, heavy with reproaches and mistakes like the low-lying ground fog. But I hate to let go of a year, too, when it has gone by without terrible disasters, and when it has had some happy moments in it, too, in case the one coming up will be worse. This year promises in prospect only pain and ordeals to be got through, and now maybe this death threat. If you could only know how the one year will be before you let go of the other.

It's funny to realize that before I got this murder idea I had been thinking, though not seriously, of suicide as a possible way out of my situation. I didn't feel actually as if I wanted to commit suicide, but, feeling sick and down after my visit to the doctor yesterday morning, it was just one of the cards I saw in my hand with a kind of impulse to throw it on the table with a wild laugh. A wild card. But now since the business of the door, waiting to be murdered has given me you might say something to live for.

My situation is not so serious, taken bit by bit. We are living here in these units, low on money, and I have the four children to take care of, and then I am sick in love with a married man, who is stuck down to a perfectly decent ordinary woman, but I know I can forever love only him, you might as well wall me up in a wall for the rest of my life, and he has sent me a death letter. In a way he has already killed me. And now this business of I think being pregnant, or maybe not, depending on the outcome of my visit to the doctor. Taken by itself, there is none of these things that is permanent or unmanageable, I know, but I don't seem to be able to manage them all together. It's a fatigue, maybe, or a failure of nerve, I don't exactly know. I don't seem to be able to rise to this.

Instead I waver between despair and dull acquiescence. I don't approve of those. You should be able to flame and fling yourself, but I hold on instead, dully acquiescing. But I try to think radiantly. Gathering my children close around me, I try to transmit radiance through my transparent skull but it's cement. I imagine if someone took my picture the face would turn out blank, overcast by darkness, or else its real expression of troubled panic, the mirror of my inner state, would show on film despite the bland smile which I have directed to the camera, to my children, to my friends. Outside I am a round-faced little woman with golden curls and round blue eyes, with round breasts and toes, surrounded by round babies; I look like a happy moon—now who would have thought I am riddled and shot through invisibly with desperate and sordid passions, raging passions of egotism, insecurity and lust? Not even I would think that, looking at me. But I am, sometimes.

I am also capable of acting counter to my principles when in trouble. Naturally. That is I think why I got upset about the door. The thing was, my period was a week late, so I went yesterday morning to the doctor to get an internal contraceptive device. My idea was that this would produce an abortion. The doctor himself had given me this idea once, by saying, "If ever you want an IUD, make an appointment to come in just after a menstrual period; that way we don't risk interrupting a pregnancy." So I lied about my period, and I was weak with fear that he would say, What's this? You're all swollen inside just as if you were pregnant. But he didn't, he just performed something quickly inside me with a little strip of white plastic. He showed it to me first, like a man demonstrating a good kitchen gadget, what a friend it will turn out to be. I surely hope so. Then he gave me instructions I hardly heard and wished me Happy New Year.

But the thing is, and I know this is silly, when I came home and saw that door, it seemed to me that it was smeared with the murdered new life; fetal membranes and blood from inside me, that was my first thought. But of course I don't really know whether I was ever pregnant at all, or maybe I still am, so I hope I am not to be pursued by this ugly guilty thought forever.

Well, I am giving myself airs about conscience, maundering self-importantly on about murder. When I get like this, I am reproached by Ev's example, for she must live in permanent and real despair. Her lovers slash and beat her, and steal from her. She expects them to. Her own brother stole her glasses, which she paid too much for besides, because the eye doctor cheated her, and probably some white spectacle-grinder cheated him. She can't ever have children. Now she is forty. She has a new wig to hide her real hair. The wig has straight black hair, because she is too old to give up being ashamed of her own real kinky hair. Yet she is tall and beautiful, her bearing grave, the bluish scars on her dark skin making her look like the vandalized statue of a great Nubian queen.

We do our best here, Ev and I. We are allies, and love a lot of the same things — men and children and pretty clothes. We have to expect reverses sometimes, I guess.

3 About the door, I didn't go to the police at first; I was too preoccupied with the symbolism of this event. I went around to the back so I wouldn't have to look at it, and called the manager, Mr. Hoaglund, who came and cleaned it up. That's the understanding here, that damage caused by vandals he cleans up, damage caused by your friends you do. I decided to go ahead with the New Year's party anyway; it didn't occur to me not to.

This was to be a children's party. I wish I could say I was the sort of good loving and giving woman who thinks up spontaneous adorable delights for children, but no, only part of me cared that the children should have a memorable New Year's Eve; the other part, the part that was not invited out in a spangled dress to twirl in the arms of my lover laughing to welcome the New Year, was sulking probably, and thinking it might as well get credit for something.

Anyway I had invited twelve children, counting my four. The littlest ones were to go to bed when midnight reached Times Square, and the rest could stay up till real midnight here in California, with champagne for all, even the littlest. In the afternoon my children and I got out their games, and strung crepe paper on lamps and doorknobs, and blew up real balloons. Real champagne in the refrigerator. I tried to keep my mind off the door. Ev left in the middle of the afternoon, dressed magnificently in a dress with feathery stuff all around the hem, to meet her man, A. J., who beats and knifes her. Tense and spoiling, Ev was, wanting to get things settled with him, but that's how New Year's affects you.

The guests belonged to Bess, my friends the Marmots and Frasers, and various families in these units. The parents were happy and grateful about not having to get baby-sitters. They brought the guests around eight, and sleeping bags and asthma medicine and pediatric cough syrup and stuffed toys and precious blankets. I told them about the splintered door, in case they would want to take the children away again, but no one did. Such things as "You should see what someone did to our garage" are what they said, and went off unencumbered into the gay festive darkness.

The only person to call while the party was going on was the phantom phone-caller, about eleven. He or she must have stayed up to see the New Year in. We are familiar with his or her habits, she usually goes to bed about ten, and doesn't try to call again until four in the morning. I think of the phantom phone-caller as a woman. I don't think she can have done the door. I don't think she knows us; she only knows our phone number and calls it obsessively. She has done this so long we are used to it. Why don't you change your number, people ask, and the answer is, I don't know why we don't.

I hoped it would be Andrew on the phone, but as I started toward it, I saw Polly grimace and make a growl into the receiver, the way the children have taken to doing to the phantom, and then hang up. Andrew didn't call. It is hard for me to understand how I both do and do not expect Andrew to call. I know he will not and that he will. I am always walking along the edge of a knife.

We played a game called Twister which got all their feet and hands tangled up thrashing about in laughing clumps with a little one or two beginning to cry. Then I read some ghost stories and got mad at the ones who hadn't learned to sit still for stories, and finally there was Times Square on television, which I thought meant we could put at least Mark Marmot and Laura Fraser to bed, but of course not, everybody was determined to stay up until the real hour. We spread their sleeping bags out on the floor in the children's bedroom—that took up some time—and then I decided to let them run outside on the lawn while I got out the party food. So they got into their coats and ran screaming outside, wildly gleeful to be out so late, so unattended, dashing madly about at nearly midnight, arms waving, staring at the sky to see some signal wonder of the New Year—what sort of noise would it make when it came, would there be lights in the sky?

Then I had a precious feeling of peace and pleasure,

forgetting everything, cutting slices of orange cake we had made, and pouring champagne into Dixie cups and arranging the table, forgetting momentarily about either Andrew or the vandal, and then suddenly remembering, with the same sort of chill of fear you feel when you are driving along and suddenly you realize you have been thinking about something else altogether, driving as though asleep and might have been killed. Like that I suddenly remembered the slashed and bleeding door, and the power of darkness to shelter an enemy, and I realized that I couldn't hear the children, but utter stillness outside.

I dashed out into the night, knowing fear was foolish, they couldn't have all been murdered at once, and I should not yield to stratagems to make me rush into darkness. I saw them standing in a silent knot at the other end by the last unit near a streetlight. Their stillness frightened me. They were staring as if a killer was holding them with his eyes, mesmerizing them with his gleaming knife like a snake.

But it was a shadow show and the unraveling of mysteries. The children were huddled whispering, giggling, nudging each other watching the closed window of a unit, I don't know whose; the shade was drawn and the light was on inside, so that there was a shadow show, adult shadows behind a window like the doings of mothers and fathers behind closed doors could now be seen: here is what they really do—broiling kisses, breasts swaying, a chase, and the woman's long hair swaying, arms slithering and waving, hungry kisses on her big shadow breasts, so that I shivered in the cold night and turned away, and said with a hurting throat, "Into the house, peeping Toms, it's almost Happy New Year."

In the house they drank their champagne and then pretended to be drunk—mad, drunken three-year-olds, wise hiccuping tens—and I herded them into the bedroom and into their sleeping bags and kissed them all on their sticky cheeks and thought of a man's kisses. It was, oh, three, perhaps, before the last whisperer in his sleeping bag subsided, paper hats and noisemakers lying all around, and I drank up the rest of the champagne and lay on the sofa in the living room to listen for noises in case the person came back with his axe and his hate.

"Happy New Year," Osella's soft, hoarse voice said on the telephone. It was still dark, I didn't know what time. I had fallen asleep, I guess, though I had meant to stay awake. "Happy New Year, white-trash whore. You think you got me fooled but you ain't. Mr. Gavvy got yo number, and so have his mama, and I'm comin to get mah babies. That nigger you got there think she can keep them away from me like she done that once, but I'm comin again. I don' need to deal with you personally, because I sees what's coming to you, and it done be real bad, I pity you, I surely do, but you shouldn't have whored and you shouldn't of kep mah babies from me. Some people jus ain't worthy. Gavvy got yo number, so let it be. This gonna be a sorrowin year for you . . ."

I only listened a little and then hung up. She can go on for hours like that. It always scares me. When she used to make these calls about me to Gavvy, he would sit for hours as if hypnotized by her. I took the receiver off the hook again and put it under the sofa cushions to muffle its complaining whine. If Osella was on the phone, at least she wasn't outside.

Well, of course, it probably had been Osella trying to get in and get the children again, and slashing the door in her fury. I could imagine her—huge, waddling, with truculent eyes, grinding her teeth, pacing some small room like a cage—and I decided I was going to do something, call the ambulance or the police if she came again. Osella is so crazy I will just have to do something about getting her locked up.

It was cold. I got another blanket from my bed and took it back to the sofa to try to sleep again, but now I kept hearing noises, car doors, revelers returning in other units, night and holiday sounds, though not the stealthy testing hands of murderers at my window latch, but I couldn't sleep. Oh, this damn year is just the same, nothing is changed about this year I saw, and I couldn't sleep but kept thinking of the man and woman in the unit at the other end rolling and panting.

But then lying warm, blanket-wrapped, hearing the faint whine of the phone just audible through the sofa cushion, and otherwise the usual constant low car motors, faraway backfires, refrigerator hum, airplane hum, the air live and electric, above all this I heard—so clearly I couldn't even think of being mistaken—a noise, rasping and rattling at the bedroom window in the room where the children were, which I flew toward, shooting out of the blanket without thought, and at this moment one of the children, a little girl, Marnie Green, began to scream that she had seen somebody at the window.

I rushed up to the window. I realize I shouldn't have rushed up like that in case the person had a gun. But I had not thought of guns until then, I had only been thinking of being killed in some intimate personal way, hands around my neck or a knife or the heavy blows of savage fists. A gun was too much; you would have to fear so much more widely, someone crouching unseen anywhere at all.

But there was no one outside the window, no one all up and down the alley. I reassured Marnie and the others who had waked up, and said she'd had a bad dream. Birth of a new year amid screams of fright.

Did she have a bad dream or not? I still don't know. But screams make you take the idea of murder seriously. And the plain evidence of the door. I feel that I must watch and listen, watch and listen. I feel that I must anticipate any practical plan this person has for getting in here into our unit for whatever purpose. Every sound I hear is jimmies and knives.

When you let yourself go thinking about the people who might want to come hurt you, the result is astounding it is so huge, it is limitless. Any Famous Inspector would at these words dismiss me as a poor paranoiac, but listen: Osella, Osella is really crazy. Gavin. Why not? Ev's husband, Clyde, who has many times done violence to her, or her man A. J. I don't trust A. J., an evil-eyed drunk. A. J.'s eyes are yellow. The whites of his eyes, I mean.

The phantom phone-caller. True we have had him or her a long time now but with a worm eating away in his or her brain, maybe finally too much was too much for him or her. How about Andrew's wife, Cookie, Texas born and bred on guns, maybe too much was just too much for her. How about someone we don't know at all, some madman neighbor who's been watching us hatefully or lustfully, us all unknowing having touched some deep sick place in him.

For instance about two weeks ago someone stole Ev's underpants off the clothesline, four pairs of brand-new underpants, and at the time I just thought, well, that is the kind of rotten thing that is always happening to Ev, somebody steals her brand-new things. Whoever it was had cut the crotches neatly out, we found the cut bits lying in the bushes like bits of pink flesh.

How do you know whether someone is sick enough to kill you? Well, you just don't. Psychiatrists are always giving people clean bills of health who then turn around and rape and strangle someone: "The accused had recently been released from solitary confinement when the doctors had pronounced him sound as a bell," and there you are.

Here is another thing it is important to decide: is the person who slashes your door and puts filth on it a killer, or does he dissipate his vital hate in little acts of filth like this and therefore render himself harmless? I wish there really were a Famous Inspector I could call about these matters. It's not just that I am afraid for myself, but I have my children and Ev to look after, and none of them will be afraid for themselves. Here is another thing it is important to decide: if someone is trying to kill you, do you maybe deserve it?

4 In spite of the disturbance over Marnie Green, when daylight came in the New Year this morning, the children all wore the knowing clear faces, the companionable smiles of people who have now been through something important together. They have been to a New Year's party and seen the birth of the New Year, and have learned for sure that nothing extra happens at New Year's and you go on being you. They were like lovers in the morning, and I was happy that this was an important night for them.

Their parents came mid-morning, as late as was decent, to collect them. Their parents, my friends, wore flushed sheepish faces. I was glad to see them, it made my night tossing feel foolish to see them so sane. One funny moment when Al Dodge came for Jessica, and I suddenly thought, I bet it's Al who is the mad strangler rapist, and caught my breath for fear. But he went away without revealing these proclivities. Or it will turn out to be some other sane, everyday person I will someday be alone with.

But I didn't remember to feel frightened when later in the day one of the principal suspects, Ev's husband, Clyde, came along to try to see Ev, who hadn't come home yet. With him was a smaller, thinner man wearing a suit and tie and carrying a plaid wool hat.

"This is mah brother Beverly," Clyde said, "would you welcome him also?" Clyde was a little drunk, not

Beverly, and I welcomed them in. I wasn't afraid of these two. Clyde doesn't seem, what, effective enough to be a hater; he seems too broken, even if I do know he has done rough things to Ev.

I can imagine Clyde did not seem broken when Ev married him and came up with him from Texas. Clyde is tall and handsome and so light-skinned that nothing bad could happen to him; that's how Ev would have viewed it. Maybe he didn't drink so much then, and he had a trade, could fix cars, not, as it turned out, the way they do it up North by sending off for new parts and wearing an overall with "Clyde" written on it, but resourcefully, with things pulled off other cars, only it turns out this isn't the way you fix cars around here, or maybe he did drink too much to keep a job, I don't know. Clyde is a gentle man, or at least a fearful one. I just don't see how it could be Clyde.

They sat on the sofa right next to each other as in a crowded back seat. "I'm afraid Ev isn't here yet this morning. I expect her back today anytime now," I told them. Clyde, his hands primly on his knees, appeared settled in to wait.

"I hope you had a happy New Year celebration?" he asked.

"Very nice. We had a children's celebration."

"Now that's a nice idea. A good idea, ain't it, Beverly?"

"An excellent idea. Kids get the short end of it too much," Beverly agreed.

"Where is the kids? I always likes to see them," Clyde said. I admitted they were watching television. I went and got Ivan, who is Clyde's favorite. He took Ivan on his lap.

"Old Clydo come to see Ev but Ev ain't here," Clyde said to Ivan.

"Ev went," Ivan said.

"Yessir, I expect so. She comin back soon," Clyde said.

"We had happy New Year," Ivan said. Clyde, appear-

17

ing to find this a memorable, a moving remark, looked significantly at Beverly and then began to cry.

"Ivan, oh, Ivan, you have a lotta happy New Years," he cried. "If I was yo daddy. I never had me no little boy. If I was yo daddy I'd do good for you, darling, but I never did have me no chile of my own. Sit still on Clyde's lap a while now. You have a happy New Year, did you? My, my, sit here now." Ivan, enjoined to sit, of course began to wiggle.

"If I was yo daddy, I'd git you a bicycle, git you a motorbike when you gits bigger, anything you want." Ivan sat still with attentive docility. Clyde continued to sob as he spoke, his eyes continued to make tears. Beverly rustled in an embarrassed way.

"Anything you wants you can ask yo daddy Clyde for, that's how I'd be. Ain't he a fine boy, Beverly? Like to be daddy to a fine little boy of my own. I'd be a better man, I know . . ."

"Yeah, he's a fine boy," said Beverly to me without conviction. Clyde set Ivan down now and took out his handkerchief, a real cloth handkerchief, not a Kleenex, mopped at his wet face and sobbed. Beverly looked gravely at nowhere, tossing his hat with one hand and catching it on the finger of his other hand like ring-toss.

"I ain't been much good, I knows, but if I had a little boy I'd do good for him, I would, you know, Beverly? If I'd just had the chance, you know that?"

Beverly looked at me. "Thank you very much for your hospitality," he said, "but I think we'd better be goin, since Evalin isn't back yet." Clyde hugged and kissed Ivan, and followed Beverly to the door. Ivan ran to me, puzzled, and called, "Bye-bye, Clydo, gonna get me a bike," excitedly as Beverly led his sobbing brother away. Well, New Year's works you up like this.

Clyde's misery increased my own, but the day wore along. I worked on my seminar papers, plagued by apprehensions of not only the outward danger which made me jump to any noise and keep the doors locked, but of my own thoughts, ugly, troubling ones: Andrew has not called, Andrew hasn't called, and I thought I was just aware of a dull pressure in my back, maybe from the new plastic thing inside me, or maybe my period at last, but nothing changed.

I can deepen the chill of my terror by deliberately letting my mind think certain thoughts: I would think them deliberately to see if an anticipated sick cold feeling would crawl over me, and it would. One way was to think of the murderer of course. Another way was to imagine Andrew and his wife, Cookie, in some spirit of new rapport rededicating themselves to each other and to their marriage. They fall into each other's arms, full of New Year's resolutions about being kind to each other, about being considerate, about finding a new sexual position. Oh, who knows. Rage and misery crawl over me. "This year will be better for us, Andy," she breathes into his ear. His body hardens with an automatic, husbandly reflex. They lock the door and tell the children to watch TV. Looking into each other's eyes, they find so many familiar memories there. I am disgusted to be prey to such fanatic passion, this passion I feel for Andrew.

Ev comes home around four, unsteady but all right, looking strange in daylight in her fancy dress, merino around the hem and rhinestone bodice, like someone wandered off the set of *Carmen Jones*. She is sullen and quiet, which I attribute to hangover or perhaps a fight with A. J. I am wildly glad to see her, glad that she is back safely. In my emotionally touchy and lorn state my eyes swim momentarily at the thought of how much I love Ev, and how I must take care of her. I do not understand the instability of my own emotions, that my eyes fill without warning, but somehow I am thinking of impermanence, transience, as being more terrifying than death. It occurs to me that though Ev can probably not conceive of permanence, having never experienced it, she can conceive even more concretely than I of death. She has experienced that, I guess, in a way.

Ev spends a long time in her room and comes out in a white maid's dress. It is embarrassing, her affectation of these dresses, which she says are simply practical (wash easily), and I feel are gestures of hostility, they seem so out of place in a public housing project. But I expect anyone seeing her out at the clothesline supposes she is a nurse to some invalid here. When she comes out of her room now, I notice a long cut on her forearm, covered with Band-Aids, "skin-colored" ones, hence showing up pale against her dark skin.

"It ain't nothin," she says. "Billie Jean and her husband were fightin and I got cut tryin to stop Billie Jean from cuttin *him*. Ain't it always the way? Them two fight like nothin I ever seen. They uses razors, they uses pokers, they done use broken bottles this time."

I look at the cut, which is deep, maybe deep enough for stitches, which I tell her. Ev is always cutting herself, burning herself, getting cut by others.

"Let it go, it ain't bad," she says, jerking her arm away and pressing the Band-Aids back down. Ev doesn't heal well, and always ends up with a terrible scar. She has scars all over her, like dark lines. "Evalin reminds me of Queequeg," some friend of mine said once.

The thing is, Ev doesn't seem to think it matters if she has a cut. She doesn't think *she* matters. Once, drunk, sleeping on a bus, she burned her own arm deeply with her cigarette. Would not someone, you would have thought, alarmed by the smell of her flesh burning, awaken her, or wouldn't her own pain awaken her? The sore lay open on her arm for months, festering and wouldn't heal.

"This is January 1st," she said presently.

"Someone came and looked in the window," I said.

"It ain't A. J., then, because I knows where he was," she said.

"I didn't see who it was. He looked in on the children, but only one little girl is all who saw him, but she couldn't describe him. She screamed, is all."

"This is January 1st, so you think you could give me my money?" Ev said, not looking at me. "Today, maybe? There's something I done promised A. J." But I pointed out it was a holiday, banks closed. She became quiet and wiped things in the kitchen. I tried to work on my seminar papers in the bedroom. We let the kids watch TV; I always feel guilty about that.

Before dinner, without consciously formulating an intention to do this, I got my coat and walked to the police station, near the elementary school on Grove. A woman in a short-sleeved blue policeman's uniform, maybe a parking-meter woman, said may I help you.

"Well, I think someone is trying to break in our house."

A policeman, the sergeant or someone, listening to overhear whether I would say anything interesting, came up alertly to ask more. But when I told him more he disappointedly told me there was nothing they could do about vandalism to doors, or about things you imagine will happen.

"Until they happen," he said. He was awfully sorry, he said—a narrow-faced man, too jumpy to make inspector, I bet, with curly red hair. So I came home again.

We feel worse as twilight comes on, fear and loneliness rising; the wind is up, too, howling but no snow. I can hear the sounds of garbage cans blowing over, scraping on the concrete behind the garages. I sit at my table trying to write the paper. Whether a transformational grammatical solution is applicable to a problem in historical linguistics: the coincidence of Middle English long open "E" in early Modern English with the reflexes of Middle English long "A." Ev is reading in the living room on the sofa with half an eye on the kids. I hear occasional scuffles,

Ev's soft voice scolding. She is too mild with them. But her languorous attitude is comforting; she is not jumpy and watching out the window for faces. Her main worry she says is that her hair is going back, and she wraps it in the polka-dot rag. The pain in my lower back has gone away. Andrew has not called, but then neither has Osella or the phantom phone-caller; we are peaceful in a way.

5 At supper Ev said, "Me and A. J. thinkin of gettin another place." I looked up staring and I saw she was happy, her headache or whatever it was before had worn off and now she appeared as if she was looking forward to something. She hardly ever has this expression; she hardly ever has anything to look forward to. Her face is a face of well-regulated serenity but is hardly ever happy as it was now. I haven't any picture of Ev; she thinks she photographs too black. "Ain't that awful," she said once, snatching away a picture I had taken of her at Halloween holding Petey and Polly in white sheet ghost costumes, like little Klan members; I thought she meant that. But she said, "It makes me look too dark, I ain't that dark."

Now I was about equally scared at the idea of being left alone with people chopping down our door and mistrustful that Ev should think of putting her happiness with A. J. again. She saw anyway my first fear.

"I'll still be around all day," she said, "just go home nights like I done that other time. A. J.'s gonna pick me up every night and bring me back in the morning. He's got this job on Bucknell Avenue where he goes right by here."

"But, Ev." This man who knocks her around in his drunken violence. I look more closely at a dark bruise on her neck.

22

Oh, A. J. got his feet more on the ground now, I think,"
she said. "He's been a lot better now he got a job. And
we're gonna look for a place over here on the west side,
with a nicer class of folks." She looked at me and all I
could think of was her drowned white satin bedspread,
from last time.

"You know how I been wantin a place. I ain't no different from any other woman," she said more forcefully.

"Why do you always say that, that you aren't any different from other women as if you think I think you are?"
We were both crossly silent. Of course I know every
woman wants a place of her own; it wasn't that at all.

It's A. J. I don't like, so unreliable and cruel. She'd
be better off with Clyde; she can't see it, though. I know
one person can't give eyes to another for seeing such clear
things. Love is like glue. Ev is just stuck down to A. J. Besides she thinks Clyde is "weak," I suppose because he is
sentimental and demonstrative. She would have hated how
he sobbed over Ivan.

"What about Clyde?" I asked.

She shrugged. "I don't want no more of that man and
that's plain. I don't know why he keeps comin round here.
When I get me some money ahead, I'm gonna buy me the
divorce, and I done plainly told him this."

"Clydo gonna buy me a motorbike," Ivan said.

"It's probably Clyde, then, coming around with his
axe," I said, thinking how I had let him in so trustfully in
the afternoon.

"Oh, I ain't gonna leave you alone," Ev said, as if reassuring a child. "Anyhow I can handle Clyde."

Ev tried living with A. J. once before, last July. They
got a room on the east side. Ev was radiant with pleasure
for weeks before; she bought a toaster and curtain material, she bought a quilted white satin bedspread of utmost
impracticality and beauty, $70 at Sears. She would take
Ivan and India out for walks and come home with strange

loot out of trashbins—a big brass platter, a bunch of dried chrysanthemums. Some things you can't tell why people throw them out, she said. She also found a very good wagon for Ivan that way, and a bathrobe for me, brand-new. A. J. would pick her up every night on his way from the job he had then, and bring her back next morning, though she missed a lot of days, and I guess those were days A. J. didn't have to work and got her to stay home with him, or days they had hangovers or were going on drunks. Living out suited her, though.

At that time it suited me, too, having her out at night so Andrew could come in; this was before the Masons moved, but they were planning the move and Andrew said he was having to clear up a lot of work at the office, typical adulterers' lies, and came to me every night for passion's sake, not work, would come talk to me while I fixed supper, and he read to the children and we'd put them to bed and make love and whisper as late as he dared to stay. We had been in love a long time, but this was the period we got to know all about each other, more than husbands and wives do, making friends, each of us emptying everything out of our lonely heart to show our friend. Oh, my dear friend.

But I didn't depend on Andrew; that was one thing I never would do, but said I would make my own way, going to these classes, and I would pass the qualifying examination. Because of this I did have to depend on Ev, for baby-sitting in the daytime, and I would grow frantic when she wouldn't come, angry and demanding. One particularly important day she didn't come; I think I was to give a seminar paper but had to stay here with Ivan and India, being very cross to them of course, when the phone rang and it was Ev, speaking fast and hysterical, with shouting and scolding in the background, sounding so distressed I couldn't scold or scream. She needed me to come get her.

"I have to clear outta here," she said breathlessly as if people were chasing her. "I ain't takin no more of this crap from A. J. and I done told the landlady I'd clear out by noon, or she says she gonna have the cops here by noon," and I don't know what else, so I set out in the car with Ivan and India to find the address, still mad but resigned because it was so often the business of my life to rescue Ev from evil.

It seemed funny to me (then) that human passions could rage evilly in the morning, on such a fresh morning, with birds singing in the lovely plum trees. Ivan and India laughed happily that we were going out while I felt all apart from exasperation, and then we found Ev's street with apprehension because it was so foul and rickety that it was bound to be full of hate and menace, and I didn't see that this could be Ev's beloved place of her own. Every so often like this I will be reminded of the actualities of Ev's life, how bitter and impossible it is, and the idea of her courage wrings me. There she was sitting in her neat dress on the steps of the worst-looking house in this slum looking like she'd been drinking or crying or both. She showed me where to drive around in back to the alley where she had put her things.

The alley was full of weeds and old wrecks of cars and a heap of indeterminate junk that was Ev's possessions — pots and pans, clothes, and ironing board, boxes, sacks, cords to things, open cartons of baking soda and salt, rags, shreds, an old chair. You expected rats to run off all these things.

"This ain't all," Ev said, and went back in the old house for more. I knew I should get out of the car and start loading but I was afraid, full of embarrassing dainty white-lady fears about getting out of my undented car in this tough place. Old hostile parked cars with orange patches on them where dents had been pounded out peered menacingly from weedy driveways and old garages at my undented car. There didn't seem to be any people around — maybe they were all at work or sleeping it off — but then I became aware first of the convergence of eyes, like in a jungle movie, then people appeared, following Ev out the back door with solemn and menacing aspect. Ev tottered with a heavy box. Two old men watched her but no one helped her. I didn't move or help; I pretended to be doing something, fussing with India's car seat with a show of maternal solicitude.

"Git outta here with yo trash," a woman began to scream, railing out the door after Ev; this was a tiny Oriental woman, old with thin hair and house slippers and a filthy dress and a little shrunken mouth. An old man kept trying to kiss her. From the end of the block I could see in the rear-view mirror two fancy black men in fake leather clothes walk slinkily toward me. Ev with a fixed expression continued to add to her heap, huge armloads of soiled, sordid, rusted, dented, unmatched things, just things, I don't know from where. Where had she, a fastidious woman, come by all these things, why did she make this huge pile of them, how would we fit them in the car: radios, chairs, irons. I sat unhelpfully.

"Look like she goin fo good," a man said. "Hee, hee, hee," a chorus of giggles. I guess everyone was drunk. Several women had by now come out on the porch, black women with bright orange hair.

"Get the fuckin junk outta here, get your ass out," the little old woman was screaming.

"Naaaaaaaahce car," said the fancy man leaning in to look at my dashboard. I had been embarrassed to be seen mistrustfully rolling up the windows, locking the doors as I felt like doing. "It's okay," I said. Just a plain Ford.

"Kiss, honey," said the old man grabbing at the old shrill woman. "Hee, hee, hee."

"Power steering?"

"This is all, I'll load it up now," Ev said, her expression still frozen so that I couldn't tell if she was afraid or angry.

"Hoooeee," someone said, looking at Ev's heap, and

then a fat old man with white hair did help her with the big chair, an ugly oak chair with a torn seat. We still have it. They wedged it in the back seat.

"I thought you was out here waitin for *me*," said the admirer of my car, and stroked its fender like a thigh, suggestively. Ivan and India gleefully scrambled among the objects Ev had now begun to throw in frantic haste onto the seat. In minutes the car was full, and as far as I could tell the mound of stuff on the ground was undiminished.

"Radio! Ev got a radio!" Ivan said.

"Bunny! Big bunny!" India screamed. Ev had a big stuffed bunny. Now there seemed to be twenty people in a loose circle around us, only Ev moving, and the old man who occasionally lifted something, chosen apparently by some deliberate process of selection from the heap, and stuffed it in the car.

Suddenly we heard a splash, a spurt of water, a tin sound of water against the side of the car, and a simultaneous chorus of cackles and shouts. The old woman had the garden hose and was wetting Ev's things with it, watering them down, drowning them before our eyes, boxes crumbling, mud welling up around a nice hat, clothes reduced to puddles of rags, boxes dissolving. Ev, stupefied, stared and then came around to the passenger's side, stared and tapped on the door which was locked on that side. I unlocked it and she got in.

"Let's go," she said, "they ain't nothin I want there anyhow," but you could see there was because there were tears in her eyes. The men who were leaning on the car stepped back and we moved slowly away down the alley, slowly to avoid the appearance of terrified haste. Then someone threw something which landed on the roof like thunder and I was startled into putting on the brake and looking back. There I saw a woman with orange hair pull out Ev's white bedspread, limp wet as it was, and drag it off away from the pile. I don't know if Ev saw that.

"That place a whorehouse, if you want to know," Ev

said presently. "A. J. shouldn't have took me no place like that. Mens tryin to get in at night." But they'd lived there a couple of months, she must have known.

Ev told me later that the last straw had been when A. J. brought another woman there, to Ev's room among Ev's things. It was that she couldn't stand. And I suppose there was much else.

"Well, I'll live in, for a while, then I'd like to get me a place on my own," Ev said after that. "I don't need A.J.," she would say, but I guess she does need A. J., I guess the way I need Andrew.

And I can understand Ev's feelings about having a place of her own, just as I could understand how if she had enemies those enemies would want to smash her lamps, and I could understand how someone must have put out that good brass tray Ev found in the trash because someone they hated gave it to them, and so on, an interrelation among passions and things unceasing. From these promptings, for instance, Andrew and I when we were first in love wrecked each other's houses. It was peculiar. I mean physically wrecked them with crowbars and such, and it seemed quite natural and called-for at the time.

When the Masons were ready to move, they began to do what was needed around their house before putting it up for sale, and when Gavvy had decided to join Andrew's firm and we knew he would be making more money and better days were ahead, we decided to fix the things around our house that seemed, like our marriage, to have crumbled; we didn't think of it like that, we thought things were getting better. We thought things were looking up, so we would replace the downstairs bathroom and remodel the laundry.

Andrew and I at the same time were already in love. We knew that but we had no special plans about it. I wonder what we imagined was going to happen. I suppose inwardly we knew that if you don't do anything about such radical disorders in your life, inner promptings will impel you some way or other. Creativity is like that, they say, and so must destruction be. Andrew and I did nothing, except to try to steal off and meet, or try to catch glimpses of each other along the halls of Briggs, Harvill & Mason or at a party. We did not for a long time make love. I mean, although we spoke of it, we did not take off our clothes and symbolize it; that was strange, because we are both greedy in that way, Andrew and I. But true love had come like a suspicious package to be inspected carefully, and when we recognized it we were respectful of it, and wished to approach such an astonishing thing in a leisurely and circumspect fashion, discussing its aspects, inspecting the exquisite minute little pictures that decorated its surface.

So we had a lot of drinks in dark places talking of love but we never discussed reality at all. Perhaps we imagined a tidal wave would sweep Gavin and Cookie away. Perhaps we imagined that our love would in some way fortify us to endure a future in which no changes would actually be necessary. It is true that when we were together we were happy, and if you are happy you try to keep things as they are, not to change them. I helped Andrew with Cookie's birthday present. Gavin offered to lend Andrew an electric saw for some shelves Andrew was making. Gavin was impressed that the great Andrew Mason did useful things around the house.

So we went to the Masons' one Sunday afternoon with the saw, and they were amidst flooring tiles and torn-up boards and cans of paint and beer, and with one thing and another we helped them tear up the old floor, tearing it right out, and the four of us were so effective at this work of destruction that the Masons offered to come the Sunday after to help tear out our laundry walls, as was only fair. That was effective, too. There we were, really home-wreckers, wrecking each other's homes. It seems amazing to me how the meaning of this clumsy acting out of our inmost wishes escaped our notice, even Andrew's and mine, we were too concerned with contriving sly absences to steal kisses.

After we had truly become lovers, Andrew wanted to make love at his house. "I can't explain why it seems particularly important," he said, "and particularly outrageous. Don't wear perfume, Cookie would smell it the second she got home." "I just want to take you into my own bed, you are my mate," Andrew said when I was in his bed and in his arms.

Why did it not occur to this woman, the Famous Inspector must wonder, that if she wrecked her home she would be homeless? One must expect a person like that to end up in a shabby dump with paranoid delusions. Everyone I have mentioned it to, even Bess, even Ev, believes I am suffering paranoid delusions to think that someone is trying to murder us.

"You are making it all up," Bess said, "imagining it, rather. You are inferring from the normal malignancy of things some flattering personal attention. I would say you are no more likely than anyone else to be knocked off by a crazy maniac, or speeding car, or atomic holocaust, or returned veteran blazing away with shotgun at supermarket, addict with shiv in subway . . ."

"No, it's all meant for us—for me, or else Ev."

"Somebody put a dead cat on our lawn. We knew they had done it on purpose from the carefully composed attitude of its battered limbs. Put it right where Lynnie would see it when she went out to school, so she would scream and cry, just as she did. Are we in danger?"

"Danger? No, of course not, that's a vicious trick, but . . ." And Bess smiled her characteristically triumphant and wise smile.

"And there's bound to be more of that sort of thing in that vile place you live," she added. She never will believe we do not live here from perversity. But murder happens all over. In the paper this morning:

AGRICULTURE PROF KILLS WIFE, TOTS, SELF

CLOVIS. Firemen extinguishing the blaze which nearly destroyed the two-story frame house of Professor Norman O. French, recovered the bodies of Dr. French, and what appear to be those of his estranged wife Dora (37), and four children, Candida (12), Melanie (10), Frank (9), and Claudia (4). The bodies were arranged in a row on the bed and the room heavily saturated with gasoline. The cause of the deaths of Mrs. French and the children has not yet been determined. Dr. French, who died of gunshot wounds, was found in the living room.

A sick man, a killer, who then tried to burn down his house, murder and destruction, no New Year for those poor little children at all.

6 I study articles like this with minutest attention because I'm trying to decide in my own mind whether Gavvy is crazy enough to kill me. Husbands killing wives—that's an especially recurrent sort of murder— estranged husband kills wife, children, self. It's always husbands. Wives never do. I don't understand the sources of male vanity and rage that turn them into killers. Who suckles them on these bitter poisons of expectation? Women, I know.

I think it is that Gavvy is crazy in respect to me, but not to anybody else. I know that sounds self-important. Yet why else would I notice things and the world not notice them, but go on right along regarding him—indeed trusting him? Gavvy is trusted with the futures and fortunes of others, after all. Yet I am afraid of him, I have been ever since he hit me, and perhaps earlier than that, at the back of my mind, since the incident of India's crib, or before that even, when he told me of his obsession.

I used to put these things out of my mind. I didn't keep a catalogue of mad symptoms. That seems so grudging, totting up madness in others, all the time riddled with mad ideas yourself. The obsession was, we were outside looking at our zinnias in a contented way and Gavin suddenly said, quite unrelated to anything we had been talking of, "I know you'll think this is peculiar but ever since India was born I've had an irrational feeling—I *know* it's irrational—that she isn't mine, not my child."

My reaction was calm, interested, rather charmed by the odd unexpectedness of this, how surprising people are even when you think you know them, what possibilities and dimensions that does add to life. But then I felt shocked and annoyed. "She looks just like you," I pointed out. He nodded and put his arm around me. We walked on. We smiled. Welling up inside me there came a feeling that now I must forever afterward reserve certain thoughts and ideas from Gavin, because inside him was an odd disorder which might fester. I tried to think where he might have gotten this odd idea, from what inner fear or pathology of his own it might have sprung. I had thought I knew him perfectly.

We didn't discuss this—if you discuss mythical events they will come to seem like true historical events, so I laughed instead. He had wanted to tell me, he said, for a long time, because his secret fear was spoiling the contentedness with which we watched off across the beautiful hills beyond our garden and so on. He pressed my hand to show me he had conquered the silly unworthy idea, that by telling me he had exorcised it. How bravely he contended with the devils of his nature, this handsome cherub.

I did wonder for a day or two who on earth he thought the father could be; I had never slept with anyone else at all, and for that matter had been more or less continuously pregnant ever since we were married. Part of me was pleased that Gavin could think me capable of such monstrous perfidy, I'll admit that.

Of course now I know where Gavvy must have got this idea, from Osella. "I surely can't make out who India favors," she must have said. I didn't understand, then, what Osella was up to.

Osella has so many ways of hating me: the hatred of the old for the young, of the black for the white, of the chaste for everybody. The hatred which is held by the powerless.

"I has powers," she would insist. "I could tell you things I knows, but I ain't gonna. Things I sees, things I knows."

"I'd rather not know anyway," I would say dismissively.

"It'd grieve you, what I sees about the children. About one of 'em. So I ain't gonna tell you, I'll bear the grief to myself."

"Yes, I'd rather not know," I would say, and turn away frightened, though of course I did not believe in Osella's powers. But you believe people when they tell you something awful will happen because it so likely will.

It took me a long time to understand Osella's need to feel powerful. It took me much too long to understand that she had any needs at all. This is because I was so preoccupied with my own, I am ashamed to say, and also because Osella concealed hers for a long time. A fat old black woman from Alabama has learned to keep her tears inside. She grins like a slave. Osella *was* a slave, and a slave was what I wanted.

This is because the children were all so little and there were so many of them; when she came, two and a half years ago, they were aged seven months, eighteen months, and three and five and a half years: that was how I had spent the six previous years. I don't know how this happened; we are not Catholics and didn't mean it to. People are condescending and doubtful when I say this, and regard me with smirks of reservation, not expressing aloud their view that I am careless and lazy, which is what they say of welfare mothers, too. I know some people think I have found my level in this housing project.

How we got Osella seemed at first a great piece of luck for us and for Osella, too. When Gavvy was a little boy, during the war, his family lived for a while in Alabama, and Osella was his nurse. Later she and her husband, John Henry, worked for some people named Spinner, old friends of Gavvy's parents, for years and years until the Spinners pensioned them off and they traveled up here and set up in retirement not far from here—California, what they had always dreamed of. But then John Henry died. There they had been, like kids, like newlyweds at the start of a new life, their own place at last and then John Henry stood up in his chair, eyes staring, and fell down unable to move or speak, so that Osella had had to call a doctor, who called an ambulance, who came and took John Henry away, and they rang back later to say he was dead. Osella got the right bus and found her way to the hospital, and they let her look at John Henry—dead enough, all right. Osella had never been on her own or alone in her whole life, never before, but she called the Spinners, and they called Gavin's mother saying would you do something for Osella, and Gavvy's mother had the good idea.

"I told her you can't pay her much," Gavin's mother said, "Gavin just out of law school and with all those babies. I think she is grateful to feel needed and useful. It will give her something to live for. Osella is wonderful with children. Has never had any of her own."

"It'll be a nice change for N. to get out and develop some interests," Gavin's father said, poor man, little knowing. I was grateful for that idea. Gavin wasn't happy about Osella or any of it, though—didn't want another person around, and, I think, didn't want me to develop interests.

I suppose I must admit that from his point of view he was right about that.

At the time I was nearly stifled by feelings of gratitude to Gavin's parents, who towed this poor uncomprehending hulk of a woman up our long steps, delivering her like white hunters. At the top of the steps Osella couldn't talk for fright and shortness of breath. She had been afraid to take her own time on the steps for fear we wouldn't want her, would think she was too fat to be any use.

"When I seen them steps, I like to died," she told me later. "I tole myself Osella you dies if you walks up them steps but then you dies if you don't, and mah heart went out of me and I just floated up 'em like I was dead and risin in grace, you done seen me." And she had seemed dead on arrival, delivered lonely and bereaved and far from home to our zoo, like some insignificant common animal barely noticeable to the keeper, me, who was more preoccupied with the misery of the delicate gazelle—me. Mine was the ordinary misery of mothers of small children. At least, I think this misery is ordinary. I can try to express the peculiar desperation of being the mother of small children but I doubt if I can make it sound serious or do anything beyond alienating the Famous Inspector. Men hate to hear about this.

You sit in parks for hours and hours. When they are sleeping, you are in terror that the precious silence will be ended by one of them waking. When they sleep too long you are in terror, too, that they have died; you are always in terror, and also it is very lonesome. You love them but you wish they would talk about something you are interested in. I for instance am interested in transformational grammar.

You must carry them. Their little arms are tightly around your throat, their sticky little fingers on your glasses. Already in their faraway eyes you see intense and proper self-preoccupation.

After Ivan was born I got contact lenses, and it

seemed to me the world had grown brighter, not meta-
phorically but literally. The world was full of dazzling
color and light bounded off pavements. Then I caught on
that this was so because the spectacles I used to wear had
always been covered with sticky fingerprints, from fat
baby fingers trying to pull them off. Years and years of
looking through a gummy film had affected my thoughts as
well as my eyes.

Sometimes I would send my mind forth, disembodied,
as it were, to read something—Chomsky, say—while my
body did the dishes, but then I would always break or
forget something, and Gavvy would scream at me, or a
child would skin its knee to punish me, would scream,
would scream.

For a while I gave up all reading but detective stories,
whose sameness comforted me, whose morality assured
me of order outside my own disorder. I would bring home a
dozen at a time, the maximum permitted, making a tiny
mark on the flyleaves so I could distinguish the ones I had
already read. I believe I also derived enjoyment from these
small acts of defacement. But then once at the library
while I was picking out detective stories, Polly found a
dime and swallowed it and nearly choked to death. You
are guilty for everything that happens. You give yourself
up. If you can understand any of this, you will understand
what Osella meant to me by coming there and being there
and why I gave ourselves to her and let her fill the house
and make it hers.

A smirk of comprehension and disgust overspreads
the features of the Famous Inspector: this is a neglectful,
a resentful mother he is dealing with, the sort that get
murdered all the time and the children put in foster homes,
usually a good thing, too. Ah, it is not reason which con-
geals the wellsprings of the Famous Inspector's sympathy,
but that he is a man. It is that inchoate masculine fear they
all have. Where does it come from? It must be that some-

time in his life every little boy baby, rosy in his bath, looking up past the warm, strong arms of his mother into her
eyes, one time sees there a strangeness which suddenly
reveals to him that she is not him, she is not even like him
but is another creature of another race, and however much
this terrible recognition may be obscured by subsequent
pats, hugs, kisses, coos, years and years of love and
encouragement—the terror and isolation of that moment,
and the fear of it returning, remain forever.

Thursday, January 2

1 Osella became our new family member, the old family retainer, and assumed at once the familiar perquisites of that role, scolded and scared us, demanded love. Her own love was focused mostly on Petey and Polly, who were old enough to listen to her stories and praise the cookies she made and sing the songs she taught them:

> Down in Black Mountain
> A chile will slap yo face—

That was Petey's favorite, such daring imputation of power to a child's hands delighted him. The actual power at our house was Osella's. We gave it to her; power seemed the least we could give her since we couldn't give her much money. Power and respect and confidence. I know now that this is a sinister sort of pact, but it seemed all right with Osella, it seemed good for us.

"Sometimes," she told me, "sometimes mah heart is so full, when I think of how I come here, findin these babies needin me so, and findin Gavvy again, for he ain't nothin but mah baby, you know, and now I done found Raider." (For this was when she had taken up with her new man, Big Raider.) "Where I done thought mah life had past, now it's beginnin all over. They say they ain't miracles. And I never looked to be so far from home as this in mah lifetime."

She took special care of her baby Gavvy, which he liked. I should have done it, I suppose, but am not good at taking care of people and pampering them. Osella would shine his shoes and arrange his underwear and always have his coffee strong enough. It never seemed to me that Gavin was nice to her; he didn't seem to love her at all, although she loved him. But of course he was always perfectly polite.

Perhaps he was nicer when I wasn't around. Sometimes he would go into the kitchen for a drink after dinner, and she would still be washing up, and they would laugh and talk in there. Other times she'd chase him away: "Git outta here, pies in mah oven, I don't want no mess in mah kitchen now I got it all cleaned up."

She seemed happy. She wore a bandanna around her head and baked cornbread and sang. I avoided buying Aunt Jemima products for fear she would resent that caricature of herself on the box, though I recognize that fear was just a function of white guilt, and that Osella probably saw nothing odd in Aunt Jemima at all, any more than I personally resent Betty Crocker.

She talked and talked. At first she talked only about John Henry, who had been her whole life, her husband and child at once, but as time went by her memories of him seemed to be developing a dusty, ritual quality, like old things taken out of a trunk, shaken out, admired after dinner and packed away again. She was especially apt to bring them out after dinner, but her quiet, pretty, small speaking voice no longer caught, fewer lumps arose in her throat. In the first weeks she would begin every sentence "If John Henry hadn't of passed," but she came to speak of him less and less. I always imagined him, as she did, in heaven looking down on us; he was glaring at us for enslaving Osella.

Unaware of being a slave, she lumbered through the house with mops, trailed by the children, whom she laughed with and hugged. We went into ecstasies, sometimes feigned, over the wonders she cooked for us: breakfasts of hot biscuits and grits and bacon and honey and eggs. But we didn't gain weight.

To our friends we became Osella bores with our countless anecdotes. Our friends became her friends, her intimates, would rush to the kitchen after parties to congratulate her on her lemon pies. She knew our friends by name and transformed herself on these occasions to a wily old darky saying very nearly such things as "How you be, Massa George?"

In fact she tyrannized. She conceived a hatred for our friend Al and said he could never come any more. She insulted a distinguished Negro lawyer whom we had earned her contempt for, unwittingly, by telling her beforehand that he had gone to Harvard, which I thought she would like. During a lull we could hear her in the kitchen loudly saying, "Harvard mah foot; his head's as nappy as a ram's ass; that coon's from Georgia or my name ain't Osella."

She tyrannized, we sighed acceptingly. She cooked, we ate. She talked, we listened. I was her chief listener, a kind of captive audience morally obliged to listen while she did my work. She had a lot of horror stories I got to like, about the folks back home: "That was Leonie, mah cousin Daniel's wife, that burnt up their baby while she was down to the fancy house pickin up a little extra change while Daniel was workin in the fields. We all knowed she do that, except Daniel, he didn't know. The baby knocked the stove over on hisself and burnt the house up. Mah cousin Daniel was the one that got his leg cut off by a train . . ."

She also talked, continuously, about her lifelong employers, the Spinners, with whom she had been as involved, to whom as attached, as to John Henry, nearly. All her loved ones, I would think, and now she has no people at all. I thought it was nice that she had our children to love, that they filled a little place in her life. She appeared to love us. I never imagined her sitting in her room at night, late, late into the night, burning her armchair with her cigarettes, stumping them out on the wooden arms, throwing the butts under the bed.

That was because I didn't understand her at all, or didn't try. She was an alien to me, so dark and fat. It was harder for me that Osella was fat than that she was black, although the reverse was true for her, I think she would have said. Her fatness seemed ordinary to her, and to me wondrous. She was like someone reflected in a fun-house mirror to inhuman width. "More than three-forty," she weighed. She did not bear this weight in grotesque folds of fat but instead was smoothly stretched, as if she had been inflated. By this logic she would be hollow, which accounted for the seeming lightness of her bearing; she skipped lightly upstairs, across rooms. Once, colliding with me as we both went for the telephone, she knocked me down. Her face is balloon smooth and shiny. She is the color of chamois, "high-yaller," with the mild brown eyes of the grain-fed.

I notice that whenever I describe Osella or think of her, it is in metaphors of things not people, or of fat animals. It is as if I did not consider her human, this fellow woman with whom I shared my children and my home and many hours, her head stored up with griefs. There was nothing in her that wouldn't sit down sisterly and share a recipe but there was something in me. I try to imagine Osella looking at me, seeing me a sour and distant little thing in the corner: what did she think? What did she think I was thinking? I try to imagine the feelings of her heart when she looked at the children rosy and loving of her.

Well, perhaps it is a sentimental untruth to say the children loved her. They disregarded her the way all children do all adults until she failed them in some way. Then they would rail. They disregard Ev that way now, and Ev, being a little afraid of them, is kinder to them even than Osella was, and buys them things at the store out of the small wage I give her out of the small sum I get. Our economics here are very shaky.

But I'm trying to confess that I don't think I experienced Osella as a human, not really. Even getting her in and out of cars, an elaborate project, rendered her a big unwieldy thing of the wrong shape, like an inner tube. How horrible for her; it's not surprising she went mad, living all by herself in a cold world of stony people who couldn't seem to see or hear her. Osella battering at us, us not feeling her at all. She would have to go mad.

But it is partly, too, that I am afraid of the very fat. I had never known anyone very fat before Osella, but seeing fat strangers I would always look away, and had always read, and still do, with great attention and a feeling of personal shame, those case-history advertisements in magazines which show huge elephant women before and after, legs bulging, repulsive chins, and then thinner in some tarty dress, recounting the personal heroism and chemical aid that led to this thin result. These are really stories of sin, repentance and redemption, I guess, always compelling.

"John Henry marrit me when I wasn't but fifteen years old. Most folks back home marries young. I didn't weigh but a hundred and forty. John Henry he liked meat on a woman, and that's what he done got. 'What I want with one of them little bitty women,' he used to say.

"A little woman like you, now, with them little chicken legs, he wouldn't look at you nohow. That's how I got all this lard. Back in our part of the country, you see, men like a whole lot of woman. Wouldn't have no use for a little bitty thing like you.

"White men got a thing for a big woman, too, even if they tole you diff'rent. Mr. Spinner had it for me, I knowed, even if he never said nothin right out. Mrs. Spinner, I think she knowed that, too, she would look at me ever so often with a look that knowed. I never said nothin about that to John Henry but I recognized Mr. Spinner in his lust."

After receiving such confidences, why wouldn't I suppose the eyes of Osella were friendly eyes, and that she trusted me, and told me woman's secrets?

Once she told me, "Mr. Spinner shown me his tool. I wasn't but a young girl and I never tole John Henry. He didn't mean nothin by it, or not too much, but it would have upset John Henry. Mr. Spinner was just a dirty man, an awful dirty man, despite bein a high-up college president and that. He was comin in from the woods where he took girls, which I knowed. I done often wondered about all them fancy people sendin their daughters to his school; they didn't know nothing. Anyways, he just took out his tool and lain it on his hand and shown me it. A white man'll do that if they's nobody around."

Was that so? I used to wonder at the things Osella knew, but I believed her. Once Osella looked at me and I, drawn into her big fawn-colored eyes, saw there an expression deep and disordered as if the brain beneath had turned on edge, and I wondered. But her voice was pitiful and sane, saying, "I done lost John Henry and maybe I done lost Raider, too, but I ain't gonna lose mah babies," and I consoled her, you never have to leave us, you never have to leave the babies, we all love you, Osella, we love Osella.

Even when she told me as plainly as this, I could not believe Osella to be as hungry and tormented as she was. She looked so well fed. I can imagine me telling the Famous Inspector this and him turning away disgusted: this broad is so *dumb*, whatever she gets she deserves it from dumbness. But anyway now I know that Osella was crazy. Was Osella crazy right along? How long was she crazy? When did she turn? Who knew? Now, looking back, it is easy to remember any number of little, little things.

Once we had a party, and our poor friend Al went out to the kitchen to tell Osella how much he liked her pecan rolls. When everyone had gone home, we found Osella still standing stiff in the kitchen with blazing eyes.

"That man don't come here no more as long as I'm in this house."

"Who? What man?"

"I think you calls him Alfred."

"Al? Al Dodge?"

"That's him. You see to it he don't come near me no more."

"But why? What's the matter?"

"He done said somethin very objectionable."

"Well, what, for God's sake?" (Gavin, impatiently.)

"'I'd like to get inside yo pants.'"

"Oh come on, Osella."

"Well, that's what he done said. 'Osella, I'd like to get inside yo pants,' and I don't take no talk like that from yo fancy white friends, think they can come out here and talk to me like that."

A babble of demurring from us: "Must have misunderstood, Al Dodge, fine man, old friend, something about pots and pans—?"

"Pants. Inside mah pants."

"You wear the pants around here, panting for more food, we'll speak to him, clear it up, misunderstanding, be calm . . ." We retreated dismayed, but giggled in the night. Maybe Al had really said these things, been drunk. Or did he have some sly streak of malicious rudeness we hadn't seen before? Or of misguided whimsey? Or have some odd hankering after fat women the way African chieftains are said to do. As Osella said that Mr. Spinner had. Impossible, of course, dear old Al—but she had had such conviction raging in her outraged widow's eyes.

"Has Osella gone through the change, I wonder?" I said. How old could she be? Then Gavvy figured out she was only forty-two. I couldn't believe this. I had thought, I suppose, that people associated with Gavvy's childhood, and who had been married to old men who died, must be of the age of Gavvy's parents. But it worked out: she had been married to John Henry at fifteen, and was a bride when she first took care of Gavvy, who was four or so, so she would be eleven years older than him and he was now thirty-one. So she was still a young woman; she could have a baby, even. That seemed impossible.

An odd thing: Osella and I have the same birthday, May 5; also we are both left-handed.

"Yes, she's probably going through the change," Gavvy said. "Maybe we should send her to the doctor for some shots. Hormones. I wish we didn't have to have her around at all."

He said this every now and then. "Osella is *too* impossible."

"I thought you liked her, your dear old mammy."

"Well, good old Osella, I do like her, but she's just plain too big and fat to be much use. This place is a mess, the kids always look a mess; I think, really, we should think seriously of getting rid of her." And then I would protest; everything would go, my loved freedom, this gift of going where I pleased. I'm going to the store. I'm going to the library, taking only such children as I pleased—one, all, none.

"Osella is wonderful," I would frantically say; "how could we do without her? Anyway, where would she go?"

And then when I most wanted her away, Gavvy would say we couldn't do without her. He said that more and more often after I went back to school, which he viewed as a withdrawal of my interest in our household, which it was, of course. But sometimes with Osella in my kitchen, filling every little inch, and the dinner all fixed and my babies all arrayed in clothes she had decided on, I would feel an excluded feeling, urgent although brief, an urchin feeling, with my nose pressed against the glass looking in at all this domestic contentment, and I would want to take a big stone and smash the glass.

"My God," Gavvy would say then, "you can barely manage *with* Osella, look at this place. What in hell would we do without her?" And since that was true, I would just turn away from the coziness and go to the library or somewhere.

2 After Osella came, and Gavin was out of law school and the babies out of diapers, I had thought things were getting better for Gavin and me, but I see now they weren't. Gavin and I were not happy. Everybody knew that but us; it escaped us—me partly because I was so busy, and partly because I don't approve of thinking about that. I don't think whether you are happy or not ought to weigh with you; I mean, you shouldn't think about it at all. Sometimes when I am in my lover Andrew's arms, the thought comes, together with a feeling from our hot skin and the dissolving feeling inside me, that I am happy. But if I dare to say that to myself then the thought will be chased by panic like baying hounds. There seem to be no words to express much of my experience of life, except love and panic.

Panic again this noon. The banks were back open so I went out to cash Ev's check and then to the library for a book I needed, and when I came home Ev and the kids were all out in the front of the unit on the lawn lying between ours and the opposite row of units, frosted and brown this time of year with gum wrappers blowing along it like tumbleweeds. They were digging, or had dug, and now stood around the dug place, Ev tall and straight in her white dress like a cemetery angel, for it was a grave, I could see that from their ceremonious attitudes, and Petey had his trumpet, which he had evidently played already, because his lips were bright. They began to stir as I watched and, India's short attention span used up, she was wiggling and saw me watching them out the curtain, so it was ended and they all came in, sober-faced.

"What were you doing?" I asked. They looked among themselves and at Ev, for guidance how to answer.

"We found a poor creature and gave it a funeral. I played my trumpet," Petey said. Ev nodded at the correctness of this.

"Just a poor creature dead," Polly said. All right, Ev had told them not to tell me, I could see that; "Don't bother your ma with this."

"Well, what was it?" I asked her when they had gone outside again. Ev looked uncomfortable, straining against some resolve of hers but of course told me.

"We done found a dead cat and buried it."

"Were the kids upset?"

"No more than me," Ev said, "or not as much. I told them it had got tangled up in its leash. You hadn't ought to ever put a cat on a leash, or a rabbit either, I told them."

"A cat on a leash?"

"A cat with a string around its neck pulled so tight its head nearly come off, layin on the step, and it never walked there. Petey he thinks it was comin to our house for help, but that cat never walked there."

"Well, there, you see, it is somebody, it's a warning, it's a symbol!" I began to gibber, feeling sick with fright to imagine a strangled cat, and Ev said, "Well, we wasn't going to tell you," noncommittally, as if her judgment on that point was now proved to be right. We don't want to panic your panicky ma, she might have said. I was embarrassed at her true view of my character.

"It's a funny thing, thinkin about that cat," Ev said at dinner, "it puts me in mind of the time I wrung the chickens' necks."

Expressions of shock and fascination from Petey and Polly. "What, you wrung a chicken's neck, how horrible, why did you do it, tell, tell."

"Well, this was when we was little and lived in Texas. My daddy he didn't always have a job, if they wasn't no cotton for pickin then, but my mama always helped at houses and she kept a little garden and chickens. Well, I won't ever forget, my brother and me kilt them chickens, all of about ten of them. I can't just remember why, chicken pie, more than likely, or practicin wringin they necks like we seen her do, and when Mama come and seen what we done, she caught me — my brother run faster — and beat me to an inch of my life, and then she sat down on our porch steps and cried, like to cry her life out, and I don't know if I know yet why she cared so much for them stupid chickens, then she locked me up in the henhouse for one whole day."

"Braawwk, brawwk, brawwk," Polly and Petey said, flapping their wings.

Taking this affair of the cat aside to think clearly: is it a sly thing like the phantom phone-caller, is it the rude prank of a neighborhood kid psychopath, the mutilator of underpants, or clever Gavvy, A. J., Clyde, Osella, knowing how to cause a panic around here?

3 Now I realize I have always been afraid of Osella, but as I said, at first I thought my strangeness with her was because I wasn't used to black people or the very fat. I would catch myself staring at her yellow dark arms in the sink; her arms were as big around as my thighs. She spoke of her limbs as her "hams." Her immensity: if you had a bellyache in that great belly, would the pain be as little as mine, a pinpoint ache deep within, or would it be a vast continent of pain? Where beneath those huge breasts did she feel her heart beat? Where did she feel her self? Where do I feel my self? Inside, behind my nose, and along my lower spine most particularly.

Perhaps finding herself arrived in this world a Negro and poor and a woman, she determined to make up for these disadvantages by taking up, by personally occupying, as large a place as she could, taking satisfaction from expanding her perimeter inch by inch across the white ladies' kitchens. She has dainty little feet, agile, which skip beneath her like the mechanical feet of a tabletop toy.

But I am trying to explain that I did not see the harm in her, none of us did. Gavin, I thought, regarded her just as a useful person who made good things to eat, and he told Osella stories to our friends, of the funny things she said, with just the right amount of unconcern to indicate that he was so unbigoted and unnoticing that he could denigrate her idiosyncrasies just as though she were a regular person, not his poor black slave.

Well, I tried to take good care of her. I made her a dress, when she began to go to church and to "socialize" afterward. It was made of wool. She said she had never had a dress of wool before. Making it was like making woolen curtains; it weighed pounds and pounds when it was done. We were glad when she began to have a "life of her own." Gavin's mother said this must always be encouraged in a live-in because it helps them to bear it better.

Osella met people at church, and afterward they

would go to a club. That's where she met Big Raider, at a club. In her wool dress and hats she had a certain massive chic. People would bring her to the bottom of our steps in old black Oldsmobile or Mercury cars crowded with people laughing and waving as she toiled up the steps late Sunday nights. Perhaps she is with some good church people now who don't realize that she is crazy or who don't care. We have never known where she went when she left, or where she calls from.

Poor, horrible woman, the only decent thing to be is full of sadness and pity for her. Where is she now? Lying on some lonesome little bed which sags shapelessly under her great weight, her furniture scarred with cigarette burns and soiled with ashes, the floor filthy. That's the way her room was when we finally looked in after she left. Her self-disgust was such that she had never cleaned her own room, which, respecting her, I had never looked into.

Yet how clean she kept us, how shiny our floors, great warm woman in her white nylon dress and powdery floured arms, warm like a Franklin stove in the kitchen. There was so much of her emitting so many calories. And her soft voice was so gentle. Osella's little voice suggests a delicate person inside her gross body, a shy and fragile soul, except when she sings. Then she sounds possessed demoniacally, as she does, too, during her ravings on the telephone. Around the house she was always smiling, had a bowl-full-of-jelly laugh, was the perfect jolly fat person. The perfect jolly darky. The baby, India, would lie on the white nylon vastness of her bosom as on a rocking sea-shelf. How she sang, mammy songs.

We never pictured her in her room, thrashing on her sagging bed, perhaps needing John Henry. Did she ever weep? And why didn't I ever wonder? Because I was too wrapped up in myself like a queen of tragedy. How fiercely preoccupying personal desperation is, even when you don't know you are desperate.

I was desperate, and grew to be afraid, but still didn't have the sense to be afraid of Osella, or even of Gavvy, and grew irrationally afraid of John Henry instead. I began to have dreams about him which I still sometimes have, nightmares with John Henry glaring down looking like God as played by a man in a movie I saw once, *Green Pastures,* black with white hair and an expression of exceeding benignity, kind of a stupid expression. John Henry's. Dressed in a suit wearing his smug house-nigger expression. That's how Osella describes on others the expression John Henry wore in his photograph, smug and benign. It's funny how Osella remembers these phrases which must have come from a hundred years ago, house nigger, and a field nigger is someone she despises. The photo had Osella wearing a ruffled dress and looking therefore like a pine cone, her face baby-young, bride to this old hat-wearing chauffeur god, and in the background somebody's big house, I suppose the Spinners', where they worked for twenty-five years.

At least it can't be John Henry who slashed our door. John Henry is in heaven looking down malevolently on what we have brought his bride, his angel, his baby Osella to.

4 My bad dreams about John Henry began after I took Osella to visit his grave. They had to bury him clear over in Roseville, segregation after death being, unlike other sorts, legal in this state and therefore insisted upon with a kind of vengeful relish. Osella put her wool dress on, though it was a hateful, hot day with brown air, late 1968, October. She dressed respectfully. I just wore my jeans, not thinking of being disrespectful, but I didn't know John Henry and didn't mean to look at his grave, only to drive Osella there. And I wasn't very nice to her on the drive over because we had gotten a traffic ticket on the way.

We had a Volkswagen then—Osella barely fit—and we'd stopped to buy a wreath which Osella would not put in the back seat but would hold in her arms, a giant wreath of lilies, roses and gypsophila covered with a cellophane bag. This wreath together with Osella filled the entire front seat, so I could hardly see, and made an illegal U-turn without seeing a cop and we got picked up. This is when I learned that if you have a black person with you, your white-lady immunity, which might entitle you to courtesy, is canceled, and the policeman will harass you as much as if you were black. He thinks you are friends with a black person. Gavvy said later a Volkswagen is nothing in your favor with a policeman, either. Anyway, this one made me sound the horn and work the lights, to see if there wasn't some defective equipment to cite us for, and called on his radio to see if we were wanted felons, and never asked about the wreath "REST IN PEACE" and the poor unmoving black woman behind it as still as if she were dead, her mind racing far ahead of her, already encountering John Henry's grave, not even noticing this policeman. I tried saying my husband is Assistant District Attorney, since this was true, but the policeman just laughed. Sure, lady. I wonder whether Gavvy's year as Assistant District Attorney will exempt him from suspicion of criminality, or whether, on the other hand, the Famous Inspector, familiar with the affinity of criminal and prosecutor, will suspect him all the more.

Anyway: the long hot drive on the expressway to Roseville, thirty miles, and Osella's wreath crackling as she shifted beneath it, her heart heavy as clods, she said, for she had not seen John Henry's grave since he was put into it, and my heart was racing with rage about the traffic ticket and fear of what Gavvy would say.

I wonder if Osella had often wanted to go to John Henry's grave and had been afraid to ask me to drive her such a long way, or whether she was afraid to see his grave, expecting, as it proved, that his baleful shade would be too palpable. She seemed stiff with fear now, her eyes staring white and frightened, as if in mortal danger, expecting the reproaches of this shade—where had she been?—it was nearly six months. Her belly swelled with audible sighs, and in the hot little car she stank in her wool dress, her own smell overpowering that of the flowers.

The Sleep in Calvary Resting Place was laid out in the cheap flat land behind Roseville at the end of a dingy tract housing development, redneck land with campers in all the driveways and blond preschoolers with trikes and wagons on the sidewalks watching a big fine funeral car come out from the cemetery gates filled with weeping black people elegantly dressed. Osella rustled tensely beneath her wreath.

"Osella, do you know where it—uh—know where we go?" She stirred and sat up; I saw that her eyes had been closed. She looked in confusion around the paths between the gravestones, which all looked big and alike, as if a whole population had died at once.

"It was near a tree, near a tree," she mumbled. "John Henry always said he wanted to rest under a tree." Her confusion became terror when she saw no trees. "It was a different time of day then," she said. But there were only a dozen newly planted saplings with wire cages around their bases, no stately cypresses or oaks to dignify these poor dead lying in this brown field.

I get headaches in graveyards, a pressure of tight tears in the head, for no one in particular. It is Margaret that Margaret mourns for, as the poem says, no doubt; but here you felt angry, too, at the ugliness and run-down aspect of the place, big showy tombstones indifferently planted by a contemptuous dealer in tombstones when the bereaved had been led away, and the dead lay unprotesting under weeds and plastic flowers as uncomfortable as they always expected to be.

When I was little, in our town there was a little grave we used to go look at, said to be the grave of Charles Dickens's son. I guess I was eight or nine and so knew that Charles Dickens was a famous writer who had lived a long time ago, in another land, and it seemed thrilling that he had really been alive, in order to have had a son who must once have been alive, in order to have died; but it was horrible to think that this little boy had wandered into our town and died there, unknown and pitiful, perhaps without his papa knowing. He was a son, I was a daughter, someone's little girl, as liable as he or anyone else, if unlucky or unwise, to get lost in a strange town and to die there.

As John Henry had done in our town. Well, we hunted for the right skinny little tree. Osella put her wreath on the ground and strode off quickly in one direction. It was I who found him, going round a tree: Mrs. Ruby Baker, Cleotha Enobarby, John Henry Barnes, 1899–1967. I hadn't realized he was so old. I called Osella and she came briskly up, directing at me an angry look I understood, that she should have been the one to find John Henry, not I. "I knowed it was here someplace," she said, and I backed off, for some reason not wanting to turn my back on this new and unvisited grave.

I went to the car and read a book I'd brought and fidgeted thinking what Gavvy would say being left with the children so long, and how angry he would be about me getting a moving violation, until finally I went to say to Osella that we would come again soon. I suppose I expected her to be standing by the grave with a reverent, pained, pensive expression. Instead she was upended on the ground, her garters showing, and the bulges of bare skin above her stockings, her fat body shaking all over, her cheek laid against the earth, her hands pounding the earth with rage and despair, rage and despair the expressions of her contorted face.

I backed away again. I didn't know what to do about someone lying shaking on the ground. And it was now that I myself felt the palpable presence of John Henry himself, invoked by her desperate fists. I felt his menace and his thirst for vengeance upon those who had reduced his Osella to this pitiable, this ludicrous, this repulsive heap of grief and rage. I was afraid, I was shocked, and hid in terror in the car again but even there could sense his malevolent glare, his fury.

I am sorry to say I felt self-pity, too, that whatever insane grieving for a man felled you to earth, set you to writhing on graves, I could not feel for any man I knew. I was excluded and defective in this, too. That was before Andrew.

When Osella came to the car, I gave her a kind, a sympathetic smile and said I would bring her here soon again. Her face, which had been somber but at peace, contorted again into a snarl as if she had been turned into John Henry's ghost avenger. She shrieked at me, wild-eyed.

"What do you know, in your jeans, wearing them jeans? You don't think it makes no difference if a poor nigger's dead. You gonna find out, you gonna find out. Just a poor ole nigger, now let's go on back to the house, you say. Mr. Spinner he sent me one hundred dollars when John Henry passed, and you don't care for nothin, don't say no prayer over him, you don't pray over nothin. You just vicious and hardhearted . . ." Here she turned her face aside to make it smooth again, compressing her lips against the many and deeper reproaches that must have been springing to them, her eyes sliding around to watch me. Overwrought, distressed, I thought, trying to appear unnoticing, and opened the car door for her. It was all true anyway; I felt hard-hearted as a stone just then, and I never pray.

5 Well, I tried to pray, as it were, let me love Osella. I knew I was supposed to love her, poor unlovely woman we were exploiting; it was the least I could do. You feel like such a sneak disliking your victim and keeping this from him, but I didn't want to alienate Osella, I needed her.

As I said, things were so much better for me with Osella there. I could for one thing leave the house. Before that I could never leave the house, unless I took the babies all with me like a mother duck. Before with my short rope I could only graze in a small circle but now I relearned what roaming was like. My heart beat hard with pleasure just to walk into a store by myself; it was like a space walk.

Osella had come in May; in the autumn I went back to school. Gavin's father suggested this, that I go back and take some classes, for stimulation—his word. Stimulation is what I got, I guess. All restless mothers go take classes; this bothered no one.

I didn't say to anyone that I took school seriously, but I did; I had a university catalogue I would read hiding away in the bathroom, in a kind of fever reading over the requirements for various degrees and certificates, intoxicated with the idea of qualification and with the prospect of the orderly acquisition of information and experience, after which I would be certifiedly qualified for something. You could become a limnologist, an archaeologist, could learn Finnish or quantum mechanics.

Reverently I stood in the long registration lines meditating registration, certification, acquisition. I fearfully watched the faces of the young students. All the faces were radiant with intelligence. I was twenty-eight. I sat on benches watching students, covertly watching the handsome young men in their tight jeans. One day, walking across the library lawn, suddenly I felt my breasts exposed. Quickly, thinking my blouse had flown open, I jumped behind a bush, but my blouse hadn't flown open; it was just the feeling of fresh breeze or something else, touching my nipples.

I was relieved when the professors appeared to find nothing odd about my presence in their classes. Only in the context of my home, where people looked coldly and without interest at my books, or complained about my absences, did I feel renegade. The university smelled of hot dogs and marijuana and coffee and flowers. I did not tell Gavin what I learned in school; at school I didn't tell people I was a mother of four, either.

About this time Osella found a new outlet, too. "Outlet" is Gavin's mother's expression. Osella had been going to the Ephesian Church of God in Christ, and now she began to sing in the choir. The Ephesian Church was a church for black and white, she told us, and the choir was called the rainbow choir, which we made a lot of silly jokes about behind her back. We couldn't understand how Osella could be allowed to sing in the choir, she sang so badly and out of tune. And notwithstanding that, she got to be the lead singer, so she said. "Just let me try out this new one on you," she would insist, entrapping us on the porch or in the study, blocking the exit with her big body and emitting the terrible yelps and shrieks she called singing, shrill and tuneless hymns enjoining the Lord to do this and that. In the daytime she could be heard practicing, louder than the vacuum cleaner, louder than the washing machine, louder than the radio; she might have been intoning from the tops of minarets.

Well, this just went to show you, I thought, people's infinite capacity for self-deception. I didn't then notice what a good example of this I was myself. But Osella had convinced herself that she was a magnificent singer, and with the power of her conviction she seemed to have convinced the other parishioners. Maybe they went to show you about collective delusion, or maybe her fellow Ephesians encouraged her not because of the excellence of her singing, which was incontrovertibly awful, but because she looked so much like a gospel singer, so huge and fervid and fat, and she must therefore be one. Or maybe, we said, different standards of vocal beauty apply to gospel singing. Maybe sincerity, for example, or volume, counts more than tone.

Well, I thought, how nice she has this outlet; how nice I have that outlet, studying linguistics at the university; how nice Gavvy is getting on so well and planned now to leave off being an assistant district attorney and was instantly snapped up by an important law firm; I was so proud. Things were getting better.

Yet they got worse. I still have no idea why, at that stage, it should have been so. I can only remember the days and hours like snatches of a home movie, silent and incoherent, showing people at their household tasks or grinning insincerely.

Well, we all know it takes two to make a marriage, break a marriage or do anything; there are two sides to everything. The Famous Inspector should know I know this and am not trying to present either Gavvy or me as the villain murdering this marriage. Gavvy and I were antagonists, that's all. Our interests were opposed; maybe the interests of men and women fundamentally are. But I think Gavvy thinks of all women as his antagonists, except his mother—or perhaps mothers in general. I was not, did not seem to him, a mother, I am sure, but maybe more a sullen teen-ager metamorphosed into the reluctant superintendent of innumerable brats whom he was required to pay for, to pay attention to. I didn't realize I was supposed to earn their keep by providing Gavin with some mysterious form of nourishment, some female brew for which I didn't have the recipe. Or the inclination or time. I can imagine what this brew would be like, sticky, sweet and pungent, tasting of its own perfume: fish, milk, musk and honey. Well, perhaps that is my own taste, I will ask Andrew; but I brewed none of this brew for poor Gavin.

That is because he was disguised as a real grownup, sitting there behind his lawbooks in his study lined with many many many books, earning the approval of cigar-smoking important people still older—the dean of the law school, judges, Andrew and his partners—and earning the tears of criminals' mothers and criminals whom he caused, in his blue blazer with the gold buttons, to be taken away. Who could have imagined he was so hungry and frightened, and perhaps, crazy?

Same with Osella. And where is she now? What does she *do?* She can't just exist a disembodied voice over the telephone. Maybe Raider takes care of her, or the good people at the Ephesian Church of God in Christ. Maybe she has stolen away to Jesus and just steals back again to telephone now and then.

I wonder if she still telephones Gavvy. She had a little game she was playing with Gavvy, without me caring enough to notice. She kept things running so well around the house I hardly noticed anything. Someone tenderly watching my babies, someone cooking supper, all the shirts always ironed—what did I have to worry about?

But her little game, talking to him, me not noticing. I still don't know when she talked to him—in little snippets when he was driving her to the bus, maybe, or when he went in to mix an after-dinner drink. I can imagine how it went.

"I wish you seen what I sees," she would say, her big face with that pale, bland, moonlike quality smiling, dawdling over the sink. "It's jus as well you don't know what I knows." She was always saying that, or, "I got minnows in mah bucket would nip you if I spilt them," this great fat bully playing with Gavin's delicate firstborn-son sensibility. When I imagine him as a little boy, it is as a blue little boy, with chattering teeth, as if he had just gotten out of a cold pool, and transparent skin. I can imagine Osella's voice now affecting him with that same shiver, him staring into his ice cubes while her sweet soft voice goes on.

"Uh-huh, well, I ain't gonna be the one to tell you. I ain't like that. I done seen a lot of things. I sees a lot. I can prophesize. Oh, I done seen a lot of things in mah day, the things I could tell you went on at the Spinners'. But that's where I learned to keep mah mouth shut, I learnt that much, with Mr. Spinner being an important man, college president and such. I guess I can keep mah mouth shut around here, too."

Gavin would not at first have wanted to ask her what she was talking about, this maid, this servant, her innuendo trickling icily down his back. Osella would know he must finally ask. By what measure she could gauge the desperate torment she inflicted I don't know, but over the years, the things she done seen, I suppose she must have had an expert eye. She could certainly see more than I could.

Finally, I suppose, Gavvy asked, would have asked, and Osella, without looking up, hands in dishpan sloshing around, voice sweet, would have answered, "Well, Miss N.—Miss N. just a whore, you know. She sleep with anything in pants, your wife do."

6 Our quarrels, Gavvy's and mine, weren't about anything so Biblical, final and fierce as adultery, of course, and also they didn't arise from insanity, anybody's, just from ill humor and irritability. They would be about whether I had gotten the shirts from the laundry, say, or who had mislaid the telephone book.

Well, that's a good example. Let's say Gavvy comes home as usual, brow smoothed from all day being a respected attorney, but beginning to furrow at the unsanitary, disorganized unruly natures of children, for which I am responsible both genetically and by example, and then there's dinner, which he criticizes softly so Osella won't hear, usually some just criticism that would have been rendered unnecessary by a word of guidance from me in the kitchen earlier. Then dinner would be over and he would, let us say, need to find the phone book and would ask me where it was. From some other room I would grow prickly because he has said, "Where is the phone book?" between tightly clenched teeth.

"It should be there somewhere," I would say between tightly clenched teeth.

Then would come a crashing and in would come Gavvy pale and angry: "You can never find anything around this fucking house."

"I suppose it's my appointed duty in life to watch over the phone book, just in case you may want it, be a phone-book guardian, a . . ." my voice rising into unnatural and affected loudness, as if I were playing the part of a shrew in a play, but it would be my natural tone of voice.

"Just any half-wit could keep track of a telephone book, it isn't too much to ask . . ."

"Well, there are six people in this house who could have moved it, and I can't keep watch over every single thing, and—"

Then he would say his favorite thing, which would always splinter me up with rage into a million fragments like safety glass: "It's inexcusable. . ."

"I'm sick of hearing that," screams the shrew. "I

don't care what you think, you are not here to excuse me, you are not a judge, you are not my boss, I am not your employee . . ."

"Is it or is it not your job to keep this place habitable?"

"It is habitable. And I am not responsible for every phone book in it!"

"There are two phone books in this house and it is not unreasonable to expect to be able to find one of them."

"It's unreasonable to get upset about it. Other men don't get upset about things like that. Why can't you just enjoy things the way they are without always bitching about everything? Why don't you care about the things that count?"

"When you want to make a telephone call, it is the phone book that counts."

And he would have a point, that's just it. He always had a point. I don't know. People don't kill people over telephone books; they call Information, I would think.

All our fights were as boring as this, even the worst one, the one where Gavvy hit me—therefore, the one I remember best. It was set, I remember, against Osella's singing practice. She was downstairs singing and I remember thinking that if he killed me no one could hear. Perhaps he *was* going to kill me, and Osella, sensing it with her powers, had set up the funereal keening already.

In fact, all our fights were the same fight, after some prefatory differences—telephone books or laundry. It was as if each successive fight, from the beginning of our marriage, had been recorded on a long-playing tape which, after we introduced the new complaints (Where is the phone book?), we would compulsively replay all the way through, acting out the parts afresh, compulsively hurling limp hashed-out old grievances as if they still had the power to wound. It was intolerably boring, at least to me. I can remember during especially long bitter ones, conducted carefully in our bedroom to avoid frightening the children, me getting so sleepy I wanted to die, as if I were being tortured by Chinese brainwashers; I would babble my responses deliriously, Gavin's prosecutor voice grating on and on into nights, into days; finally I would pretend to cry into my pillow so that I could just sleep, anything to sleep.

The fights were all conducted in the same phrases but each phrase was just a formula, stood for pages and pages, a very long list, of hate and pain. I didn't understand this at the time, I admit. I didn't understand for example that every time Gavin said, "And then you bought that fucking chair," which he did say obsessively in the course of every fight, he really meant, "You defied me and went and did what you wanted just as you always do, causing me to feel unimportant and wretched and unattended, unlike my mother, who does what *I* want, which makes me feel manly, and, because it is an ugly chair which I hate, you are also assailing my comfort and my position in the household, making me feel unwanted and uncomfortable here: and by buying that hideous old secondhand chair when I had said not to, you were reproaching me financially, you were complaining that we couldn't afford a new one, another way of saying, as you constantly seem to, that now that we have all these loathsome brats I ought to disregard my personal development and think about earning money for them, something a man is not obliged to do, as I infer from my own family, where my father's career was sacrosanct and my mother's whole concern was my father, and instead you stick me with all these brats whom you don't even take care of properly, witness their dirty faces and wet pants, and have the nerve to complain to me about needing help and freedom when I did not ask you to bring all these brats into the world and when I did, good-naturedly, help you bring the chair home and help you upholster it, that's when I stuck the upholstery needle in my eye you were not sorry although I could have been blinded which is another way of saying castration which is really your game isn't it, isn't it?"

There were a number of other formulas: why don't you ever play with the children (me to G.); why don't you ever clean up around here (G. to me); you are rude to our friends (me to G.); you neglect our children and home (G. to me). We would trot these and others out at each quarrel like dominoes and line them up on the board. I was really dumb, I never did understand the game; I would dump over the board, screeching, "Why are you always bringing up that chair? Can't you forget it? Why do you want to ruin our family about some old chair, what a crazy obsession, sometimes I think you are crazy," and that's when he hit me, that one time, thunk, backhand across the face, the impact coinciding with a raucous shriek from Osella, "O Lord God, forgive us Lord."

I made no sound. I was too astounded. Nobody had ever hit me before. I guess Gavin had never hit anybody, either, because he looked as astonished as I, then slyly pleased, then full of sober apologies.

"It's all right," I said. "I'm all right," and went into the bathroom, and it was true, my face was all puffy and red. Thunk, something else had been knocked into place in my brain, too.

It's funny, with all the fights, that we never said the real things behind the things behind the things. For instance, I never said, "I hate the way you look. I hate the way your face, formerly charming, has become contracted by your inward fury and disappointment. I hate how you have grown so thin, and I don't care whether you suffer or not, I am not sorry for your personal pain, I even hope it gets worse. I hope your pain gets worse. I hope you wizen and shrivel still more. And then I hope you will die. Well, give us some money first, so we can live, then you die. I hope you die." I didn't even know I thought such things.

Maybe Osella knew I thought them.

"I has powers," I heard her say to Gavin. I had known she must be saying such things to him, but then I heard it for myself: "I knows."

"I don't want to know, Osella."

"I ain't gonna tell you nothin, but I knows all the same."

"I don't want to know *nothing*," Gavvy said, mocking her.

"It's *yo* wife, it ain't no never mind to me."

I heard this and then Gavin came out of the kitchen, his pretty face clouded, and, seeing me, startled. Then, shaking his head toward the kitchen in mock despair, he shrugged. I didn't realize then that she talked this way a lot, spreading poison like butter on his cornbread, sending smoky smirks along her narrow glance after me as I left rooms, or long looks of sorrow and sympathy, deep mystical sad looks for the children and Gavin. I didn't understand, but I didn't have anything on my conscience then, either. I was still thinking that things were getting better. In me I could feel an unfolding, a stretching out, to do with Osella being there to help me, our lovely children, my studies, Gavin's upcoming new job. Happy prospects. Gavin had grown thinner that year, his shoulders suddenly frail, and bought some new jackets for his new job—a blue blazer with bright buttons, and a tweed coat, and new spectacles with horn rims, which made him look older, and serious—and let his sideburns grow. "His hair jus the color of gold when he a baby," Osella said. "Jus like Petey. Them girls they got it, too, but it ain't a good thing in a girl. John Henry used to say a man got a blond woman got nothin but a sick bird gonna peck him and faint in they cage," and she would clap her hand to her mouth and laugh at my hair, which is the color of a broom.

Well, there were two, just two, possibly crazy incidents, which had frightened me, but not for very long: I did not consider that people are always being strangled or shot by people whose craziness they have not believed in. I wasn't scared enough.

The first time I had been upstairs, I remember, crying in the bathroom, I'm not sure why. Our bathroom had a fuzzy white rug and I would sit on it, my head between my knees like a patient in a madhouse, weeping as quietly as possible so as not to worry the children, with tears trickling down my legs. I had once burst into tears in front of them and, from a stricken horrified face of Petey's, had seen I must never do that again. It was the first he had realized, from his mother's tears, that a future of unbroken felicity could not be relied on. Being grown up was not what he had thought. I know they have to learn this, of course, but I wanted to keep it from them as long as possible.

I sound like I was an awful crybaby and I guess I was; I never cry now. But the point of mentioning it is, that's why I crept downstairs and outside as quietly as possible, so no one would see my puffy red face. I crept out the kitchen door leading to the path which passed below the window of Gavin's study. The bright glass of the window was almost opaque with the reflection of the garden, greens and streaks of violet, and beneath this mirrored brilliance, like shadows, like a glimpse into the spirit, like the shapes of the real beyond the forms—it seemed to me I could see the shapes of Gavin and Osella: Gavin sitting on Osella's lap.

A chill of terror caused me to stumble and lose my glimpse. I stepped quickly past the window knowing I anyway could not turn back to look again to see if it was a true sight I had seen. For it had, simultaneously, the unreal quality of a reflection, or perhaps of something in my own mind; the dark window was like a strong membrane between two views of reality. But surely among the

reflected flowers I had seen the figures—sitting, surely?—
in the big study chair, and some motion, I thought, of rocking, though even today I'm not sure, and it scarcely could
be true—Osella enfolding Gavvy in her huge arms rocking
him on her lap as she might Petey or Ivan.

Oh, the terror of the real beneath the form. I had only
been afraid of Gavin like this once before. Now as I
hurried on the path toward the play yard and the swings,
where Ivan and Polly were in the sandbox, my terror
diminished as swiftly almost as it had settled upon me.
I was not so sure after all that I had seen what I had seen.
I sat on the swing and pushed myself back and forth with
my foot, trying to recapture the exact configurations of that
glimpse. The more I pried with all my brain after that sight
and its meaning the more I got used to it, so that it lost its
terror and oddness and came to have a kind of reassuring
quality. Reassuring to know that Gavvy was in good arms.
At the same time it couldn't have happened, I knew, so I
tucked the sight away and swung in the swing and pushed
Polly and Ivan and didn't think of it any more.

But it made me remember the crib incident, which had
happened maybe a year before, and which I know I had
seen right. India had had chicken pox and we had moved
her crib out of the room she shared with Ivan into the hall
by our room. Gavin got up in the night to go to the bathroom. I, half asleep and half listening, heard the steps to
the bathroom and returning, and then the rattle of the sides
of India's crib and odd grunts as of an adult doing a difficult gymnastic. I thought he was picking her up. But
then came a long silence, which frightened me awake;
I went into the hall and there was Gavin lying curled up
beside India in her crib, his arms wrapped around himself without the coverlet, his eyes looking at me.

I screamed, stupidly. Osella's door downstairs
opened. "Get out of there!" I screamed. Gavin did; he just
climbed out and went silently back to his own bed. I lay in

mine for hours with open eyes, afraid to go to sleep for
fear of what this mad somnambulist might do next. But
then the next day he was all reassurance; he must have
been sleepwalking, had done so as a kid, didn't blame me
for being startled, was relieved he hadn't rolled over on
poor little India and squashed her. Office strains. The
Cameron case. Some much-needed rest next weekend.
And so, as always, I put it out of my mind, sort of.

7 Oh well, I don't suppose I need to go on about all
our quarrels, our estrangement. In most ways I
suppose they are usual and predictable. A Famous Inspector could chart by heart the stages of a disintegrating marriage—I suppose he would be a great student of human
nature. It makes me uncomfortable to find that the biggest
drama of my life should turn out to be like others, so alike
it is not even interesting to look back on it. With what feelings of singularity you lend yourself to each thrilling act of
girlhood, marriage, to the growing troupe of exquisite
babies with their tender fingers, like the beautiful mother
in a diaper ad you are, and then it begins to seep away, the
picture is torn off the billboard and torn into little bits and
these bits washed down a drain, a whirling vortex of dis-
appearing candlelight suppers, vanished pet names, ca-
resses down the drain. All gone. Shorn wet bodies shiver
slightly in the chill of the real sour air, their garments of
deception gone. The air smells of madness, and ill nature.
I avert my eyes from the sight of the engripping despair of
my former bridegroom, who is congealing without knowing
it. Embarrassment is what I felt, is what I feel.

The situation can be looked at from Gavin's point of
view, too. He told me a dream he had: there is Gavin, his
mind streaming tears, in a room filled with female figures,

with masks over their faces, their hands folded in their laps, bellies swollen, their forms quivering alternately bright or blurry through his tears; the room is filled under his feet with objects, treacherous wheeled things, plastic cars that crunch sharply under his feet, toy dogs uttering anguished shrieks, something slippery—baby oil—that nearly brings him down, and, his vision impeded by tears of both self-pity and rage, he must make his way across this alien and dangerous floor amid the rocking fertile female creatures who ignore him. Their unintelligible hum seems mocking. He thinks he will stride through the room bravely anyway to get to the refrigerator, but when he does there's nothing in it but bits of disgusting things he sees they are saving for him to step in.

He may hate these females, he may fear them, but what decides him to kill them? That's what I don't understand. From the newspapers I have figured out that most murders happen one of two ways; with the first kind, people are arguing, growing angry and angrier and angrier until their hatred is intolerable and someone reaches for something and puts an end to it, bang.

The other kind of murder is premeditated, brooded upon, done for revenge or gain. The first kind is commoner, but estranged husbands, I have counted up, do both kinds. They lurk, they brood. Here's one in the paper tonight:

FATHER KILLS ESTRANGED WIFE, CHILDREN OUTSIDE CHURCH

MINNEAPOLIS. A father of five waiting outside St. Anthony's Catholic Church in bitter winter weather shot his estranged wife and four young children as they came out of the eleven o'clock service while horrified bystanders and priest . . .

When Andrew and I became lovers and after Gavin and I were separated, I used to think that Gavin would come and shoot Andrew and me. I expected him to but he didn't, and the worry gradually went away until now. I know this is a foolish worry, considering that Gavin is a sane lawyer and Osella is literally mad. I know—but how do I know?

Whoever it is, I don't like waiting for him these evenings. With the settling dark the danger seems more immediate, and I remember things and hear things. I asked Ev not to watch the TV because I am afraid we wouldn't hear over its noise the noise of the stealthy hand fumbling our latches. Our murderer, to my mind, has supernatural powers. Walls will dissolve away, locks melt with the force of his malice. His malice can murder through walls. Our ears strain for footsteps outside, his hesitant scuffling, a murderer walking up and down unseen outside, finding chinks in the wall where he will put his fingers and push it in. A ratlike rustling chills us; we don't know if it's a person or not out there. It's just dark, we have had supper. I am writing this and Ev is reading a *True Confession* story, "I Need a Man Every Day." I think it's funny she should seek vicarious thrills when real ones threaten. "It ain't half thrillin enough," she says, "to take my mind off that poor cat with his eyes bulgin out." I am afraid to go to the window, and ought to be writing my essay on long "A." Will time forevermore drag silently and slowly like this, mind like a metronome ticking off the details of our persecution?

This afternoon after lunch when Ivan and India went down for naps, I took Polly and Petey with me to Bess's. I couldn't bear staying home, is all. We went along to the car, which was parked in the usual place in the open garage. On the windshield was another foul mess, apparently vomit. My own stomach lurched precariously but this was, after all, the second time for this; you get inured. If this sort of thing is all, I can bear it, I thought.

"Braaaagh, blaaagh," Polly and Petey said, excited with this second deviation from perfect peace occurring in their day. They were happy that we had to go to the car wash; I was glad, at least, that the gas tank was almost empty. If you fill up with gas at the car wash, your wash only costs 49¢ instead of $1.50. I am developing a core of calm resource and thrift, I told myself.

The men at the car wash looked impassive and un-judging as they washed the windshield, as though they were used to all sorts of human frailties splattered across the windshields of the world and it was their business to clean them, not to inquire.

But I was afraid, this new thing made me more afraid. Of course. I saw the world as through that windshield, through a film of someone's hate smearing everything over. But it was good to be reminded that our danger is real, the threats are real; I must be serious and serene, must pro-tect, must prevail.

Sometimes I scare myself with this idea: you are alone with someone you love and trust, whom you have always known, whom you were a child with, maybe, and have seen each other cry, and are known to one another's mothers. Now you are grown and it is a cloudless day, as blue as the eyes of your friend. The two of you are away in the coun-try, I imagine lying under a pasture tree surrounded by all the innumerable pleasures of exquisite days—fragrance, the grass to lie on, blue flies singing, your picnic lunch in a basket and the friend smiles over you at this moment of perfect repose, of perfect rapport; leans toward you smil-ing, and then his hands are around your neck, crushing your neck, but even when you are dying still you cannot see anything in the blue eyes that you had never seen be-fore; they are the last thing you see, illimitably familiar and strange.

"I know who it is," Bess said when we were safely at her house and had told her about it all. "It's the checker you insulted at the market."

I *had* insulted a checker at the market. I suppose I ought to note that incident. Had gone to the market—this was a couple of weeks ago, just before Christmas—and I was worrying about not having heard from Andrew, so it must have been at least that long ago, before the letter. Anyway, had bought a whole week's worth of groceries, feeling surly and detached, and depressed also about the approach of Christmas. I'd assembled an enormous grotesque cartload of food and was waiting in a huge line, numbly shuffling along, listening to idiot conversations on every hand and viewing moronic assemblages of disgusting TV dinners in other people's carts (I am trying to reproduce my frame of mind then); finally got to the check stand, piled up my provisions on the conveyor belt, had written out my check except for the amount of purchase, and was standing patiently. Impatiently. But the checker, a lively handsome brown Mexican girl, kept not checking me out. Someone came and asked for change. Someone came and asked to buy a pack of cigarettes. She rang up the cigarettes and used the last of the cash-register tape. Had to change the roll. Another checker had to come help her. Then another checker asked the price of something and they began a conversation about it. At this, something inside me, some spring of impatience and frustration, sprang, and I tore the check in half; "Forget it," I said, and stalked away leaving the torn check and all the groceries heaped up in front of her, thinking even as I did so what a dumb thing that was to do, now I have to go to another market and go through the whole stupid thing over again, what was the point of a stupid gesture like that, and so on, so that I hardly noticed until I almost bumped into her that this girl, in a livid fury, me having evidently violated more deeply than I knew some Latinate code of civility, had flung herself from behind her counter into my path with her hands outstretched toward me in claws, hissed something I didn't properly hear and then pulled back, turned away with the other checker screaming warning. The other customers stood all around in a silence of embarrassment or disapproval, naturally angry at me for the extra delay while she cleared away my pile of groceries, no wonder.

And as I slunk out I noticed the two torn halves of my check in her apron pocket.

"Yes, Inspector, we knew the deceased, a well-known troublemaker in the neighborhood stores."

"Of course that's it," Bess said, laughing. "It's her way of saying you make me sick."

For Bess the perils of the world are nothing, speaking of their power to terrify and kill, compared to the perils you encounter in the dark abysses of your mind, strange powers there which drive you straight into the arms of murderers or under the wheels of buses. I've never been able to guess the sinister powers Bess has met in her own mind, through being psychoanalyzed, but she claims to have met them all right; she talks of them with the genial candor of the psychoanalyzed, but I've never been impressed. She was molested by a baby-sitter or something, is all. It seems to me her real problem, Lynnie, is tangible and external.

Bess is Bess Harvill, that is, wife to Joe Harvill, senior partner in Briggs, Harvill & Mason, and she has been a true friend to me when it might have been expected she would henceforward after our divorce have attended only to Gavvy, junior member of the firm, and in the interest of her long acquaintance with Cookie Mason deplore the adulterous currents which threaten to rend the flawless harmony of Briggs, Harvill & Mason, or to deplore it in behalf of good wives everywhere, or just to keep generally to the safest social sailing, but instead she has been a good helpful true friend to me. So of course to me it seems that however riddled her heart is with dark secrets, and however riddled *mine* is—for she tells me, doubtless correctly, that I'm not aware of a hundredth of them—anyhow I am very lucky in having this friendship.

Bess is impervious to fear because her heart is pure; her strength is as the strength of ten. My impure heart is what renders me so craven, so craven I am almost enjoying the fearfulness of the past few days. Is that true? Well it's exhilarating, and to the extent that it's a reflex of my own feelings of guilt (for I'm not so unsophisticated in these matters as Bess and maybe the Famous Inspector may think), it is a worthy state—even noble, like the fear felt by freedom fighters in countries run by cruel generals. I feel I have done right to sin against the Law. I am fearful yet resolute.

8 This state of mind, fearful yet resolute, has gone on a long time, and I know the exact moment it began, luring me to crime, if you can put such an immodest name to my pursuits. Entering into fear and liberty is exhilarating and elating as it must be to fly in an open plane, but also the thin air makes you giddy and liable to error.

My error was to think you can do as you please. My life is not a good argument for this view but my heart believes it. Maybe my life is ashes but I still believe it.

I believe sometimes things are shown you by symbols and predictions. Standing before a picture in a museum, you are suddenly overtaken by tears, or you have cut yourself and a bloody gash lies across your palm. When I was still married to Gavin, at the end, I lost my wedding ring; I had grown thin. It slipped off my finger and sank into the sand of the play yard and could not be found.

On this day, early morning, I looked out into the leafy tree that screened the window of my dressing room and someone seemed to look back at me. I thought at first it was a person, a person with a black corsair eye which glared at me, a beaked face, hooked like the nose of a dream lover glaring reproachfully at my pale life, but, also, recognizing me as someone greedy and desiring.

But it was not a person, it was a bird, and this was

more shocking yet, chilling—an immense bird of yellow and green. A parrot, in fact. I was soothed for an instant, a parrot escaped, a poor baffled creature. I could look in the paper for the owner. But this reasoning thought did not still the racing of my blood, nor could I wrest my imprisoned stare from his staring eye. He knew me. Then he flew away, on immense wings, like a hawk. Unclipped wings.

When I told Osella, she was not surprised. "Imagine, a parrot, wild, flying free in North America," I was saying, and she looked at me with an expression full of signification and said, "Oh, it's you, is it? I been wonderin. I might have knowed. Well, then, I expect you did see a parrot, you sure did."

All that day and all the next my head was full of parroty phrases of wifely love and obedience and motherly concern but my voice developed an odd croak as I said them. With my keen parroty eye for spotting little running rodents far beneath me, I saw the creatures of my household newly. Poor Gavin had grown so thin. How could those attenuated little arms embrace me? That other one was so fat; perhaps she was consuming him? Why doesn't she keep her kitchen cleaner? I spied into drawers like a contemptuous stranger.

The day after that I stopped parroting affectionate phrases. I glared with lidless eyes. To Gavin it must have seemed that his wife had left, and he told me later that it was about this time that he started going by himself to "Adult" movies, embarrassedly, furtively, not himself knowing why. He would call and say he was working late; then he would stop at such a movie, blushingly shove his three dollars at the ticket girl and duck in, and there be filled almost immediately with shame and dash shamefully out.

Me, I felt myself to have grown bright green wings, and to have grown them to some purpose, so I flew home one afternoon about three weeks later with one of my professors, as I had been wanting to. A mild owlish bachelor accustomed to seductions, set up for them with an apartment in the Heights, fancy, with soft sofas. There I allowed myself to be undressed, explored, me watching him all the time at his explorations, with my beady bright eye studying his responses as attentively as I might hang upon his opinion of my seminar papers. How pleased I was that I could make him pant and quiver, that I had, evidently, my share of female power beyond that which had been conferred upon me legally by the rite of marriage. And I had an appetite, or the beginning of an appetite, after that long time in a cage. It was terrific. I loved it. And there began my life of crime.

My life of crime had nothing to do with falling in love with Andrew; that came later. Falling in love with Andrew reformed me, or has ruined me forever. Well, they say no one is so earnest, so convinced, so fanatical in his rectitude as the sinner reformed. I have the reform view of True Love now. Now I can't imagine the embraces of another man; Andrew has got my body and my imagination both. I am in a smaller cage than ever.

Well, thinking about it, I suppose that calling myself a criminal and a hawk is a bit grandiose for what was after all ordinary adultery. Bess would laugh, and a Famous Inspector, too, if he had a sense of humor, which on the whole I think he hasn't but takes a traditional view of such things. But it's funny that seeing a parrot should have set me off. You never know what will set someone off. I beleaguered my friends with talk of omens.

"Death," they usually said. "Birds presage death." But my presentiment then was not of death.

9 My life lit up like a Christmas tree. I had gotten the idea that I had the solution to it, to getting through life with Gavvy and the children: I would have lovers, discreetly; by lovers be put into a kindly frame of mind to be good to Gavin and the children, made more cheerful. I had been freed, I thought, by that parrot sight, by it somehow enabled to see that although everybody could not expect in this world to have a perfect marriage, a resourceful adult could adjust, could come to terms with life. Lovers would just be one of the terms of mine. I *know* what a detective would think about this. But I am obliged to tell it. I would have lovers at least until I had satisfied a deep, deep feeling I had, I think it was of curiosity; it was the same hotting up of the blood I felt when I went to the library, though of course more intense, something seeming to pump the blood around in my veins noisily when I even thought about the warm future peopled with strong-hearted, witty lovers and covert lunches. I thought no nonsense about love, but about charm, affection, long furtive afternoons of lovemaking, except Thursday afternoons when Osella was off; then I would stay home and tell enchanting stories to my children. All this would have to be enough. Most people, after all, did not have so much —did they?

I still don't know how Osella knew. She dropped dark, smirking hints into his drink, along with his ice cubes, in whispers in the kitchen, or whenever it was she told him.

Maybe she could smell sex. Sometimes when I came in she would look at me so long and keenly that I would look away, and she would expand her huge chest with a deep breath and exhale and sigh and turn and shuffle off, her shoes, where she had trod over the backs, flopping against her bare pink heels.

I don't know whether Osella has a need for or a horror of sex. Perhaps something horrible had happened to her. Maybe something with Mr. Spinner. She made up fears about sex. For instance she would say, "You better watch Petey, you don't want him doin nothin to his little sisters.

I knows about kids," or, if the children rolled and scuffled, "Don't you let him get up top a her that way," this when they were about five and seven.

Maybe she had been raped by her brothers. But I could never think that Osella's feelings about sex could be personal, except for her clearly quite personal interest in Mr. Spinner's tool. Because of her giant body you could not imagine her having so much awareness of its needs. "Imagine fucking Osella," Gavvy said once, and we squirmed with horror. But now—I wonder. Perhaps she felt a greater, a huge need, the whole of her feeling, as I do, the smooth swelling, the pulsing throat, the need for a man's hand stroking my belly, his lips there, a man hard inside me.

But I would conceal from a police inspector my need for a man. It wouldn't dispose him to look any farther for our murderer. An adulteress in her blood, by her nature, must seem worse than an adulteress from principle or circumstance. A wanton woman is her own murderer, having first slain womanliness, delicacy, virtue, isn't that so?

Maybe Osella knew, and maybe Osella tried to warn me, but I didn't catch on. I remember one afternoon I came home from my adventuring and Osella sitting at the kitchen table rolled her eyes around on me, eyes wearing an expression of groggy fury I had come to see there more and more often, not recognizing it, though, for madness.

"I sees things," she said.

"What've you seen today, Osie?" asked I gaily; I felt happy.

"I seen Mr. Spinner in the woods once," she said. "I wasn't but seventeen or so. Me and John Henry been marrit a couple a years but I dint tell John Henry. I had done gone back there to get some crab apples, I believe. This was summertime. Mr. Spinner he a very high-suited man, spent lots of money on them fine clothes he wore. That man was a fine preacher, too. When I heard him practicin these speeches—he give them at the college for they commencin activities—I always like to shouted myself. He had a gift.

"Miz Spinner she cried to him nights. I heard them once in a while. But she never had nothin to cry about I could see, as they was rich, and that man never lif a hand to her, and he was good to they kids. A dignified man, bein a college president.

"So I went back woods to get me some crab apples, and I come up on a glade and there I seen Mr. Spinner with one of the girls from the school, red-headed, looked like she didn't have no eyebrows or eyelashes. I seen her close up once after that. Nekkid, both of them was. This girl was layin on her back with her knees stickin up and Mr. Spinner was kissin her knees.

"That did seem passin strange, now dint it, kissin knees? Just lovin up them skinny knees. I stop back in the bushes and just watched in amaze, only one thing ever did make me feel more strange since then." A long sly glance at me.

"Oh, Osella, how embarrassing, did they see you?" I asked.

"Nobody sees Osella if she don want to be seen," she said, smirking as if she had been invisible watching me naked that afternoon.

Well, among these innuendos, grimaces, distant silences, we all—Gavin, Osella and I—lived along like this awhile. But like canaries in a mine we sickened on the sour air of our household, and one after another we began to show the symptoms of the toxic poison, Gavin next. It was about a week after this that Gavin came up to bed one night and said, "I've decided to get myself fixed."

I was reading in bed and looked up surprised, not knowing what he meant, or thinking he meant fixed, healed.

"God knows we've got enough kids and I never want

any more." Then I understood but I just stared. I suppose I should have been pleased, since it was I who had to wear the diaphragm or else swallow pills, which made me queasy, or have the babies and care for them. But it sounded like a terrible idea.

"What if I died, or we got divorced and you married someone else?" I said.

Suddenly he was screaming. "Why do you say that? What a horrible thing to say!" he screamed. He was white. Then he became controlled: I wouldn't want any in any case; it's a simple operation, it doesn't affect the libido; social responsibility, sensible.

"I know," I said, "they do it to you in underdeveloped nations in the train depot."

"You have to sign this paper," he said, handing me a paper, spreading it out on the book on my lap, and putting a pen in my hand. "To avoid subsequent litigation."

My hand hung.

"I can't think of any objection you could possibly have," he said.

"I'm signing, but I don't like it. It seems like something we should discuss. We should have long discussion . . ." But I signed, because I was frightened. I thought he had figured out my real objection, which was what if I got pregnant, then I couldn't tell him it was his.

This recollection lends a certain congruous irony to my present situation, I think. Actually, about Gavvy, I do not know if the operation was ever performed.

10 Like canaries in a mine, in the sour air of our household we continued to sicken, next Osella. On a Monday morning she said to me just as I was leaving to take Polly and Petey to school, "You and me has to talk serious about my burden."

"Your burden?" Why were people saying these bewildering things to me?

"It's gettin too much. Two years I borne it. I has to
let it drop, if you don't cooperate. If I can't bear up I'll
have to leave, and then you know what would happen, or
maybe you don't know, the children would all die before
they was twenty-one."

"Run out to the car," I said to the children, who were
looking, naturally, rather alarmed.

"What do you mean talking that way in front of them,
Osella?" I said.

"I'm tellin you I can no longer bear mah burden," she
said more loudly, and I noticed that her eyes were that way
again, drugged and narrow. "Two years I borne it now."

"I know things are difficult around here," I said. "You
can see that. Gavin and I—strains—we should give you
more money, but—Big Raider?—strains—" I don't know
what I said, exactly.

"You want me to spell it out?" she said. "You think I
don't know what's wrong?"

Now my heart absolutely stopped with crafty attention. How could she really know? Did she? Why was she
saying all this right now on a busy morning? What *was*
wrong, when it came to that? Were things not getting
better?

"Spell it out," I said with unconcern like a princess.
I imagined she would accuse me of deceiving Gavvy and
then I would deny it and sweep out insultedly.

"Right, all right, then. I knows you is witchin," she
said. "You think I don't know about your witchin? All the
strength I have is holdin you back. Oh, for a while I didn't
know as it was you or Gavvy, which one. But I knowed it
was someone, someone here witchin. I could feel the evil
upstairs and now I ain't goin upstairs any more. Mah
strength is gone."

"Oh, for God's sake, we'll talk about it later," I snarled

and rushed out exasperated; what new stupid thing was life going to bring now? Witching was I?

In fact some pictures in our bathroom were witch pictures, little drawings on bark used for witchcraft in Mexico. I think I had told her that. So I put it right out of my mind for then, witching indeed, and I went to my class and then to the library until time to pick Petey and Polly up again, refusing to employ my mind even one minute on this new nutty thing of Osella's any sooner than I had to. That's how I was in those days, more force and resolve, and not, like now, maundering and irresolute.

So I was so blank-minded when we came home and up the steps and saw a litter of charred wood and paper burning and smoldering on the kitchen doorstep that I couldn't even think what it might be. Closer up, we could see it was of course the pictures—you could make out bits of burnt paper and broken glass and the charred frame—but also there was a slightly charred doll dressed in a scrap of cloth from a dress I had sewed myself. This doll had mostly escaped the flames, so I saw what was what.

There was Polly's doll Mabel, dressed in my dress, her legs burned off, finishing in melted stumps, and a paring knife stuck through her belly. I picked up Mabel, mostly to hide her from Polly, so Polly wouldn't see her, and put her in my book bag.

Angrily I stamped in and called for Osella. She was coming down from upstairs, I listened impatiently for her fat slow steps. Then she lurched strangely into the kitchen, madness streaming off her like oil, madness showing in the swaying gait, in the white rolling and smoldering of her eyes, so that I could only think in a sick sudden panic of the burned bodies of Ivan and India; Osella had gone mad. Where were they? And I began to scream and scream for them, backing sweating away from Osella, Ivan, Ivan, India, India. Then I could hear them upstairs squeaking "Mommy's home" serenely.

83

"I smelt somethin burnin and it was them devil pictures," Osella said, her voice sounding normal and calm in spite of her deranged aspect. I stopped backing away in that craven fashion and stood forward to deal with this. "Go outside," I told Petey and Polly, but they didn't; they lingered behind me. I was shivering.

"I done smelt somethin and I knowed to expect trouble so I went up there and right before my eyes they done burst into flames. I had knowed they was ready, but I didn't think they was ready yet. I don't read that close."

"Osella, you burned them." Maybe she was drunk. She looked drunk. Ivan and India were clumping on the stairs and Osella was blocking my way to them. Her huge body took almost the whole space between the counter and the kitchen table.

Osella looked at me. "*You* burnt them," she said. I saw that she believed this. It was then I really understood that Osella was raving mad. I had never seen anyone raving mad before; there is no mistaking it when you look close. What did you do? And *then* I saw that in her hand beneath her apron she was carrying the bread knife. She had had it upstairs with her; she hadn't picked it up since she came into the kitchen. What had she been going to do with it? Maybe slaughter Ivan and India, and I felt faint.

"Osella," I said, so scared but walking around the table within her reach, slowly inching around to get to Ivan and India, "I forgot we have to go visit Mrs. Harvill. I promised to take the kids over there. We're late. I'll go up and get India and Ivan." Around the table safely, Osella swaying, hand still on bread knife but not lunging toward me. Ivan and India dragging junk down the stairs; I grabbed them up by the arms, one little kid on each side, them screaming with outrage, scuttled down the hall with them, through the living room, and put them out the front door: you stay out here.

Back in the kitchen, Osella had stood unmoving this whole time at the kitchen table, her one hand outspread on it, leaning on it supporting herself, in the other hand the bread knife and in the eyes that look, that helpless drugged crazy look.

"Petey and Polly, go out to the car," I said to them in that reserve fierce voice that children do obey; they opened the kitchen door and backed out like timid little visitors, and I backed out the stair passage again, watching Osella, until I could get out the front door. India and Ivan, disconsolate tots, brightened to see me, and they giggled excitedly.

"Osella made a big fire. It went whoom up to the ceiling," Ivan said.

"Walk with Mommy," I said, picking up India. Petey and Polly were already scuttling down the garden steps toward the car. Osella had come as far after us as the open kitchen door and now began to emit loud terrible howls.

"I done saved them babies!" she screamed. "Them pictures was killin them. I tried to keep you off." Now her voice became an exhausted whisper: "Mah strength is gone, mah strength is gone. I done told Gavvy he haf to hep hisself now. I done tried. Gavvy he so blind. Well, Gavvy a blind man that's gonna see light. I been carryin this weight, but mah strength is gone."

In her hand the knife. Slowly walking toward us. Scurrying, stumbling, down the steps to the street we went, and I threw the kids in the car and got in and locked the doors around us. It wouldn't start. I suppose I flooded it. Osella put her face against the windshield, glaring in at us through the window as if we were fish, the children laughing but scared, patting the glass her nose pressed against, or she was the fish, her mouth going and going, bubbles of mad rage coming out which we could hardly hear but only could see her opening and closing mouth.

"We will not look at her," I told the children. "We will

pretend we cannot see or hear her. Then if she goes away we will open the car doors and jump out and run to Lynnie's house."

In the end that's what we did. After about ten minutes Osella seemed to tire of us, or to become confused and to forget what it was she wanted of us, and she wandered off back up the steps and stood at the top looking down on us. There was a chance she meant to trick us into coming out, fancied herself swooping down like a revengeful witch, but we could outrun her; she couldn't do stairs fast. At the agreed moment children and I burst from car and began to run away. At the top of the steps I saw Osella lurch but whether in pursuit I don't know. We just ran.

It is strange to be fleeing for your life along your own block with no one noticing much. We slowed to a walk, walked as fast as we could, me carrying India. Did we wear harried excited faces? We passed people walking their dogs, and at the sight of them I would get a big confessional lump in the throat wanting to tell them that although we looked normal too, hurrying along the street, it was really that the maid had gone crazy and was trying to kill us with a bread knife. But then I would turn my eyes away and sidle past them, ashamed to be a person someone wants to kill. Maybe you think the stranger will turn against you, too. Each new person that we passed increased our terror.

I can imagine running down a long street, and someone gone berserk, a knifer or a rapist, is chasing you; you are too frightened to scream but all your power is concentrated in your heart, pushing you along in a frenzy. But you are getting tired; you are running more slowly, and his steps are closer behind you. Then, thank God, from an open doorway a figure steps out with a face of calm mercy and beckons you to shelter and safety. This happened to someone, I read about it in the paper: a figure steps out with mercy and you rush to him, fling yourself into his haven. Then as you look at him the warm flood of relief is checked with a gasp, a cry, for he is laughing at you with mocking malicious eyes. Together your assailant and your rescuer press you into the doorway, laughing, with the points of their knives against your belly. In my imagination they both look like the Famous Inspector, who in turn looks like my lover Andrew Mason. Funny.

But anyway then, swiftly as they always do, madness and terror passed over like cloud shadows and we were at Bess's sane house, and I rather relished saying with great aplomb, "Osella has gone crazy, I'm afraid; there's something strange about her eyes and she's burnt me in effigy." The children were laughing; Bess, too. After fright comes such elation. We thought we could hear the sound of dim shrieks from the direction of our house.

"But from here it sounds much the same as when she's singing," Bess said. "Maybe she's just singing." And other noises on the still afternoon air. It was just possible she was smashing things up. Something would have to be done. I called Gavin, who surprised me by saying he would come home. You never knew with Gavin; he had not come home when Polly broke her leg.

Bess minded the children. I know she minds my children for me more than I mind Lynnie, but she likes to, because they provide normal company for Lynnie.

Gavvy and I went back to our house, hesitating outside, hearing from within not shrieks but a lot of heavy thumping, and things being dragged around. "You stay here, I'll go in alone," Gavvy said, which made me laugh, it was so like a line from a movie. Indeed the whole thing was. Self-consciously we addressed ourselves to the unreal actuality that our maid had gone crazy. Gavin went in and came out almost immediately carrying the kitchen knives. "You're right, she's had some kind of break," he said. "She's packing her clothes but we should try to get her to a hospital. You go back to Bess's and call an ambulance."

But it was too late. Osella put all her clothes into a taxi and was driven off, the black taxi driver ignoring Gavvy's remonstrances, protectively driving her off. The ambulance came and went away again empty. This was the first time I completely understood that you may live with someone peacefully enough for a long time—years, maybe decades—and then one day they can look at you with eyes of blazing hate and go away in a taxi never to be seen again.

In the night when Gavvy was asleep, deep breathing and he always seemed so sweet and at peace then, I crept downstairs to the kitchen where I had left my book bag and took Mabel out. Twisted melted stump legs, knife in her belly, a dress made out of my dress. I looked at Mabel's dress, neatly sewn. Little sleeves, it had, even, and a snap to fasten it at Mabel's neck and a rent in front over the belly where the knife had savagely gone through.

11 I have never seen Osella again. For me it is as if she had died and her disembodied voice comes back from the spirit world along the telephone wire carrying whispered words of hatred. Sometimes she calls every day, sometimes not for a week or so. Where can she have hidden herself, in her hugeness, her madness, but in some demonic place to sit beside John Henry's malign corpse plotting things? I mean, I can't understand how she could be, say, in an apartment at Stockton and Twelfth and singing in her church choir on Sundays. What is she doing for money? How does she avoid being carted away by the first person who really looks in her soft deranged eyes?

She did come back once, when I wasn't home, and talked to Ev through the kitchen door. That was before we moved to this unit; I've never seen her around here.

"Hello," she said to her black sister, smiling; "I come to see if mah babies wouldn't like to go for a walk with they ole mammy Osella. I been walkin by." Ivan and India crowded to the door with noisy shrieks of joy to see her, but Ev saw Polly's scared eyes, I guess, for Polly remembered, and Ev said, "No, they can't come out today, N. expectin them to stay in."

"Lord, woman, jus down the street, Osella's goin buy 'em some ice cream. Let 'em come out in the yard here."

"Ice cream! Ice cream!"

"No," Ev said, "you get along from here," in her polite voice, and shut the door.

"Nigger slut!" Osella shrieked, and then, they said, she stood quietly outside the door for maybe fifteen minutes, holding her big plastic pocketbook, and then waddled away down the steps.

I don't know if Gavin has ever seen her again. He tried to find her at first. When she began her phone calls with "things to tell," he would try to talk her into meeting him somewhere so he could catch her and get her to a doctor. "Yes, I want to hear these things you have to tell," he would say to her on the phone; "why don't you meet me?" But she was too cagey for that.

Instead she told her "things" over the phone, lies so excessive I stopped worrying whether Gavvy would believe them. She was working for a movie star. She was soon to be married to the famous Big Raider. She was being kept in a house with seventeen rooms and a swimming pool until her marriage. She had been offered a singing career, and, endlessly whispering it, "Miss N. just a whore, you know, you ought to see what she do; I seen her in the woods, with a man between her knees," and Gavvy would listen endlessly, rocking patiently to the monotonous sibilance, telephone held loosely as if he wasn't listening at all, making faces to communicate his boredom.

"Maybe she'll say something that'll give a clue to where she is," he explained, but she never did, but just called and ranted and Gavvy listened.

And shortly, oh, in not too many days at all, while we were dressing to go out, Gavin said, "There are marks on your neck." I looked in the mirror. There were; so what. I picked up my hairbrush.

Calmly he asked, "Who are you having an affair with?"

The scene is very clear. I watched it in my mirror: my eyes flying open in innocent astonishment. Various denials springing to my lips while Gavvy stares over my shoulder into the mirror, into my mirrored face, and fixes my gaze with his own knowing and deep eyes which seem to contain both the blood-and-bone knowledge of the cuckold and the practiced, courtroom knowingness of the Assistant District Attorney. I mentally review my case and my chances.

"Don't be silly," I say, and go on brushing my hair.

Gavin traces with his finger a scratch on my back I cannot see but can feel the soreness of, and I shrink, not from pain but from his touch. He senses the nature of my revulsion and smirks unpleasantly at this confirmation of his guess.

Then I attack him: "Ask Osella, she knows what I do, I tell her everything. She'll be happy to tell you everything she knows." I turn to walk away. Gavin opens his mouth, steps back; I essay an amused sarcastic laugh at the whole silly discussion.

"Osella is crazy, but what she says is true, all the same," Gavin said. "She knows things intuitively, and I intuitively know she's right. I realized when she started talking about it over the phone. She used to hint and I didn't pay any attention. Now that she raves, I somehow know she's right." And I intuitively knew that he knew that she knew, so there we were.

Then there followed a long silence or else one of those split seconds which expand in recollection because of the number and complexity of the many thoughts and considerations the mind reviews, perhaps simultaneously — truths, possible lies, consequences, probabilities. I saw images of Gavin's anger superimposed upon his presently calm face, I felt a certain leaping of excited blood, as before a battle — all this and more, however long it took, us swaying there, and finally I said, "Well, if you know already, why ask?" and turned indifferently away.

Now Gavin stepped around in front of me and I saw that this did not end the matter; this was no friendly chat. His face seemed to be dissolving in ripples, as if someone had dropped a rock in the middle of it; his eyes swam. I caught a glimpse of a sort of seaweed of demons behind them. It occurred to me crazily that I had gotten the curse of seeing into people's brains through their eyes, but then the glimpse closed over. I couldn't understand his face at all. I had no sense of personal danger.

"Oh, my darling," Gavvy said in a mumbling way, as if his teeth had dislodged. He breathed deeply and put a hand on each of my shoulders as if we were going to have a man-to-man talk. I was just in my slip, I think, because my shoulders were bare.

"We've had a lot of trouble," he said, "too many kids, all those years of my law school, neither of us is an easy person to live with. I suspect most couples face this moment some time or other."

A courtroomy quality had crept into his voice. My vigilance relaxed, was replaced by a distinct cold feeling at the base of my spine which climbed it like mercury and diffused into my shoulder blades. I did not understand this sensation but attended to it minutely, distracting from what Gavin was saying, but he was giving a peroration about our marriage, its trials and difficulties, about commitment and understanding, about unity and our children, about trying, about the sanctity of the home, about his great love for me and for our children. Gavin a veritable marital Clarence Darrow. Mutual forgiveness. No one is ever blameless. He for example was not blameless. And he knows he had not been as helpful, as supportive as he might have been. I, on the other hand, must know that I have not been all the things—enumerated—all the things I should have been. Gentle, urgent voice speaking searchingly into my face, hands gripping my shoulders, his pretty blond curls rumpled, face all earnest dimples. Blue shirt.

"I won't press you about it, and I promise I won't bring it up again. Just give me your word you'll break off this affair, and that will be that. We'll start over. Sometimes, I think, these shocks can be healthy, can bring everyone to a sense of what he has at stake, to reexamine the relationship, or to galvanize the situation. That was probably your motive at some level—did you ever think of that? To bring about a confrontation. And I *am* shocked, in the best sense. I really have come to my senses about a lot that's been happening between us; how destructive Osella has been, for example. I see what we have to do. We can do it. Tell the person—I won't ask who it is—that it's over. Break it off. The important thing is *us*. I've really awakened. It's worked, it's no longer needed. But you can understand that I would have to know the affair is over. You can understand that. I won't pry, won't ever ask, just tell me when you've broken off and together we. . ." So good in court, it is said of Gavvy, so earnest, boyish and convincing.

"No," replied an inner witch insolently in my voice.

"No?"

"No, I won't break off. No, that is, I won't stop doing whatever I'm doing if I've been doing anything, which I by no means admit. I will do what I want. Stop bothering me, and stop telling me what to do. I will do what I want," or other words like this spoken with a thrilled and rising abandon.

"Of course, if you've found somebody who really matters to you, that makes it more serious," Gavin said, preserving his judicious tone, "but I doubt, when you consider carefully, that the reality situation . . ."

It was that I had identified the chill in my backbone; I had understood it was my deep dislike for Gavvy. I don't like you, I don't even like you, over and over in my head like going over railroad tracks with all the excitement of wild dashing. And then the inner devil or brattish child began to scream in my voice, quite insanely, I suppose, "I *will* do what I want, I *will* do what I want!"

At this, dearly beloved—I can hear the mellifluous tones of some Famous Inspector instructing his flock—here, my children, here in this corpse you see the embodied or rather, unhappily, the disembodied perils of erotic self-indulgence and willfulness. Of these the principal sin is willfulness. A person cannot do just what he wants.

But I think I only meant, I will do what I want now because that is more honest than to do as I ought. Trash, Osella always spoke of, and it is trashy to live with someone you dislike and pretend to like him and pretend to love him and talk to him and feed him, when all the time you love someone else.

Then Gavin ran mad, his face a field of throbbing knots. I thought, well, here is the second, maybe the third person to run mad here recently, counting this outburst of mine, but I had myself subsided and watched blankly as he raved and went through my dresser drawers "looking for evidence," he said, and packed his own clothes and piled his thousands of books into the car ("What's Daddy doing, what's he doing?" "Moving his books") in a kind of efficient frenzy, and I floated dim-wittedly about on the driveway, confounded by my sense that although something important was happening here, I was not adequately grasping it or coping with it. The children were infected by the excitement of it but not, I hope, by the deep poison of hate and finality that had seeped into the air. They did not seem to sense it, and I'm glad of that.

"You were very stupid," Gavin said, following me back into the kitchen. "I made you a generous offer, to forget your infidelity. I can use this against you, you know. I can take the children, I probably will. How will you live? No judge on earth would—you made a mistake—I was very generous . . ."

I don't suppose I said anything back. I was beginning to be scared that he wouldn't go after all, but he did, drove away in his car, and when I went into the kitchen with the children, there was no Gavvy, just as there was no Osella. They had left. Was I a sinking ship? There was, I remember, a feeling of deep deep peace.

The deep deep peace, the balmy, lidless solitude of the deserted. How I hate it now and how I loved it then, not needing to speak to anyone or answer them, or answer to them. Cold reality of course set in, but not then. Then I locked the doors and windows ceremoniously, with my little train of children went around the house locking everything; this was a female house now; and then had a serious talk with Petey and Polly about Daddy and Mommy. "Now you can get his pillow," Polly said. Then we made fudge.

An odd thing is that Gavvy in a way disappeared as entirely as Osella; I have never really seen him again either. Oh, we had to meet at the lawyer's, and I can see his outline in his car sometimes as he waits outside for the children, but he will never look at me, and so I can't really see him.

12 Well, it wasn't that I was so brave, but I had a prop in Andrew; I suppose the Famous Inspector always looks for the lover waiting like a stage prop in the wings. Not that Andrew was tangibly solid like a wall, because his life was wobbly and sliding and he was trying to keep his own balance. But the *idea* of Andrew was supportive, and also the pleasure we took. Pleasure does a lot to keep you going.

But I did worry about telling Andrew about this change in the practical reality of my life arrangements, for fear he would feel a challenge to his own.

This has nothing to do with Andrew, nothing to do with Andrew, I said over and over, arming against the blinding acquisitive dependence that would smite me when I saw Andrew and would want to rest in him, never leave him, be with him always, all that. As it was, we met in a dim murky place, little bar near Roseville, so I could hardly see Andrew for the first moment but just his tall form leaning on the bar and then his smile when I came in and told him that Gavvy was gone. He smiled a happy and gentle smile like the quiet pride of the parent of a successful child, or, perhaps, of an idiot child who has learned some elementary skill easy for others, heretofore thought to be beyond it.

"So you're really going to do it?" he said.

"Yes, it's better to. It's necessary to. Yes, thank heaven. Yes, I am immovable," putting the torch to every bridge with every word. Telling others you will do something is just a way of making yourself stick, of course. But I didn't want to frighten Andrew into thinking this was a game and I was now saying your move; I wasn't.

But Andrew told me later he was thinking it *was* his move, because it was. That was the admonition of his own heart. We were like children on the bank of an icy pool, and there is always one skinny fearless little fiend who plunging in shames you and confronts you with the horrid cowardice and fleshly reluctance which control you, and you'd better overcome them. I had, in the phrase, taken the plunge. This was kind of a new thing for me. Usually I'm the one that shivers wracked with aversion and ambivalence on the bank, as I have said.

But anyway I made sure that Andrew knew I wouldn't, like a marine monster, drag him into this and drown him, and he on the other hand reassured me that he was pleased, that this was an important step for us, that some-day, he knew, things would work out for us. It is hard to have conversations like that one, avoiding every concrete noun but only mentioning things in adverbs: then, some-day, when, if, only.

But also we weren't so strangled in tact and polity that joy and glee did not break through this discussion, too; what a harvest of love swayed in the foreground, and no motels and creeping hiding and kissing in cars. Our talk was like going on a train that gathers speed, excite-ment.

I left it to Andrew to organize the practical problem, for him, of looking at Gavvy at the office every day and carrying that off; he still had a month before moving to the new office in San Francisco; that was a day I didn't want to think about. Our impending separation was too dreadful to think about, or ever to talk about, but lodged in our reticence was the hope that this upheaval in An-drew's life—his new eminence—would free him, too. The moving trucks would gather up all his furniture, kids, cats, wife, trundle them eighty miles, down would come the tailgate, out would come furniture, kids, cats. But no wife; Cookie would have just disappeared on the jour-ney, by magic.

"So you're really going to do it?" Andrew said in the Roseville bar, warily, maybe, for Andrew and I might never be such dangerous friends, so wary, as then. But he was charmed, too, charmed and excited by this new evidence of passion and license all around him ruling the world, arranging lives when he had thought that prudence was the organizing principle.

What had happened to Andrew was that he had discovered he was a passionate man. He had been too modest to think this of himself before; he had thought of himself as just smart and effective, or he suspected that should the occasion arise he would be capable of much, but he knew it wasn't going to arise, the way a man may deeply know in a peacetime generation that he would be a fierce, gallant soldier but there wasn't going to be a war. Life does not arrange experience like the leaves of a fan that can be extended at will to its full range; life is more an apothecary cabinet with some closed drawers marked skull and cross-bones not to be tasted out of, at least not by you.

Andrew says he liked the thought, when he had discovered his own nature, that other people were as mysterious as he, well-barbered, hiding inside their clean shirts and dark suits hearts unruly and defiant, cherishing bad thoughts and hot love. Andrew has never done much criminal or family law; he is a corporation lawyer.

Well, if you ever do find out your true nature, you don't sit up in bed all at once electrified with self-knowledge; it comes on you slowly. It came on Andrew when he became a full partner last year, such success at such a young age. Before this, he had his burning ambition to heat him up, to make his life warm and cozy; but now ambition was satisfied, the fire was banked, and now little chill drafts came streaming through all the chinks in his life, and now he had nothing to keep him warm, no love for instance, and now life instead of being warm had become cold ashes.

Andrew, when he asks himself about himself, which I don't think he does very often, gets an honest answer anyway. He'd asked himself about love before and the answer was always, Well, you might have liked to have a

Great Love. It is known to exist; great literature proves that there *is* such a thing. But from books we know that great love dies. There is something fatal in it. Great lovers are fated, too, always die; perhaps the breed may even be extinct, so why waste time worrying about not being one?

Also Andrew thought he wasn't a very good lover in bed. He was philosophical. Some men were good at track events or could mysteriously hold their liquor; bodies were strange chemical compounds whose responses differed imperceptibly with the amount of salt in the cells or something. Some quite little men can jump prodigiously high. Andrew, handsome and athletic, seemed formed to love women, as even he, with all due modesty, could see, but love didn't seem to be his special skill. Cookie seemed to like it well enough, always on Friday nights and sometimes in between. He would have preferred it oftener but had come to terms with their different natures; Cookie was cheerful and cooperative even though she was not herself a strongly passionate woman. She was getting better now that she wasn't so afraid of having babies as she was in the pre-pill days.

I remember Andrew once standing up after making love to me, and he was naked, and I saw him see himself naked in the mirror; I saw him recognize something, not the weak nakedness of a man without clothes, clothes put on like power to disguise poor hairless weakness underneath and taken off reluctantly to perform animal functions, man hiding in his vestments. The reverse, the reverse—naked and powerful and beautiful, regretting he must put clothes on his body and go around disguised as Andrew Mason, prominent attorney, quiet-minded and courtly; I saw it pass over his face, his recognition—no, his admiration for his naked self, and that pleased me. I understood how he minded putting clothes on and covering up his power and beauty.

I'm sure Andrew is grateful to have discovered his

physical powers, but I am not so sure that his discovery of emotional powers is not hateful to him now, hateful. It isn't better to let your soul get stirred up all the time. Maybe he wishes he had worked harder instead or taken up golf instead of getting stuck with this hot, hot center like the hot center that is imagined to lie at the core of the world, very deep buried and impossible of quenching, burning there while the world turns round in its ordinary way.

13 Now tonight a third thing, three blows in one day raining down on us, the cat, the car and now real blows in fact raining down on Ev, just about eight o'clock. She went down to the laundry room to take the clothes out of the washer, not worrying about this because the laundry room is locked at night and you get into it with your key. It is kept locked because of just this danger, of people lurking in it, and also people were urinating in it for some reason, some undeniable prompting called up by the sour urinal cement smell of the floor perhaps.

Ev went down carrying the clothes basket, turned her key, picked up her basket and pushed open the door with her hip, and went in sidewise, her back, therefore, to one wall, and not looking behind her in the dark. She was going to set the basket down and turn on the light when a shape came from behind and beat her, struck her a number of heavy blows on her back; she couldn't scream because the first blows of the heavy fist or object between her shoulder blades knocked the wind out of her. She dropped the basket and was driven flat against the soap-dispensing machine by the blows, where she struck her head and fell down on the floor. She doesn't think she was knocked out, but just hit and hurt by somebody she couldn't even see.

She thinks the person laughed or grunted, and ran outside. Ev didn't look to see but sat slumped on the floor blind with tears.

It wasn't so much the pain, she said, but that she couldn't *bear* being hit and beaten, it was too much. I can understand that. Ev would not turn and scream and fight this person but accept the beating thinking this is too much, because she has borne so much of this and it *was* too much. She sat sobbing and then got the clothes out of the washer, loaded the basket and came back to tell me.

"I'll call the manager," I said, frightened but knowing we had no chance of catching the person really.

"Oh, whoever it was done it is gone now," she said, recovering her philosophy. We waited for the manager, Mr. Hoaglund, and I strewed the wet clothes over the backs of chairs to dry, and Ev, taking our danger ever more seriously, checked the doors and windows again. Then she lay on the sofa, just undone by this, morally crumpled, looking up at the ceiling.

"In a way I'd just as soon," she said.

"What?"

"I'd just as soon he come on. Jesus, I feel so dumb jus waitin for whoever it is, and jus walkin up on him that way in the washroom. I'd jus as soon have it out."

"I wouldn't. I don't think he means to fool around, whoever it is," I said.

"It's *somebody,* and that's kind of a relief," Ev said. "I mean, it's somebody and I don't mind that so much, I can handle somebody. What I can't stand is anybody, that idea it could be anybody, God sendin down on us or whatever."

"Depends on who the somebody is," I said. "Anyhow it's the opposite with me. I don't mind the malice of God so much, or the idea of bad luck, but I really hate the idea of some particular person hating just us."

"Well, I don't know," Ev said. "It works out the same, don't it?"

Mr. Hoaglund, a thin straw-colored little man, the manager, with his big ears and Adam's apple, came along presently, and he and I went down to have a look in the laundry room. Together we looked at the cement floor, clean except for a gum wrapper, and at the corner of the soap dispenser where Ev's head must have struck; we envisioned feet standing where the feet of her assailant must have stood. But, really, an empty room is an empty room, empty of clues. Mr. Hoaglund shrugged.

"I'll report it to the police that we've had another incident. But I don't know that there's any point to it, they won't be able to do anything. Your girl's a nice quiet girl, isn't she?"

"Yes," I said, "but terrible things seem to happen to her."

"They seem to turn on their own kind first," Mr. Hoaglund said. "You read about a black getting hurt, odds are always it's another black. That's certainly the pattern in these units.

"You've been troubled with strange events, haven't you?" he remarked as we walked back, his tone a mixture of solicitude and disapproval.

"There seems to be so much of it about," I said, not wishing to seem to him a person who is the special target of trouble, and we contemplated in silence this daunting and squalid fact: so much of it about.

Ev has gone to bed now. We spent the rest of the evening trying to guess our enemy; this has become our favorite parlor game. Ev stayed up, I think hoping A. J. would call. I stayed up hoping Andrew would call, but neither called, only the phantom about ten-thirty, right on schedule. It's about midnight now but I am not sleepy, I may never sleep again. I keep watch while Ev sleeps.

14 Ev and I have only been together about ten months but it seems longer, as it would to shipwrecked persons adrift together. We have become old friends, our affection predating our acquaintance.

Ev came a few weeks after Gavvy left. At first it had been bliss to be deserted, but soon it wasn't bliss at all, it was impossible. I had to go to school, there was no one to look after the children, there was no one to help. Mostly it was that there was no one at all, except of course Andrew. There were the hot delicious visits from Andrew, but they were like the Arabian nights or a dime novel. I mean they had nothing to do with reality; I couldn't say to Andrew, oh, God, what am I going to do about the washing machine? Well, I could have, I suppose, but didn't want to, because I liked our love to be like the Arabian nights, and because that is the kind of remark that would remind him of Cookie.

I couldn't admit it to Andrew but there came—I will not say a despair, but a low feeling when I thought I'd been mistaken about everything. I should have been better to Gavvy, I should not try to be a free and independent person, I should not have done—any of the things I had done. I was a living warning. All my deeds were mistakes, but worse than that, I also knew I was going to compound my mistakes and prosecute more, error upon error unending, and that I had passed into a state where good sense had ceased to function; it had calcified, rigidified, and I was not going to admit my low feeling to anyone, not even Andrew. Especially Andrew.

My spirit I could now measure in grains and it was running out faster and faster onto the sand whereon my house was built instead of rock—well, you understand— real, not pretend problems: no money, and what to do with the babies so I could go to school so I could learn to do something practical so that I could take care of the babies —a circular difficulty seemingly impossible of solution, and the roof of the house, that principal symbolic structure, actually leaked, and all the machines, the washer and toasters, rusted and stopped as if they had been oiled before on Gavvy's money. There's nothing bleaker than when your machines stop, when even machines desert you, and also the telephone rings in the cold night, and salesmen, somehow knowing about you, seedy salesmen assault the doors.

I found out about the salesmen; they look you up in the divorce list in the newspaper, bullying failed men puffed up on the ignorance of defenseless women. Nothing would work right. A swarm of termites came up one day through the windowsill and lay in the sun shedding their wings. Such arrogance, you are so powerless even frail insects defy you. But my children seemed to trust me as before, held my hands when we crossed the street, didn't seem at all to know I had no powers any more.

I called an employment agency, one that advertised "no fee to employers," because there wasn't any money except what was left out of the $500 I had rushed to the bank to get the morning after Gavvy left. I had half expected to learn that Gavvy had got there first and taken it, but he must not have thought of that till later. I would have taken more money if there had been any, and done any other larcenous thing that might have served, but couldn't think of any; the Famous Inspector should have no illusions about my principles.

Anyway, Ev came out from the agency, a tall, grave woman standing quietly at the door. The first thing I noticed was that she was terrified; her voice had a quaver like a terrified public speaker. She just stuck a paper out at me, a thing she had filled in at the agency, which gave her name and age, 40, and birthplace, Texas, and answers: "Smoke?" No. "Drink?" No (lies), and her name, Evalin Wilson. I asked her in and tried to think of interviewish questions, to which she just nodded. She is beautiful; her hair was cut as close as a man's, her dark skin was perfect except for the new scars on her face and arms, which looked still painful. She wore a smart suit, like a secretary, and smiled at the children when I presented them, and I was terrified she wouldn't say she would come. But she did, and we walked to the door together. We were like two halves of a mirror. In her was a deep unspoken fear. In me was a deep unspoken fear. How implacable our eyes. We were both struck silent by our fears, but the person worse off has to speak first; that is the rule of desperation, I guess. Ev was the more desperate; like me, her husband had deserted her, but she was also Negro and didn't even have a quarter for the bus ride home.

"I wonder if you could loan me the money to get back on the bus," she said. "You out beyond the line, here, and I had to take a transfer I didn't figure on. I gave all my money to my husband, you see."

I was surprised, I suppose, anyway was silent, so that she felt obliged to go on: "I mean, he done took all the money when he left, he's gone to Georgia to see his daddy, and then I worked three days for this lady cleanin house, but then she didn't give me no money at the end, except for five dollars. She said I didn't do it no good, but I did. Then I give the agency the five to buy me *this* job, and the agency woman give me the bus fare, but she didn't give me enough to ride beyond the line. So it wasn't enough to get back."

Well, I, at the time, had what was left of the $500 and a fine house, did I not, and a host of spiffy clothes, and credit cards, which they don't take away from you until the slow machinery of their computers catches up to you; I was well off compared to Ev, and so I gave her five dollars.

"You can take it out of my first . . ."

"That's okay," I said, and she promised she'd come back that same night. I wasn't sure whether she would or not, but it seemed crucially important that she should. Ev's return was vital beyond the mere convenience of having a baby-sitter again, I mean. If Ev came back, that would mean that the flaws in my spirit did not show, that I presented to the uncritical eye—and poor Ev's was certainly uncritical—a seamless disguise, disguised as a brave facer of the future. You can trust this winning team—dear little children, cheerful competent woman, pleasant sunny place where they live in comfort lacking only you (Ev) to make them happy.

Ev came back that night about seven in a beat-up maroon Cadillac that let her off down at the corner (I was peering from my bedroom window); some man helped her out with a couple of suitcases and then drove off, leaving her to struggle up the long steps. I rushed out, wreathed in smiles like the witch from her gingerbread house, and she has been here ever since, except for intervals when her various life troubles have kept her away. By "here" I mean, of course, first there in my old house, and then here in this unit. I don't think she minded moving here; she says she finds more people to talk to during the day. The children like it here, too. I am the only one who hates it here.

Friday, January 3

1 Now that Ev has felt real, bitter blows, and has come to believe in our enemy, she is afraid. She thinks Clyde is after her and is afraid when before this she has always said, "I can handle Clyde."

Perhaps it really is someone after Ev, not me; these blows suggest it. Well, I still cannot see how she or anyone can be afraid of Clyde; even I am not, when usually I am afraid of black men, a little. If I am walking toward one down a quiet street, not even a dark street, I feel some extra apprehensiveness. I know this is supposed to be sexual, something about dark super extra potency that stirs in you a female fear and longing, and I can understand that sometimes. But mostly it just comes from what you read in the newspaper. Social realism, statistics. Some people are more likely than others to grab your purse or stick a knife into you or drag you off into an alley. You know they hate you with an extra hate.

But Clyde is so broken, so pitiful, swaying there in his

old man's coat-sweater, tears in his brown unfocused eyes. He doesn't have enough character left to kill us. Sometimes, evidently, Ev has taunted him deeply enough to pain his manhood, poor atrophied sensibility though that is in Clyde, so that he hit her and knocked her head against the wall. He was always doing that — that's why she left him — but he couldn't kill anybody, I don't think, and he wouldn't crouch in the dark in the laundry room.

But why would anybody do that? It could be anybody. You simply don't know. It could as easily be Big Raider — he has his share of funny obsessions, as we found out. He is a popular entertainer, a successful, well-paid man, the opposite of Clyde and A. J.; maybe he would have to indulge his rages in the dark. But why would he feel rage against Ev? Maybe I don't understand rage at all, but I would have thought I did.

We are surrounded by the enraged. Ev's boyfriend A. J. She says it couldn't be him, but why couldn't it? A. J. out there scaring us so Ev will come live with him again, A. J. grimacing in at the windows at us, his enemies, scaring us with dead cats. Maybe all this will stop if Ev goes to live with him again. A. J. wouldn't hurt the children, he wouldn't hate us personally, just impersonally, as members of the oppressor race. Still, you can hate the oppressor race a lot, and then, too, maybe I have underestimated the extent of his personal grudge, which he has borne me ever since the business of painting the house.

A. J. is a rangy, thin man with yellow eyes and light mud skin, an evil man, like a killer, with oddly bright lips, smiling when he's sober — when he's drunk, too, but then his hate shows in his long teeth.

"A. J. done been to junior college," Ev told me. "His daddy and mama rich, own a funeral parlor, and A. J. he could have all they got but they think he's a no-good."

Ev loves him, I guess. "I needs what he give me,"

she says, laughing. "Every woman need that." Even this seems a strange explanation. I can't see what she sees in him. I have investigated my heart on this point, searching there for any inadvertent thrills or secret lust I might myself feel for A. J., but no—A. J. is scraggly and drunk, like Clyde. I feel sorry about this, that I am somehow failing Ev in yet another way, by not even finding her men worth coveting.

Besides sex I can't imagine what else A. J. gives Ev, but I think she loves to hear him talk hate. I can hear them outside sometimes, his rasping voice going on, what he's going to do to them, and Ev's loud laughing, something deep in her gentle nature enthralled by his witty brutality.

"I'm goin to take that little squirt and send him through his own car wash, drown that pest, scrape him plain to death with them brushes." A. J. works in a car wash. Ev laughs and laughs.

"Shit, I ain't gonna cut him. Anybody know it's a black man done it then. I'm gonna wax him to death, and they're gonna think it's that other honky, Jenks." Gasps of laughter from Ev. But A. J. doesn't hurt anybody except Ev, his woman, leaning on his arm as they sit in his car drinking Colt 45 Malt Liquor, or gin.

What gleams beneath A. J.'s cold smile is intelligence, bitter intelligence, which must make his life much harder.

A. J. hates me because Ev tells me things. "Don't tell no honky your business," he says. And he hates me because I keep Ev here with me, and because I wouldn't let him paint the house.

That was when I still had the house, thought I could hold on to it, and I had become filled with some need to fix it up, to get the plumbing and the roof mended and so on. Gavin and I had let the house crumble; even with Osella there cleaning it, it had rotted in the emotional climate like the steamy tropics. And the man across the street, Mr. Probst, had come over about it.

He came very confidentially into the kitchen in a way that made me think he was going to make advances, which often happens from unexpected people when you are divorced and alone so didn't even surprise me in Mr. Probst, when he came closer, closer, with an ingratiating and expectant smile that said he was going to do something nice for me. They don't see their bald heads and paunches, I was thinking, and backing off, Mr. Probst advancing, coming closer, and finally speaking in a low propositioning tone.

"My dear," he said in an urgent way, "*if* you were planning to get your house painted, what with improving your property values *and* improving the neighborhood, and protecting you against looking, well, run-down, which no offense, but a woman in your position can't be too careful. Well, I have a good man and I could put you on to him, he does a lot of work for me around my place, he would give you a good price, I guarantee. You probably don't notice, got a lot on your mind, but looking over at your house from our place, Mrs. P. and I notice, it's pretty obvious. You got to keep a place up or there goes your investment."

I had to have a new kitchen sink, I said, and fresh paper in the children's room, I knew that.

"Ah," he said, "that's a mistake a lot of people make. You leave the inside go for a while. That's one thing I learned from my mother, rest her, if she didn't teach me nothing else; it's what shows that counts. People conclude their conclusions from what they see."

He said many's the time he had gone to school with no underwear back in the Depression, but his mother, wonderful woman, had seen to it they had snappy new shoes and neckties and that way nobody tumbled to it that they were hard up. It bothered me that Mr. Probst's mother had told him the exact opposite of what my mother had told me. Were mothers so various, so unreliable? Was I then perhaps handing on false lore, lore not universally received, to Polly, Petey, Ivan and India? Passing on my opinions only, and my own deviance and eccentricity.

Anyway, Mr. Probst aroused these and another apprehension in me, a fear that people could see from my seedy facade—the peeling sills, chipped siding—the seedy condition of my soul; so I developed a passion to have the house painted. Borrowed the money, got the painter's name from Mr. Probst, and then A. J. came to see me. I guess Ev had told him I was thinking of this project.

"I've had plenty of experience paintin'," he said. "You let me paint it for you. I'll give you a good price, and you know you can trust A. J." He smiled, the whites of his eyes all yellow, swayed, drunk, confident but watching, and I could tell that someplace inside him, beneath the racy smirk, was a fear that I wasn't going to give him this job he needed, and I wasn't; nobody would, nobody could trust him, it wasn't his fault; or it was his fault, his mama so disappointed in him, been to college and working in a car wash, and didn't he know he could get a crew together, buy the paint, paint this big place. Him and Ev discussed it. No, I said.

"You let A. J. take care of everything."

"No, I'm sorry," I said, "but I already asked this other man, and, um . . ." But A. J. knew.

Another reason A. J. might hate me is Ev's car, but I think he saw the justice of my position about that. He always wants to borrow it. He is so persistent I almost think that's why he keeps after Ev. The car is her lone and best possession, but she doesn't in fact know how to drive it, and A. J. keeps wanting to take it, which I won't permit until it's paid for, because I guaranteed the purchase. It was bought from Mr. Probst, across the street from where we used to live, and I signed something saying Ev would pay $25 each month until it's paid for, or else I would, because she wanted it so much, had always wanted a car so much.

"Tell you, I know if I have it I'll learn to drive it,

otherwise I never will learn, and when I do, then I don't have to depend on no man for rides. Cost me sometimes five dollars a weekend buyin rides back and forth out here, and I can almost buy a car for that." It's her friends she has to pay for rides, friends more expensive than taxis.

There's no question that the car, a 1965 Pontiac, added to her allure for her friends and relations. Clyde came around, ever so nice, and her sister-in-law Billie Jean, and who knows who else, and especially A. J. with endless inventive excuses why he ought to have it. Ev knows, Ev understands, but Ev loves A. J. There's no accounting for love.

I ought to apologize for pontifical remarks like that. I'm no expert professor on love, that's for sure, the mistakes I make about love. If I had to explain about love to someone from another planet, I would tell them about Andrew, because that's all I know of love. I must seem like a loony professor with a disproved theory writing "Andrew Andrew" on the blackboard trustfully, in front of a skeptical class. Now I know love is just a state of mind and does not imply a permanent physical situation, like a warm room, say; and it is not an action like a play. Well, I suppose there's not much use any more in going into my love for Andrew. If what you thought was true turns out to be a lie, then you thought wrong.

I guess what I mean by love, besides desire, is confidence, a confident state of mind, a clear and reliable feeling. Your heart is clear, knowing that when it thinks about the person it loves it won't surprise itself by stumbling unaware on some ugly reservation, some knowledge that must be suppressed or excused. The heart is glad just to think about its lover, is suffused in gladness.

2 There's no accounting for love; now that is a true statement. For instance, you would have thought Osella would be the last woman on earth to find romance, a balloon fat woman "risin forty-five" by now, but she found romance. For a while there it looked like a real triumph, but I'm not sure how it turned out. Her boyfriend, amazingly, was Big Raider, the jazz singer.

He was playing a cheap nightclub—the Zanzibar—downtown. He's a better singer than that, and famous, but I think he owns a piece of the Zanzibar, and that's where Osella met him, at this club. He sings his famous song, "Hangin In"; everybody has heard that.

We were all crazy about Mr. Raider, as we called him: call me Big he said but we didn't. Raider is huge, like a dream of Othello, only elderly and portly and balding. Six feet eight at least, at least three hundred pounds, a huge man. Big, black and shiny he calls himself, self-hating but true; under the lights on the stage his black skin shines blue, his eyes glare, the top of his head shines. He has creases along the back of his bald head as if it were a forehead. We couldn't guess how old he is because he told lies, fish stories about his life, now one thing, now another: he had been raised down South, had been a lumberjack in Washington, or played for the Chicago Bears in 1959, and his stories would be full and complete with names. "Me and Jim Brown nearly scared a man to death one night. It happened to be a snowy dusk in Chicago, me and Jim happened to be wearing identical overcoats, black ones as a matter of fact, and we went round the corner up against this little guy comin toward us,"—and the point was that the little man looked up at these giants with their white eyes looking down at him and burst into screams, screams, screams. But then someone mentioned after Raider had gone that Jim Brown played for the Cleveland Browns, not the Bears. You couldn't tell a thing about Raider. But he seemed to love Osella; he was officially her man.

On Sundays after church supper she would go to a club with her friends and on this one night Big saw her, an immense splendid woman in her wool dress and a smart feathered hat. Osella had on occasion an inexplicable but undeniable glamour. I cannot think how this could be so, but it is so. Great presence. Big made wide-smiling jokes to her from behind the microphone and then came down and talked to her and asked to take her home, which she didn't allow until the next Sunday, and thereafter on Thursday and Sunday nights Big would call for her at our house and take her to his club.

There all evening Osella would sit like a queen laughing out her girl's laugh at his jokes, sipping a little Scotch. "I ain't no drinker but you has to be sociable," she said. Big Raider, an old-fashioned, delicate man, didn't like a woman to take too much whiskey. People joshed and courted her, saying, "a whole lot of woman," and Big made up a song with that line. Osella hummed it around the house.

Being famous, Big Raider came easily in to talk to us and our friends if any were around. Everyone liked him, he was easy, he was attractive, "used to whites," Osella observed, and "in show business they don't make no difference, black or white." Gavvy and I, like the parents of a backward child, rejoiced in what we saw as her gain in personal self-respect, in confidence, from this new experience of a black and white world.

Also we didn't feel so guilty about paying her such a low wage. With her new freedom, we presumed, came offers of other jobs, lures of money, people telling her she ought to be making more. She could earn double in another family. Big Raider, we imagined, would tell her to get a better job. Perhaps he did tell her that; perhaps that was another tension in her life, between loyalty and common sense: she stuck with us against common sense.

Sometimes Raider would say outrageous things. One

time looking at Gavvy's mother he said conspiratorially to her, "People don't give us old folks any credit that we still like a roll in the hay from time to time, ain't that right?" And Gavvy's mother didn't at all stiffen frostily as we expected, she just turned a pleased pink color and said, "Nooo, indeed, where there's life there's . . . as they say . . . hum."

But the odd thing is that Raider apparently didn't like a roll in the hay. "Imagine Osella and Raider screwing," Gavvy said, but they didn't. "Raider's a funny man," Osella said. "He don't want any of that old stuff. I done asked him. Only after marriage is what he say." I wonder if Osella had asked him because she wondered if he found her desirable, or whether she aches for love the way I do.

"Itch for it," Ev says. "People gits the itch at different ages the first time. Me I done got it when I was twelve. I done gits it now ever so often where I has to have a man no matter who, if you don't mind plain speakin. Course I notice there's usually somebody to hand quick enough." She wants me to imagine the itch settling over her just any old time unexpectedly and her turning into this beautiful prowling cat, showing her teeth, rippling her shoulders, walking along alleys. But I think she may be making it up, in scorn for what she imagines to be my pallid sexuality.

Anyway, I get it, too, not an itch exactly but a burn. I feel rooted like a tree and my throat closes up and my thighs are wet from a thought or memory. But I've only been this way since Andrew became my lover. I don't know what's the matter with me.

I don't know what's the matter with me; I am a grownup, almost thirty, the mother of four children, educated, civil, responsible, how can it happen that I have these feelings of desire inside me like wild tigers that must choke me if they don't melt into tears and stream out, my body always streaming with desire and woe?

Sometimes it maddens me that I am not as beautiful as a goddess, but only me all arms and feet too ordinary to make love as love deserves. I worship love and also feel for it a profane relish. Sometimes when I'm longing for Andrew and he is absent, I feel like a statue of lead, with great heavy limbs; I grow sleepy, stifled with lethargy as if a giant were standing on me between my shoulder blades pressing me down. Other times I can hear my blood rush like the sap of a tree. When we have made love, the deep peace of our sticky sleep is the sweetest thing I know of. Maybe oblivion is the important thing, not pleasure. I don't know anything about love. How did I become so old, marriage, children, reading books from the adult sections, "X" movies all this time, and still not know about love until now?

Well, I know about love now, and I still can't feel it is a lie. It's as if this horrible thing, Andrew's letter, had not really happened. How can it have happened? It is incongruous, like ugly words defacing a solemn book. Or it is more like an accident which has happened, for which you can only blame impersonal powers.

3 The powers impersonal or personal that hurt Ev in the laundry last night have hurt her worse than we thought, because this morning she could get out of bed only to crawl to the bathroom to be sick. She hurts, she says, in the same old place in her back, which has me worried because the back pain is from her damaged pancreas. Since we have lived together, she has had two serious attacks of acute pancreatitis, both requiring hospitalization, and she was hospitalized another time for pelvic inflammatory disease and had to have a hysterectomy.

But the pancreatitis comes from drinking, the doctor

said. "You have to lay off the sauce, old girl," the doctor told her when I brought her home from the hospital, but to me over the telephone he had said that she could die from this disease. Why didn't he tell her that? If it were my pancreas, I would expect him to hold my hands, to look into my eyes, to warn me solemnly of my mortal danger. But perhaps the doctor, like the Famous Inspector, is a moralist who reserves his sympathies for those who don't drink themselves into dying states or screw themselves into unwed pregnancies or live in sordid places. Or perhaps the doctor is a fatalist who believes that the owners of alcoholic pancreases won't quit drinking anyway.

Ev says she doesn't drink. She has always remained true to her original lie. "A little beer on weekends," she says.

"Ev, you must never have liquor, that's what gives you these attacks; please, promise," I say.

"If a little beer weekends goin to kill me, I'm just as well off dead," she says, sniffing.

Along with my concern for Ev I'm obliged to admit I feel mad at her for letting this happen just when everything is chaos and I need her and depend on her. How will I get my papers finished, how study for the Qualifying Examination, but also how could she allow someone to hit her like that, why couldn't she have looked first, why do these things always happen to her?

I had been planning to go to the library today but had to stay home instead, to look after the children and Ev, and so tried to work on my papers here. Papers due Monday. The children are carrying on through all this with trustful cheerfulness; they seem not to have noticed anything at all, which is peculiar, because normally they notice without knowing and will react to tension or anger by fighting or wetting the bed. They reenacted the cat's funeral, and I caught them trying to make India play the part of the dead cat, and I lectured them hysterically on never put anything around your neck or anyone else's neck.

Poor Ev—who could work with her groans and the feverish smell that hangs over a place where someone has thrown up? But I did get some work done. Because I am so full of dreads: dread of our murderer, dread of sickness and pregnancy on the one hand, but dread also of failing my classes or getting Incompletes which would keep me from taking the Qualifying Examination at the end of January, and dread of failing this examination. This last dread is sometimes paralyzing like being embedded in a block of cement and sometimes it is like people with whips shouting behind you driving and scourging you.

Also I have a new dread: it began last night with Ev lying there demoralized, just staring up at the ceiling, wiped out with chagrin at this thing that had happened; something quite unrelated came into my mind, the idea that we had gotten botulism from the canned string beans we had had for dinner. I don't know where this idea came from, but suddenly it was there, risen up from the submerged repository of dreads and horrible notions that I keep festering there, wherever it is. Botulism, said my mind.

It seems perfectly logical. I remember that can was dented and there was a stain on the label, and the beans tasted funny. My idea—I still have it, my heart is pounding with panic even at the word—is that Ev, who is more delicate that I am, has reacted to it first; that is why she is sick. The children and I will come down with it later. I have looked it up in the dictionary and learned that the incubation period is up to three days. I know there is some vaccine you can take for botulism if you take it before the symptoms appear, but I am constrained from calling the doctor by the sheer foolishness of my idea, since I know we haven't got botulism. It is just that I feel that we do. So it is like suicide to sit here doing nothing—suicide and murder, both. I'm afraid I'm going to have to call the doctor for Ev, if she doesn't feel better pretty soon, and I can slyly ask him about botulism. My pain, my anguish was so intense over botulism that late last night when everybody was asleep, even in my fear of the murderer I stole outside to the garbage cans and rooted about in the disgusting mess looking for the bean can but couldn't find it. Is it possible that our murderer poisoned our beans, then took away the can? You see how the poisoned mind behaves.

I ought to consider, instead of suicide, madness as an optional form of escape from my situation. This has occurred to me in connection with the phantom phone-caller, who called both last night and this morning, getting the chance because I didn't like to leave the phone off the hook. I told myself this was because the number might go out of service and then wouldn't function in case we needed to call for help, if the murderer came or if Ev got worse. That is partly true and partly I suppose I am still hoping that Andrew will call. The line has never gone out of service before and I have left it off the hook countless hours.

In a way I envy the phantom phone-caller in his/her madness. No doubt a state of terrible personal distress, of mental anguish, but at least his/her mind is all safely bound by its obsessions; it is not free to be always inventing new ones. All its horrors are known already, arrayed for review. My mind is continually taking me by surprise with new inventions. Our murder, botulism, what will be next?

Ev felt better this afternoon, sitting up in bed looking pretty in spite of her head tied up in old rag (symbolizing her hatred of her hair), wearing a gorgeous nightie, symbolizing her respect for femininity and decency. At first, to my shame, I used to find these nighties strange, but what it was is, you have seen a lot of pictures of pinkish skin showing through filmy lingerie and the effect is quite different. I myself wear ugly flannel nighties and none, of course, when with Andrew. My theory is what you wear relates to maternal instruction, and I am in line with Mr. Probst's mother on the matter of nighties, but Ev is in line with her own mother and mine, that even clothing that can't be seen should be new and dainty.

I know the position of Ev's mother on this because when Ev had to go to the hospital the first time, her hysterectomy, her parents came by. This was when we still lived in the big fine white-folks' house, and Ev's parents were plenty approving. Ev's mother was taking Ev a "decent" nightie, meaning a pretty one, and stopped by for her overnight case. Ev's parents are a timid, nice old father and the round, fierce, serious mother, who said, "I hope you goin to keep Evalin's job available for her. I done tole Evalin she got a good job here, and she shouldn't throw it up account of what no man tells 'er." And "Ev surely loves you-all, I done tole her you ain't gonna go givin her job away while she sick, ain't that so?" And she slewed her eyes all around looking at the pretty house and narrowly at me, thinking, I guess, will she, won't she, Ev better hold on to this steady deal, this white woman like to hear about love, I bet.

"Yep, Ev really loves you-all," her dad assured me.

4 I suppose in spite of dread, murder, botulism, basically I am expecting still to be alive at the end of January for the Qualifying Examination, for I continue to work and study as if I were. I suppose, dying of something, you would forget your death from time to time and catch yourself thinking of the future with yourself in it. Anyway if I am alive at the end of January, I have to take the Qualifying Examination which, if I pass it, means I have a Master's degree and can go on to study for the

Ph.D. If I don't pass this examination—what? I would have to become a typist or a telephone operator.

A typist, a telephone operator or a nursery-school teacher are. what Melvin Briggs suggested to the judge would be good things for me to become, in reply to my idea that Gavin should give me some money until I can educate myself to some profession. Melvin Briggs, the son of the senior partner old Briggs, does the firm's family law and represented Gavvy. Melvin said, "Mrs. Hexam should try to be more practical. With a bachelor's degree she can get a number of good jobs, for instance as a supervisor with the telephone company, or with a few additional courses she could get a certificate to teach elementary or nursery school, which would be consistent with her role as the mother of young children." And the judge agreed, saying that I was already better educated than most women and should be contented with that, but that he was sure that a young woman like me with motivation and initiative would take night courses to further herself, even while working at the telephone company. A little child support is all they thought necessary, and everyone around Briggs, Harvill & Mason, except Andrew of course, considered that Melvin had done very well for Gavvy. Andrew says the hardest thing for him has been not to strangle Melvin, and I appreciate the frustration of his position, but it isn't of much practical help.

Well, of course the judge was right about motivation and initiative—here I am studying. But he was wrong about my ability to become a teacher or a telephone operator, because I couldn't possibly; I won't, even if I do fail the Qualifying Examination. I wonder about all the poor women, the whole world full of poor women— men, too, of course—who have to do jobs they don't want to do. Ev for example, I'm sure Ev didn't want to grow up to be a cleaning woman working in other people's houses, her mother either, despite telling her to hold on to that job, love that white lady, recognize a good thing when you got it, toe the line. What does the woman at the laundromat think, or a waitress? When I think of the moral stature of these women, I am chagrined and ashamed to be so complaining and unresigned, but I know if I were faced with the choice between working in the laundromat or going on welfare I would go on welfare. I don't know if I would go on the streets exactly, but I wouldn't work; I would choose to become a charity case.

I spoke of this to Bess, who said, "Of course you wouldn't become a charity case; you have *children*, you'd get some sort of job."

"Oh, no, I wouldn't. That's a characteristic of my sort of demoralization—I wouldn't. And if I felt I had to for their sakes think how I would hate them."

"It's good that you can face these feelings," Bess said vaguely, and was underneath it shocked. I've noticed that the psychoanalyzed can face some things—sexual feelings, say—with utmost equanimity but have a special inability to face the really nasty shocking things like feeling hostility toward your children. It's as though, assaulted by the disease of self-knowledge in its most elementary form, they develop antibodies which keep them from finding out anything important.

"You only talk this way because you have a scholarship," Bess insisted, wishing to cling to her wrong notions of motherhood and good and love. "It's all very well to be paid for being an intellectual. It's the intellectual pride of the academy—intellectual pride—and it's unbecoming. You'd change your mind; of course you would work as a waitress, if you had to."

"Well, the more children I had, the larger my welfare check would be," I reassured her. "So I wouldn't resent the children, I would value them."

Though I couldn't convince Bess of it, I know I would become like the other welfare mothers in this unit, adding children from year to year to my fatherless brood, not working, because what would be the point? A job would just be one more terrible enslaving insult. Perhaps I should submit myself to sociologists as an experimental case for them; they could see if they could inspirit me, then they might have a clue how to go about it with others. Mrs. H., our most resolutely demoralized incorrigible case. This is if I fail the examinations in late January.

How I hate Melvin Briggs, first man to illustrate to me—I guess I had been overprotected—the power and malice of the rules by which men help and protect each other and turn on women they have no reason to turn on because men are loyal to each other. I'm sure Melvin didn't give a thought to fairness, but only tried to do his job, which was saving money for the new junior man, Gavvy, without a thought to my future or to what is fair. Why would you do a job that led you into defending wrong and injustice? That's a question I have asked Gavvy and Andrew both. "When he becomes your client, he becomes right," Gavvy said. "You wouldn't," Andrew said, meaning he, Andrew, wouldn't, maybe; but for all his fury at Melvin, Andrew couldn't or didn't speak to him about it, there's that.

But it still seems funny that Melvin Briggs, say, who has nothing against me at all, has met me plenty of times at parties and always been charming and civil, could get up in court with a face like plaster of Paris and say he could see nothing fair about Gavvy's four years of college and four years of law school and it being my turn now. Because I am a woman and a mother, I am not to have a turn.

And then, of course, women will do each other in, I am guilty of that myself; men are loyal to each other and women will do each other in. I'm thinking of my behavior to Cookie Mason. The last time I saw her was the last party before Gavin and I separated—I guess I must have seen Melvin Briggs there, too—and Cookie and I talked. Then I felt some charity and pity, instead of, now, the hate I feel for Cookie, too. What a mess. Usually I tried to avoid talking to Cookie, because it was embarrassing when I knew about Andrew not loving her and she didn't know. But this last time she knew about his infidelity and I didn't know she knew, so the advantage and feelings of embarrassment, or of satisfaction, more likely, were hers. She knew I was Andrew's mistress and that every word she said was woe to me, and she kept going on and on about them moving away.

"We've found *the* house at last. So charming, Victorian of course, in Pacific Heights. Exquisitely preserved, still with the original wooden drainboards and embossed tin ceilings. When I called my daddy to tell him about it, he said what in hell do you mean, wooden drainboards, get Formica put on. That's Texas, isn't it? My Lord. Actually it isn't as big as our present house, but it has an unfinished lower floor Andy can panel. The best view is from the master bedroom, which takes up half the top floor; we could almost divide it in two, if we needed another bedroom, but the space and privacy will be nice, and then the garden . . .

"It's a new life," she said, "a new house, a new city, this wonderful challenge and opportunity for Andy . . ." A new start together, a renewal of their marriage. I knew perfectly well what she was telling me. If she'd been Ev's sister-in-law Billie Jean, she would have slit my throat maybe, and no one would have blamed her; instead of that she tells me about her well-preserved kitchen, which is I suppose as useful and accurate a symbol as any of her hold over Andrew. She looked thinner at that party. I suppose she had been dieting. I was pretty confident in those days of my big breasts and of the way I could make Andrew laugh.

I didn't hate Cookie at all then; I suppose I shouldn't

now. I'm still not sure, whatever Bess says, that you oughtn't to suppress your hate. Hate is a bad thing when it gets a hold on you. I know I don't sound reasonable about Cookie, that's just natural, but I should try to be fair; Cookie is a desperate woman, too, after all, with justice and reason on her side, and plenty at stake, too, she must feel, a sixty-thousand-dollar meal ticket, peace, harmony, her self-respect as a woman. Can their marriage be saved?

It's just circumstances, woman's war. I am unwillingly the enemy of this perfectly pleasant although rather dumb woman I wish no harm to, but just inadvertently in the course of leading my life I've become her enemy and she, very naturally, has lined up her sights and taken action—why not? With justice and reason and moral rectitude on her side. I know it is Cookie who made Andrew do what he otherwise would not have done, I mean the terrible letter. The terrible terrible letter. I'm sure she made him write it. I'm sure she must have dictated it standing over him.

But you can't blame her. But I didn't think Andrew could do such a thing to me. It was the letter that made me think of suicide; that was only ten days ago, imagine, and now seems a year ago, a year besieged in here meantime by a crazy murderer. I know these things don't happen, but that doesn't keep them from happening, and I am afraid of a lot of things.

5 In a way my doubts about the reality of sinister events are vanished by Bess's new attentiveness: she plainly believes now that something is happening. She sees I could not have made up a vicious attack on Ev, she sees poor Ev lying bruised and dashed. Bess came by this afternoon, still wearing her hospital volunteer uniform, to cheer us up. She has been doing this nearly every afternoon, and I am more grateful than I am able to express to her. Perhaps she is the exception to my generalizations about female loyalty.

In addition to being grateful to Bess, I like and respect her. She is a brave woman who has a lot to bear. She is a tall, smart blonde, looking, if you can imagine it, like a shopwindow mannequin, same rather immobile serenely set face, same heavy rope hair. She was childless for fifteen years, during which time she was a Democratic State Central Committee member and a city councilman, and then, a surprise, she had poor Lynnie. Then she got psychoanalyzed, now she does volunteer work at the hospital and at Lynnie's special school.

"Perhaps all these strange events are a projection of your own anger," she said as we were speaking of my troubles. "That can happen, you know. It's well documented. Poltergeists for example are a form of psychic projection. It isn't known how the psychic forces determine physical events but it's been shown they can; hate can break a dish up on a shelf, or open a locked door. Unexpressed hate can. If you could express your anger, maybe then . . ."

"I *can* express my anger, I do express my anger, I strongly tell you how furiously, inwardly, outwardly angry I am," I insisted, tears rising in my voice because this is so true.

"That's right, let it out," Bess said soothingly, and this made me laugh so much that I laughed myself into tears that were suddenly real tears, into a great unseemly hiccuping eruption of emotion, and suddenly I was babbling, "I don't see how Andrew could do such a thing, he must be crazy, I shouldn't let him ruin his life like this, someone else should tell him this, if only I knew where Osella was, I can't stand this world so full of malign people lurking around, if I could just see them, I just want to leave and go away where no one can find us . . ." And much much more, quite incoherent, and went on quite a long time, so that poor Ev, nearly doubled over with her pain, got out of bed and came to the door of her room alarmed. The children were outside with Lynnie. I never let them see me cry.

My outburst served to show me that although I understand and respect and love Andrew just as I've been saying, and forgive him, too, I do really also feel anger, bitter rage at his betrayal. He has betrayed my conception of love. "Big deal, how arrogant and puerile she is," I can hear the Famous Inspector saying, "to imagine that she had any right to the one illusion that nobody else has."

But if you can't trust in your own instinct about things, in your own feeling of rightness, in the things that you know, in your deepest intuitions — then where are you? It's as if you were flying along in blackest space in a craft from which all instruments are taken, all gauges and indictators, the thing that tells you whether you are upside down or not. Nothing outside to go by but the black hole of space. It's this derangement I can't bear; it's not, I hope, just that I resent the man who has made love to me and made me pregnant and taken up all my affections and made promises and then gone back to his wife. Well, that *is* an age-old story, isn't it? I wouldn't have any right to complain if it was just that. Anyone would say I should have known better.

Actually, Andrew has never made any promises to me and I wouldn't want them. A love has got to arise somewhere other than from the scruples. Andrew is too scrupulous for his own good anyway. He would always keep his promises, however resentfully. His scruples, probity and promise-keeping are just what have led him to make a mess of his life, so let him remain in his icy cell, to hell with Andrew, I wouldn't want him to wreak his scruples on me.

"At least you should call him and tell him your period is late," Bess had been urging when I hadn't heard from him in those long days before the letter came, long silent gaps of days. I was excited by Bess's idea, by having an excuse to talk to him at all; I tortured myself with the silent phone in front of me, but I didn't do it, and now I wish I had. Now to do it would seem like a trick, and a trick that has been used on him before. Well, I suppose it wasn't exactly a trick, before, when he married Cookie, because she really was pregnant, and that was eighteen years ago when people were more likely to feel that they did have to get married in those circumstances. But Andrew says they had planned to get married anyway.

With Cookie, as with many women, pregnancy is the Old Reliable, a means of getting something you want. For instance, it happened again after Cookie found out about Andrew and me, or it almost happened. Andrew called one night from his office, working late, and said in a choked inaudible voice, "Cookie says her period is a week late and she thinks she's pregnant." I was shocked silent and then a rage welled up, and then I snarled something—"Oh, Andrew, how could you let *that* happen?"—never doubting it had happened, either, because it made such perfect sense, it was what you would expect.

It made me mad, too, that she had been *exposed* to pregnancy. Though I had certainly not discussed with Andrew the details of his connubial duties, I guess I thought—I don't know what I thought, because I didn't let myself think about it at all. But of course unfaithful husbands do make love to their wives right along, just as I did with Gavin while I was being unfaithful. It's morally disgusting but a practical necessity. The truth is, you are so used to your husband you don't much notice; he is a cipher, it is a non-act. But this did sully—I can see now—the intense, blinding, white-light purity of our love, a love which neither of us was ever in doubt of.

"How nice, a darling little baby," I remember saying in a dark raging quiet voice, and Andrew misunderstood me and thought I was serious. "Are you mad? It's terrible, terrible." He was upset, but he saw fatherhood before him, I could tell that.

Maybe she could have an abortion, I suggested eventually. "On account of her age. Childbirth would be unsafe for her." What depths I have occasionally sunk to over Andrew.

"She wouldn't. I'm sure she wouldn't, she must have done this on purpose. A new baby to bring us back together, that sort of thing. I don't know but what I'm kind of touched," Andrew said. "Cookie hates babies, but she wouldn't get an abortion."

"Oh, I don't blame her; I wouldn't get an abortion, either. It seems like wicked murder," I said. Ha, see how I lied, and thought I was truthful, and how quickly I rushed off to the gynecologist, thoroughly excluding from my mind all thoughts of murder, all consideration of new life, as soon as I got in trouble.

It's a nice point for the Famous Inspector to sermonize upon: legitimacy. "Andrew's wife, being legally married, although he loathes her, has a right to bear his child, while you, being unmarried, must bear one at your peril."

"Suppose, however, that I had become pregnant at that time instead of now, so that Cookie and I were both pregnant at the same time. Would Andrew, like the father of twins, have dashed from, say, Cookie at the Holy Angel Lying-in Hospital to the Magdalen Home and me, bristling with cigars, and cheer and kisses for all?"

"Certainly not. He would have dutifully observed the responsibilities of paternity with Cookie, his wife whom he loathes, and to you, whom he loves, he would have insisted upon abortion. You could refuse, of course, but that's what he would suggest, without regard to your scruples. He would pay for the abortion, naturally. Cookie is the legal wife, the legal, legal, legal wife. And, you might remember, you were once a legal wife yourself, with all the perquisites thereunto pertaining, until you so impulsively and imprudently tossed it all up in the name of principles which you have not as yet elaborated comprehensibly."

"That's because I can't remember what they were. I thought I knew: honesty, physical purity, the freedom of the soul."

The Famous Inspector politely hides his involuntary small smile behind his hand and nods good day.

6 It occurs to me that if I am murdered and found to be pregnant, an investigating officer might well conclude that the murderer is Andrew. Desperate married man murders pregnant mistress. Noted jurist in dock. A rather Victorian sort of murder, to be sure, but these Famous Inspectors are morally conservative and would see the world in those terms. And he could find out who my lover was easily enough from Ev or Bess. If I let myself dwell on this idea, I can almost make myself imagine it *is* Andrew, gone unhinged in some undetectable, Victorian gentlemanly way. Andrew could never go unhinged in a berserk, unruly way, he is too elegant.

Actually Andrew and I have discussed murder. I told him about the time I thought of murdering Gavvy. This was about three summers ago, just after India was born. We bought a tent and drove back to the mountains of Idaho and Colorado, beautiful cold high country with little lakes and clear streams running through marshy meadows between peaks where patches of snow remained. We camped in valleys so thick with mist in the mornings we could barely see the moist little pines around us, and then the mist, rising, would reveal those beautiful peaks in bright sunshine, the most astonishing wonders I have seen, like the vision of heaven in some apocalyptic painting. It was very cold mornings and I would lie lazy and cozy in my sleeping bag while Gavin stamped around camp making fire. I would lie there watching the beautiful mists uncover the mountains until it was too delightful to lie there any longer and I would bound out to breathe and eat. I mention all this beauty, the exquisite peace of these places, because of the oddness of an idea of murder intruding there.

We had made camp at the edge of a river which ran below at the bottom of a gorge about ten feet deep, narrow, perhaps only fifteen feet from one bank to the other, so that the stream, compressed into the little channel it had so diligently carved itself from the rocks, was full and rushing, and at first I had been frightened that the children might fall into it, but they showed a great reluctance even to peer over, and instead scrambled among the rocks hunting for chipmunks to feed, and lizards and terrifying spiders which I would have to look at and say whether they were black widows or not. We were so happy. We were dirty, had given up baths and settled into our clothes as into our skins. We lay on rocks in the sun.

I lay on a rock in the sun watching Gavin cast a long line into the turbulent stream which I could hear rushing beneath, pushing rocks and sticks which cracked against the boulders jutting up. I could hear things being carried rapidly along, could hear the children's chatter, Gavin swearing with contented irritation when his hook got caught. He was having good luck, filling his creel nearby with glorious fish we would soon eat. Then it simply occurred to me to push him in the river, to walk very quietly up behind him and give him one firm push into the water. And then my next thought was that it might not be deep enough—that he might climb out. Would I be able to make him think that I had accidentally fallen against him? How could I feign this? But it was a fast and battering river, surely it would wash him away. A ranger or a policeman would come to tell me, the poor distracted widow frantic back at the encampment. "He was fishing, he fell, I heard his cries, saw his bleeding body swept away," I would sob. "Daddy, daddy," the children would shriek. My own body, lying in the warm sun against the hot rock, became heated with a physical sensation like moist voluptuous desire thinking these thoughts. I remember so well that rich, desiring heat.

Then, of course, like a civilized person I felt a polite corrective sensation of horror interrupting this guilty fantasy: poor Gavvy fishing, his unsuspecting trustful back to us, fish for his family. I shivered with chill shame for the wayward human brain that will thrust such unbidden notions upon you. Of course you wouldn't kill anyone. We were so happy in the still peace of this beautiful place . . .

But, remembering the pounding power of my first impulse, I have never been sure why I did not push Gavvy. What is the real reason? I wish the real reason would be that I am an ordinary, sane, non-homicidal person, even the sanest of whom must sometimes be aware of homicidal thoughts, and these were mine. But there was some extra urgency in my first calculating judgment that will always make me wonder or darkly know that I only hesitated because I thought it wouldn't work.

This uneasy conviction has driven me several times to mention my experience to people, sympathetic people I trust, in hopes they will come up with a similar experience; for instance I told Bess, who since her psychoanalysis takes it for granted that the human heart is so riddled with larcenous, incestuous, homicidal notions it barely has room for any others. But Bess was not helpful, not really. She only said, "Any husband that makes his wife camp out with four small children for four weeks deserves to be murdered."

Andrew, however, my best friend to whom I can tell anything and who himself possesses a high order of emotional honesty, or innocence, Andrew says he quite understands because he has often found himself wishing Cookie would wreck the car, or, when she went back to Dallas once, that her plane would crash; and once when she had rushed out of the house distracted after a quarrel it occurred to him she might commit suicide and this would delight him. This is murder in a way, we agreed.

It's this knowing what a shallow grave deep notions of hate and murder lie buried in that makes me believe the warnings of our murderer, these notions not dead but only sleeping in your brain, easily awakened, awakened now in our murderer and beginning to prowl so softly, so stealthily that no one hears them except him, and me.

Another thing I try to figure out from newspaper accounts is whether people who are murdered—estranged wives in particular but in general any victim who is murdered by someone he knows—whether these victims are people who *believe* in murder, and therefore in some way accept it into their lives, or whether they are those who disbelieve in murder and are therefore taken by surprise. I hope the latter but cannot be sure. I believe in murder.

I can imagine women and their lovers, husbands and their mistresses, very companionably conspiring to do murder. Everything seems so new and reasonable, all the thoughts you thought that only you had had, when your lover has had them, too. Andrew and I had such heart-pourings, long conversations in each other's arms in the night. We thought we were so new.

I guess we had been just lonesome, even with all our friends and colleagues and spouses and children around. And there does come a moment when you realize that you have not been granted an infinity of youth and beauty and time, so you have to do something. Or maybe love is something else. I know it had to do with the way I can feel Andrew's heart beating inside his chest, though I cannot feel my own, when he is wrapped in me.

7 Like Gavin and me, Andrew and Cookie married young, when they were in their early twenties and Andrew was just starting law school. The bride, like so many brides, was pregnant. Andrew had wanted her to have an abortion. I don't know whether this was to avoid the embarrassment of a seven-month child or to avoid the shadow of the shotgun that would otherwise hang between them. That consideration would be more typical of Andrew. They planned to have an abortion and then get married, but the abortionist got arrested or something, so they just went ahead the way they were. The shadow was eventually bodied forth in the form of their very agreeable child Maureen, and the first few years went pleasantly enough. I hate it when Andrew says this—I want him to say every minute was misery but of course he can't say so, and Andrew never will lie. I didn't hate every minute with Gavvy, either, I suppose. I can't remember. It's funny but I cannot remember any details of our years and years of everyday life. I remember it only as if it were childhood, by knowing that it must have occurred; my amnesia is almost total, with little tears in the veil of obscurity here and there through which to glimpse a hand tightly closed to show white knuckles, rooms, beds we had, a grimace, my own hands holding a platter and hurling it at the enemy, the hated enemy, which must have been Gavvy, whose face I have nearly forgotten.

Like Gavin and me, Andrew and Cookie cannot pre-cisely detail the degrees by which they became enemies or enumerate their grievances. Andrew cannot, that is; Cookie does not think of him as the enemy but as the beloved, the beloved with a live streak that has to be put out. "When I try to explain what's the matter with Cookie and me, to her, even to myself, it doesn't sound so bad," Andrew says. "What sounds bad is my own character, shown up as de-manding, impatient, desiring." Cookie is dutiful. She serenely knows that she has always done her duty. But she has misunderstood what that is.

"At least Andrew and I don't have *sexual* problems." This is what she told Bess once. "Sex has never been a problem with us. Andrew doesn't pester me at all, he's very understanding. The nights I don't feel like it, he just goes to sleep without a word of reproach; we have a very good adjustment that way."

Also, Cookie is someone who believes what people tell her. That's about the worst that can be said of her; she believes what people tell her and won't change her mind ever. She has never asked a question on her own. At parties she is always supporting strange views, contrary ones, and in a contentious manner which is unexpected from such a bland person. You can see her views must have been formed from her mother and father, in childhood, or some-times they come from Andrew himself, but she will slightly misapply them in some illogical way, or they will be opin-ions he has discarded, and he must uncomfortably with-draw from discussions to avoid embarrassing her with public contradictions. She is interested in vigorously de-fending such propositions as "Religion is the opiate of the people," as if people cared. I'm afraid she is a little stupid, but that's the worst that can be said of her. But it's hard for me to be fair and objective. Someone recently mistook her for Andrew's mother. Oh, I don't know. All the pretty houses are full of women like her.

135

How usual everything is, how predictable. She must have been pretty once but has gotten plump, hair gone gray early and she doesn't seem to mind, lacks the vanity of a sensuous person, or maybe has designed this kind of revenge on Andrew, that his kisses must fall on withered skin; that will fix him for not opening up his soul to her.

Her response to his infidelity was just what you'd expect: she lost weight and learned to play tennis and tried to inform her mind according to the usual prescriptions. She doesn't see Andrew as an anguished man, only as prey to the vagaries of the dangerous age. The reliable myths about men in their forties have taught her to expect a little of this, have not really shaken her confidence in his ultimate place by her side, with the terms of their life sweetly reversed to justify her good patience. Andrew will come to need her, in their old age or whenever. No doubt she has endured pangs during all this, but Cookie knows it is an old story with a dependable outcome.

Meantime she's *trying*, Andrew says. He can't seem to stop her from *trying*. "Let's talk about us," she is always saying.

You can't talk about unhappiness, Andrew cruelly says. The subject is diffuse, the attempt is self-indulgent.

"We *are* happy," Cookie will whine. "You just won't let yourself admit it. You don't try. If anyone was unhappy, it should be me; you never talk to me, you're always away and *I* don't complain."

But Andrew is constrained from revealing his complaints. One reason is for fear she might actually correct some of the things he views as faults: she is childish, frigid, selfish and dull, and he is reluctant to say so for fear she will change and he will have to keep her. "That would spoil everything," he admits.

Well, it is I who am saying these things; Andrew is a gentleman and doesn't tell me Cookie's secrets or complain very much; I don't ask, either. He is scrupulous and gallant, and takes the blame on himself. He is cruel to her, he says, withholds the praise she seems to crave (nice dinner! pretty dress!) and does not talk to her. "The silence at our house is a wondrous, unfathomable silence full of gripping and pulling. And at that the silence is better than her talk," he said once.

In a way his attempts at politeness to her are cruelty, too. If I cared to improve their life together, my handsome gift to them would be telling him why this is so. If he would express his real complaints, maybe she could fix things up. Maybe she isn't aware of a lot of things. She could feign passion if she doesn't feel it; if she has to, she could sigh and scratch; but maybe she just hasn't realized how he longs for love.

"Oh, well, have your fling, your little honey, if you have to," she has said to him with a sarcastic, knowing smile, and one important time she said, "All right, I've had it now, God damn it, it has to stop. Make your choice," whereupon Andrew walked out and moved to a hotel.

He called me to come to San Francisco to spend the weekend with him, and I did, but it wasn't any good; it was too soon, or his heart was not yet easy, and so we sat like strangers on a bus. His gloom aroused my fury, which I would not speak to him about; he was like a gloomy prisoner, and that was not to be blamed on me, so I left, even sicker from love than I am now. Complete despair is rather restful, I'm finding now. How I paced and raged then and forbore to make a scene. I wanted to say go back to your wife, why don't you, or else, God damn it, smile.

He did go back of course, a few days later, and a few days after that he was in my arms again, but I was damned if I would listen to his account of their tender reconciliation, so I don't know what they said. I was just happy to take him into my body again; this is all I care about anyway, I told myself and him.

What an old story. Nobody knows anything about it,

not statisticians or marriage counselors or sociologists or
old wives, either. It's one thing to talk complacently about
the vagaries of men at the dangerous age and another to
feel the anguish of these lovers who wonder what will become of themselves and of the exquisite and desperate love
that they feel. When Andrew left for his new life, the day of
the moving vans and the family trek, coming to me in the
morning, we wept, trembled in each other's arms like children, drenching our naked bodies with our tears as we took
our pleasure, at the poignance of this parting, and we did
not even think of it as final. That strong man weeping,
that must have been the real Andrew, mustn't it? That must
be the Andrew he feels himself to be, suffused with love
and tenderness and passion. Yet there is the grave and
handsome staid Andrew who goes into Briggs, Harvill &
Mason carrying his briefcase and his briefs, saying good
morning, of whom the secretaries or his colleagues maybe
whisper behind his back, "Have you heard he is having a
little thing, straying a bit?" and some people feeling sorry
for Cookie, and others saying they always expected it.

Andrew says that until we fell in love he hadn't
minded missing what he'd never had, but then when he
discovered he was not a cold and distant man but a passionate and lonely one, he was excited; still the new, ar-
dent, open, confiding, sexual tiger, Andrew rather enjoyed
going around disguised as the old, reserved, composed,
poised, polite and just about average Andrew. It's a good
thing Andrew discovered these powers, for the world
would have missed a great lover in Andrew. But what I
started to say is that Andrew and I took seriously, as a
serious love, what onlookers probably did not.

But that's part of the old story, isn't it? The man at the
end of his thirties, beginning of his forties, his professional
success assured, having propitiated the ghosts of his fore-
fathers and accommodated the hopes of his mother, looks
around at the dismal wreck of his prosperous life, looks

within, falls in love—is perhaps imprinted with love for the first woman who walks by after the scales have fallen —takes a mistress in whose arms his sexual powers have never been more astonishing, this belying the first gray hair at his temples, soars on wings. And then must engage with reality—his promises, other people's version of him, his own habits, mortgages, the disappointments of his children.

And what is the end of this story? Well, I know, I think, and I hate it, I hate it. Everything Cookie has been told will turn out to be true. How is it that some people are provided with the correct information right from the start and from others it is scrupulously kept? All I have ever learned, if I have learned anything at all, I seem to have learned by catching people by surprise in horrible shaming attitudes, by snooping around like a bad, banished child who is subsequently caught and given a bruised apple to eat in silence in the alley.

Saturday, January 4

1 A day never dragged like yesterday, poor Ev puking in the bathroom and my hand dragging out slow words across a page with no sense that any of them meant anything, stomach revolving in sympathy. It is surely only coincidental that the contents of stomachs have become the motif of our persecution—the mess on the door, on the car, even this insane dread I have developed of botulism; and the hideous retching agonies of Ev kneeling on the bathroom floor emitting sick, croaking, inhuman noises from her dry stomach, her head in the toilet. The children trying to peek around the bathroom door, which in her rush she had left open: you see what can happen to adult humans, their frightened looks said. They were frightened at this frailty in Ev, and so was I.

But her stomach had quieted by yesterday afternoon and she was able to drink a little tea. I took the phone off the hook before dinner so she could sleep undisturbed by the phantom phone-caller or Osella, and that showed how

I had given up on Andrew anyway. Today Ev is definitely better, so it isn't botulism, I guess.

When you've been sick like Ev was, making plans for the future is a sure sign you're getting better. After dinner Ev came out of her room dressed in her turquoise wrapper and announced that she had decided to take driving lessons at night school instead of depending on A. J. to teach her.

"I think it be too hard for a man who is someone you know. It's just better to get a regular teacher," she said. I agreed with that, because I'd gone driving with her once myself, only once. She drove up on the curbs, and it was too scary to do again.

"And I might try takin English again," she added. She took an English class once before, Standard English as an Alternative Dialect. It involved a workbook and a lot of boring sentence diagrams I couldn't understand, either, and one night she just said, "Shit, I'm speakin it, ain't I, peoples understand what I'm sayin, I just don't grasp them dumb lines you has to draw," and that was that. But now she came out and sat on the sofa full of that and other plans, and restored the telephone and had a long conversation with A. J. while I was giving the kids their supper.

Later we got to talking and wondering what our murderer was going to do next. It was possible, I thought, that he had scared himself off, or else accomplished his will, by beating Ev. After all, nothing more had happened in a whole day, and that was some record. "I wish he'd come on," Ev said again. "It's sneakin I can't stand." But we couldn't agree on how he was going to come. Our windows and doors were carefully locked; he would have to be witty and crafty. What would he do?

Of course we found out soon enough, at about nine. I had decided that you can't just always cower inside, and I'd been in cowering all day, and now I thought I'll just drive up to the liquor store and buy some wine. But somebody had slashed the tires, all four tires, on my car.

I wasn't surprised, but I was upset, because that's

very expensive, and I didn't know if my insurance would cover it, and how would I go about getting new ones, and from where, and how would we escape from here with no car? It seemed like part of the plot all right, to flatten us here. Also, I'm kind of ashamed but I really minded not having the wine, I almost minded that most of all.

The murderer misjudges the effects on me of attacks on the car. I don't consider the car an extension of myself the way a man might. This argues for the murderer being a man, A. J. or Clyde, who admires cars, but not Gavvy, who wouldn't make a mistake like that about me. Gavvy on the other hand would know how peculiarly unnerving I find vomit, sickness, physical dissolution, the threat of or sight of illness, things reminding me of cancer and death. And now, after this morning, I more than ever don't know what to think about Gavvy.

I slept on the sofa again last night, but fitfully, awakening at noises, at dreams, at the dread which comes rushing over me when I think of death, my own death or my children's. Sometimes I feel I am going to die soon, sometimes never, maybe at the hands of a murderer, maybe not. Either he is tormenting us with all this vandalism and symbolism before he does his worst or else all this petty viciousness will satisfy him, and I don't really know which; my mind reels endlessly in the nights about the probabilities. Maybe I will die from just losing heart.

2 Yesterday was interminable but today is going by like an arrow, like a newsreel, good news, bad news, news of human interest and you don't know what to make of any of it. Good and bad events like angels and demons sit on your shoulder looking deep into your eyes, each urging that he alone reveals the true pattern of human life. What is the pattern of human life?

This morning Ev was a lot better and had toast and walked around, and that was something to be thankful for. Then we were hit immediately by a strange event which could perhaps be construed as a good one. Perhaps not. We got the children ready for their weekend visit to Gavvy and his parents. They look forward to this except when they sleep at Gavvy's house and he sleepwalks—that frightens them. It frightens me, too. First hearing about it from Petey, I called Gavvy's psychiatrist, who said that although he really wasn't supposed to say anything, he would reveal that I needn't worry, so I try not to. There's no way I can prevent him from taking them sometimes, so I just try to depend on the psychiatrist's judgment. Psychiatrists have to be right sometimes, I guess. I suppose I have always been afraid, after the crib incident, that Gavin would try to hurt India.

Usually Gavvy's mother and father pick the children up, but sometimes Gavvy does. He telephones first, and Ev walks them out to the street to meet him, or, infrequently, he pushes the doorbell and then walks away across the lawn, lounging at a distance, not looking toward us, and we send the children out. I can watch through the curtains their hugs and greetings. They are always glad to see him. The slender distant stranger embraces my children and takes them away, carefully not looking at me, as if I were a powerful Medusa.

But this morning at ten, the appointed hour, when the doorbell rang, I sensed with a shock that Gavvy was still standing on the other side of the door. Intended to come in, perhaps, otherwise why was he still standing there? Odd how you can see people through doors. Now is Gavvy the murderer or not was my thought, you'd better decide. So I opened the door of course.

And of course it was just old Gavvy, my old husband whom I hadn't seen for a long time, standing there looking handsomer and heavier, for he had gotten too thin there awhile, and now he had new clothes on, clothes I had never seen—well, which stood to reason—a checkered coat, I think. I was so flustered but just derived an impression of checks and expansiveness. Was he now come to confront us and finish off the thing that was in his mind?

"What happened to your front door?" he asked. "It looks like it was clawed by some lion trying to get in."

"Vandals," I said. What was it lying behind his smile, mockery? Knowledge? Triumph? Or was it perhaps the bland surface of a genuine smile, for that is what it seemed.

"Well, anyway, come in," I said, assuming, I hoped, a brisk implacable tone. He surely wouldn't do anything in front of the children. But: estranged husband kills wife, children, self. Ev peeked around the hall door, and, seeing him, whom she disapproves of, withdrew. I caught the flicker of her scowl.

But Gavvy's expression was the friendly impersonal one of someone come into the house by accident, perhaps the face of an announcer on a television screen, floating into the living room smiling and handsome. Polly, who loves him especially, ran into his arms; they none of them seemed to find it odd to have him standing there. Petey came out of their room lugging the weekend case we had packed.

"Hello, Scout," Gavvy said, giving Petey a kiss, too, an affectionate man among his children, not looking like a savage killer, a mauler of doors. Yet was he looking around, memorizing the placement of the furniture maybe? Could he tell from the pillow and blanket still on the sofa that I slept there? I watched his eyes move around noticing. I can't tell what my feelings were really. There was just dismay to see him at all.

"I have been thinking that it's better if we transact this weekly thing in a normal friendly way," he was saying in an affable voice. "Better for the kids and better for us. We can't *be* friends, it would be phony to try, and neither of us wants it. But we can acknowledge the facts of our circumstances and learn to live with them."

It had that rehearsed sound Gavvy's speech has. My mind frosted over. But Gavvy was not interested in my reaction and was stooping down helping India into her coat and listening to Ivan, who was raving on, Ev's sick, Clyde gonna buy me a bike, we found a dead cat, on and on, and Gavvy was laughing with him. Chatter filled the room.

"Yes, that's so, well," or whatever I was murmuring to Gavvy's speech, and Gavvy, standing up, said, intimately: "Rancor is destructive, it brings people down. There should be no room for rancor in our lives. The poison of rancor." He pronounced it conspiratorially, carefully, "ran-cor," as though it were a code word, over the children's heads, denoting, perhaps, a surprise for them.

I suppose I was staring, startled and bemused as I was, for he smiled at my surprise.

"I'll keep the kids tonight, and then take them to Mother's in the morning, so they'll be spending tomorrow with my folks, and they'll be bringing them back tomorrow night." Yes, good, all right.

"Are you all right here, getting along all right? I've never asked you that," he said as they were leaving. "I hope you're getting along all right." Yes, good, yes.

So. Well. You just don't know what's lurking in people's hearts. Though you don't know when people will turn bad on you, you don't know when they will turn good on you, either. Either way it makes you feel uneasy. That's a lesson to learn. Someone you thought was bitter and sick is struggling in his heart to overcome the poison of rancor and break through to joy and harmony, and you are just a rock or stone in his road; he must get round you, or he must coat you over like a pearl. I had the feeling Gavvy was coating me over now and I was just round and non-irritating to him.

Or maybe all this was a trick and a deception to make me think he is safe and doesn't hate me.

Perhaps it was not heartfelt, his aversion to the poison

of rancor, but maybe this was a maxim learned from his psychiatrist: my son, do not let the poison of ran-cor poison your life. Repair your bridges. Coat over the irritating bits and make your life into pearls. Well, that's good advice, and he would have maxims for me, I know: do not let the toxins of fear, guilt and vanity plague you, either.

I find it irritating, though, to think of Gavvy coating me over. I am not through thinking about Gavvy; how can I be, with this death threat lying in the bushes along my road? I am not sure about him, and it rankled, his face of lustrous serenity, pearly with philosophy. So he had come to terms about me, had he? I find it infuriating to have Gavvy settle his mind about me before I am ready. Yet of course I am happy if it is true. It would be so much better for the children. But oh, what a final cruelty if Gavvy and Andrew are going to go off and leave me holding all the hate myself. I must try to make my mind into a pearl.

Trying to understand the personality: it is so mysterious; it is like being stood in a closet, baffled and fearful, with dark strange-smelling coats stifling you, and then someone reaches a slim hand in, takes out his coat, and beyond you see a normal bright pacific world. People peer in at you; the world must seem a dark and stifling place indeed to you, they say, choosing to stand in that closet in that odd way.

I mean that where Gavvy is concerned I am reluctant to believe that things can become orderly and benign; I want to come trustfully out but can't seem to bring myself to. I do not quite trust the angel of order.

3 The dark view, the demon's view, was urged again, at about eleven this morning when the mail came. After Gavvy and the children had left, the mailman brought a couple of bills and a manila envelope addressed to me.

In it was a folded color page from a magazine, *Look* or *Life*, which I took out and trustfully unfolded and spread out on the table, imagining it to be an ad. But it was a photograph of an atrocity in Vietnam, a little thin woman lying dead, burned and bloody and smeared over, with dead children, bits of them, strewn around, and one tiny child left alive, crouched in the angle of her outflung leg, staring at the camera. That was all there was in the envelope, addressed to me in an unfamiliar hand.

It worked as I suppose it was meant to work, or perhaps better. I looked at it at first as if it were a glossy advertisement, and then really saw it, understood its subject, tried to look away and could not look away, but stood staring at the burns, at the indeterminate bits of human beings, at the child, at the dead woman, all bloody in color, and how pleased the sender would have been; I began to grow faint, I began to grow cold, my skin became icy, my ears rang. This is how you feel when you are going to faint, some first-aid-book memory said, and I sat down on the floor and put my head between my knees until the room stopped rocking and my stomach stopped. I shivered with chill sweat.

Ev came in to get something from the refrigerator, and, seeing me, asked in a frightened way what the matter was.

"Just a funny spell, nothing," I said.

"Girl, you green, I never seen such a shade of color before," she said, really frightened, and began to remonstrate, and then, her eye falling on the picture, she became silent.

"Someone put that in the mail to us?" she asked.

"Yes."

"Oh, Jesus, ain't that awful, what next," she said, and closed the refrigerator door without taking anything out and went back to bed.

It's funny that this impersonal photograph seen by

millions of readers, of these things which are no longer people but just pieces you can't identify, a pitiful thing with thin burnt little arms, effigies everyone is supposed to have gotten used to, pictures like this in the paper every day—it is good that such a thing could make my ears ring, could shock me worse than the letter from Andrew which my whole life hung on. But I'm glad that I do not always put myself first, but sometimes get things in the right order.

I suppose I had always expected the letter from Andrew. But it came on Christmas Eve, and I didn't expect it on Christmas Eve, so I thought the one that did come might be a love letter. I don't think Andrew would design a letter such as this to reach me on Christmas, but maybe Cookie would. Anyway I read it just as a jet was going overhead, so that the jet's loud roar seemed to emanate from my head, otherwise I was calm:

Dear N.
I'm afraid it has to be over. You are young and beautiful and you'll be okay. I'm sorry.
                              Love, Andrew

It was such a bleak plain letter, on memo paper from his San Francisco office, from the desk of Andrew Mason bringing you this death stroke.

But anyway, my God, how can I even be comparing mere erotic disappointment with the horror of the death of these poor burned people; thank God my sensibilities are not that deranged, that I can still make distinctions and got sick at the stomach about the proper thing.

I know I will get over Andrew, but it's just that I don't think I ever will. I could try harder to get over Andrew if I could get myself to believe it. It has been almost two weeks—no, more now—with no word from this man I used to talk to every day, in whose arms I have lain hundreds of times, with whom exchanged words of love of the most sacred kind, with whom begun, perhaps, a child—how could I believe it? Of course I cannot. It is simply not like Andrew to be so bitterly cruel and I cannot believe it.

Today I have to think of other things—Gavvy, Ev, and about how to get the tires fixed, and who sent this photograph. Should I literally fear a bomb thrown in our window or arson?

Well, that letter from Andrew made me numb but not surprised. Part of me had always expected that letter. Summonses and regrets and sentences always come that way, in neat envelopes, and I never thought we would get away with it anyway, Andrew and I, for one thing because we were causing pain to other people, that's partly why, but also, if love like ours—true, relentless and complete— really existed, why does no one seem to have it, or be in it, or however this thing is to be expressed? Where or what is it? We must have made it up.

The day after it came, Christmas Day, I couldn't believe the letter, though, and had to keep pulling it out of the drawer where I had quickly hid it out of my sight. My Christmas present, and that's what it said all right. I almost called him then. I had almost worked myself up to call him before the letter came anyway, to wish him happy Christmas and to mention that I was a little worried about my period being late, but then I hadn't. Well, I knew they were embroiled in Christmas; Cookie's old parents always come up from Texas. Cookie is the youngest daughter, or "baby daughter," as she always puts it, of a former governor of Texas. But now, after Andrew's letter, I could never mention my period; it would just seem like a trick.

I just wanted you to tell me yourself, I could say. So I could really believe it. How could you expect me to believe what is merely written in your cold handwriting; *that* doesn't tell me anything, tell me in your voice. I wonder if he could.

Then I got mad thinking well, the silly fool, does he

really think he can turn back now, he has burnt his bridges, Cookie will just torture him now one way or another for the rest of their lives; what a defeat for you, Andrew. You are more conventional and timid than I had thought — worried what people will think, no doubt. It was scorn that kept me away from the telephone.

But I love Andrew, I really don't want his life to be ruined. Even if he doesn't spend it with me, he can't spend it with Cookie, he's been too cruel to her. Doesn't he know anything? As for me, I realized this was the payoff, the Other Woman getting hers as she so richly deserves and decent wives have all foretold; all right, God damn it, and I wouldn't touch the damned telephone, I can get along, but I still have the soul of an Other Woman and I always will, too.

Someone told me that once, a psychiatrist. It was at a party — I didn't *go* to a psychiatrist. Well, once I had to see Gavvy's psychiatrist. I told him all the strange things Gavvy had done to me and none of the strange things I had done to Gavvy. Did not tell him I ran around on Gavvy for fear he would try to cure me. Yet he seemed to understand me very well and did not suggest cure. Neither did this party one, who was making advances and smiled and observed that I had "free libido."

"What?" And he explained it. Didn't seem to belong to anyone. Andrew had an unowned quality, too; perhaps one lets this show at parties, though Andrew seemed to me to be behaving at this polite gathering with perfect decorum and mostly talked to the men. But Bess claimed she could see it, and said, "Some little typist will walk off with that man before the year is out," and at the time I couldn't see how she could say that, Mr. Mason over there chatting quietly at the side of his big agreeable wife to some friend, but even obtuse Bess could see some hunger in him.

It truly was not our hunger that brought us together, I don't think, but our affinity. I don't think Andrew could have loved just anybody. It seemed to have something to do with me. We were just meant for each other, simply. But we were both relieved to find out it was real love, that it wasn't just the pleasure of betraying Gavvy and Cookie that led us on. Andrew never did think it could have been that: "I don't hate Cookie, I'm very fond of her," he would say. "I just wish she would disappear." He didn't then believe in hate. Even then I wasn't so sure.

Our talk was of passion and also of daring. We had each separately discovered the pursuit, in which we were now evil companions, the knowing of thyself enjoined on you by philosophers and poets, or that's how we loftily conceived it—weren't we silly? Sometimes, our lips pressed together, our hearts beating together, it would seem to Andrew and me that we were much smarter than other people, or much luckier, to be let in on the great secret that you must sometime dare and risk all you have. If once you see your choices clearly and you draw back, you'll never recover. I mean, if you once admit that your life is wrong and you know why and still fail to change it, then you are doomed forever. That is why I left Gavvy. Looked at one way, Andrew and I were rather conventional adulterers, and looked at the way we looked at it, we were great lovers sternly conscious that all our lives and characters were risked, as in some pilgrimage. And what you risk you sometimes lose.

4 The new envelope containing the photograph has come, to the day, on the two-years anniversary of the consummation of our love, Andrew's and mine; that is, two years ago today we finally went to bed together. The present symbols, death and ashes, are too ghastly to be anything but coincidental, I guess. Or maybe not.

Those were happy times. We had been meeting Wednesday mornings all those months on park benches and wooded walks, hiding our cars in alleys, kissing frantically in anonymous outdoor places and telephone booths and library stacks, and talking about love, about us, about our great desire—truly felt, but we were warned by some indefinable sense of propriety, some precautionary tenderness, that the time was not right.

Then one morning Andrew said this is the morning. We went to Bess's; the Harvills were away for Christmas and I was watering her plants and feeding the animals. We were too apprehensive to talk about it as we drove there; what if after all this time it wasn't beautiful? Maybe there was something the matter with Andrew, to have put it off all this time, or maybe I would not please him. I was insanely fearful the whole way to Bess's that my body would be engraved with elastic marks around my waist and breasts from panty hose and bra when I wished to look like a statue pale and smooth.

We went up to the guest room. I hid my hot face in Andrew's collar. Oh, I remember the suffocating power of my desire to have Andrew inside me, and our terror, to subject our desperate and sacred emotions to this treacherous activity, to our unreliable bodies. Our skin flamed profanely. How meticulous we were, how workmanlike our carefully regulated lovemaking and how surely our true passion transported us. And there were funny parts; for instance just at Andrew's climax Bess's cat Widge at the same moment jumped onto his naked back all claws. A memorable sensation, Andrew says. Also there was a moment when, with my arms around my naked lover, our hot bodies and our mouths pressed close, etc., I looked over Andrew's shoulder and saw an embroidered sampler on the wall of Bess's smart Early American guest room which read, "A ROLLING STONE GATHERS NO MOSS."

Mostly what I remember is how gallantly we both behaved, with this first time something to have gotten behind us, and we were overtaken with pleasure all the same: it augured well. We have laughed as much as we have cried, Andrew and I, and my God how I wish to laugh with Andrew now, or to laugh with anyone, at anything: the laughter has gone out of us around here. I would settle for having Andrew to weep with, even; my tears are close enough, all the time tears at the ready. I can sit here wanting Andrew, wanting and wanting, with all my whole force, concentrating all my will, and nothing, nothing happens.

5 Happy times, or so they seemed, those first few months of my affair with Andrew. And it was at this same time that Osella was getting along well with her man, Big Raider, so the household was warmed temporarily with erotic radiance, complacent egos, good manners. My satisfied good nature prompted me to be courteous and equable to Gavvy for the time being, and Andrew, he said, was attentive to Cookie. What did any of us think we were doing?

The sunshine of Big Raider's personality lit the place up with interracial harmony, but that was more of a problem than a blessing. Poor Osella, so innocent, so dependent, had always been sheltered by John Henry, had spent her life in quiet kitchens. I used to wonder whether her discovery of my infidelity to Gavvy was what shocked her to madness, but I don't see how, after her experiences with the Spinners, it can have been that. I think it was the awkwardness with Mr. Raider that sent her over the edge.

We all thought Big Raider wanted to marry Osella; it was an accepted thing, an idea fostered by him as well as by Osella. He would say to us, "One of these days she's coming to take over my kitchen, you know," or, "Has my bride learned to cook anything fit to eat yet?"

I had mixed feelings about this. Part of me wanted her to make this important marriage; what happiness and triumph, what a comment on life itself that it could sometimes reverse its shabby, ugly coat for people who had not despaired when they had every reason to, and that it could provide surprises. Part of me was worried about what would happen when she went away and left me to the squalor and bewilderment of my former life. I used to try to get Osella to tell me if she and Mr. Raider had made definite plans but she would coyly avoid my questions—only to tease me, I thought.

But her friends were baffled, too; her stout, slow-moving, heavy cleaning-women friends with their eyes that have seen everything, these were worldly women—Lutherine, Lola Mae, Bobbie Jo. Osella was popular, and her friends came and sat comfortably around the house. I suppose they wouldn't have if it had been my house instead of Osella's. They paid no more attention to me than to a shadow, and sometimes indeed they spoke of me—that little bitty woman—when I was in earshot. Other times they would speak of Raider with cagey banter in their obscure metaphorical style.

"When you gonna land that man, Osie?"

"It ain't no man, Raider jus a peach, a big ole peach."

"He done hung on that tree a mighty long time."

"Well, he high up on the branches, mighty high up."

"Heeee, heeeeee. The frost done got at him, you ask me."

"Oh, no, he been hangin there ripenin, but he was camoflagged. Now they done got me a 'lectronic ladder I'm gonna clamb up there and pick me that peach."

"Heeee, heeeeee, hear the woman now. Wish her good luck!"

We thought we were being hospitable and we were pleased to think Osella felt at home enough to have her friends in to this liberal, this democratic, this unprejudiced place. We gave ourselves a good many airs this way and got what we deserved, a good look at ourselves. It was an embarrassment for us, but for Osella it may have been a disaster, and I think it was this which sent her mad.

One night Gavin and I, Bess and Joe Harvill, and another couple, after a concert, impulsively stopped in at the Zanzibar where Big Raider was singing. Raider was good, with an easy manner, reaching out his big arms to his audience, making them laugh, filling the place with his large creamy voice when he sang. He was pleased to see us and made some public joke about the place being raided by the D.A., even though this was after Gavin had left the District Attorney's office and gone into the firm. Anyhow, he sent a free round of drinks, and dropped by the table, making us feel embarrassed but pleased with the glamorous attentions, and people watched us from neighboring tables as if "Happy Birthday" was being sung to us. The Zanzibar is pretty sleazy, full of slicked-up teen-agers and serious drinkers and Black Panthers at outside tables not listening to the singing.

The next afternoon our phone rang and I answered it in my bedroom. Big Raider.

"I'm just calling to tell you how pleased I was that you and Gavvy come out to the Zanzibar last night. I appreciate it," he said.

"We enjoyed it, too, Mr. Raider."

"I did want to tell you something else, too, N., are you upstairs? Good, well, it's just that I wanted to say that when I come over there to your house I sense a certain excitement when you're around and I wondered if you felt it, too."

I was puzzled and didn't understand what he meant and just mumbled some politeness.

"Yes? Well, it's you," he said. "I just wanted to tell

you. I don't suppose I could see you? My heart is so full, could I see you?" Plain enough, and yet I still thought he was wanting to tell me something about Osella, of whom his heart was supposed to be full, wanting perhaps to make me his confidante.

"I was thinking maybe we could meet someplace. Your husband's going out of town next week, maybe we could have dinner. Maybe before he gets back. Nothing sneaky. Some quiet place where you aren't known. Maybe out to the Airport Inn," and as I was realizing what he was getting at, as he was saying this, I also realized that Osella had come into the room and was standing behind me— arms clenched into fighting fists like a boxer, face blanched with rage—and looking at me with puffy eyes.

"Tell the man you'll be there," she said.

"Uh, well, I suppose I could," I said to Raider, mystified. "The Airport Inn? What time?" And he told me and we hung up.

"Why did you want me to say that?" I asked Osella.

"I has mah reasons. Let him cool his heels out to the Airport Inn awhile."

"I suppose he wants to talk about you; he probably doesn't realize it might look, that Gavvy might . . ." I didn't know if she thought I'd been angling after her peach, her prize. Unluckily she had picked up the phone downstairs to answer it; that's how she came into this. Now she gave me her glance again of slumberous rage and waddled out and said no more, and that might have been the end of it.

But instead all hell broke loose, a hell of silly shame, discomfort, telephone calls, whispered conversations so Osella wouldn't hear. It started by me telling Gavvy and him telling his mother. Then I compounded it by telling Bess.

"You'll never guess who made an amorous advance," I said.

"Yes, I would, Big Raider," she said. She could guess

because he had called her up, too, and when we checked we found out he had, sure enough, called the third woman, Angela Hood, and he had said the same thing to all of us. "Different trysting places, at least," Bess said. "Nice of him to insure that we didn't all meet each other, all gussied up, in new hairdos and slinky clothes."

"Him hiding behind a potted palm," I said. What had he been up to really? We discussed it endlessly. You just don't know what people will turn out to have in their hearts.

"You simply can't have him in any more," Gavin's mother said. "But how awkward to drop him. But you can't have the man calling up every woman he meets. How distressing!"

It seemed distressing at the time, but now I have no idea why. It was curious. Did we object to being tricked? Or were we hurt that he had called our friends, too? Perhaps he had an obsession, but then so do lots of people about different things and you still invite them over. Instead we turned on Mr. Raider.

I wonder what I would have said to him if Osella hadn't come in. "My dear sir," I would have said in haughty tones. At least that is what Bess and Angela assured me they said. We agreed that Mr. Raider was now *de trop*.

But why? Because he was making advances to one, or three, married ladies? But an advance from a man usually improves him in one's view, even if just a bit. Because he wasn't serious about his advances, as inferred from the fact of his making them to three ladies at once?

"*Three* married women at once is hardly the work of a serious seducer," said Angela Hood.

"Or else of a very serious, dedicated, energetic seducer," I said. Perhaps we now despised him because he was a silly trickster, a crank phone-caller—it only just occurs to me to wonder about him as the phantom phone-caller. Raider! That would account for the late night hours and for many other things.

Haunted liberals, we searched our hearts; was it because he is black that we now despised him, and because he was the maid's boyfriend and had stepped out of line?

I thought it was the latter reason and that we were snobs.

"*I* think, frankly, that it's because he's black," Bess said. "I think we have to face our prejudices honestly. If he was an elderly white gentleman, we'd be amused. We'd chalk it up to show biz, or eccentricity. But here we are hollering rape, like Southern belles."

"You can't have the man making a pest of himself," Gavin's mother said.

"I think he shows excellent judgment, three such lovelies," said Gavin, much amused.

Osella only mentioned it once, but from her words I inclined to think she blamed me, and we didn't tell her about Bess and Angela. She lectured me.

"I'm tellin you one thing," she said, "I don't say Raider done right, but I'm tellin you, you got to get hip. If you go roun to these clubs, people gonna talk that way to you, and you got to know how to turn them off. If you goes around to these places, people is always comin up with things. 'Go long now, you gettin too big fo yo pants,' you says, or sometimes you plays 'em for a while. A lot of that ole stuff goes on and you got to get hip."

I figure she thought we had led Big Raider on in some way, but she didn't let him off altogether. I heard her one day on the telephone saying, "You wonderin whether I'm upstairs or downstairs?" in a sweet voice, and then in a deep, menacing one, "I'm tellin you I'm downstairs, and what you mean callin upstairs around here?"

And whatever humiliation she felt must have been deepened when her friends found out. I think Gavvy's mother told Lutherine. So now the talk would go:

"When you gonna land that man, Osie?"

"Oh, I'm gonna clamb up there and pick me that peach one a these days."

"You done forgot you gotta give that little bitty woman some of that peach."

"Oh, sho, I'm gonna cut it in two and give her the rotten half."

"You done forgot about the seed in that peach."

"Give her the rotten half of that, too."

"Maybe that little bitty woman don't like peaches."

"She like peaches, grapefruit, pears and apples." Much hilarity.

Osella, voice rising: "She like peach ice cream, peach shortcake and peach pie."

Lutherine: "Now, that's one pie I never would take a piece of."

I wish I had paid more attention to this enigmatic but most serious talk.

Anyway, we didn't ask Osella not to have Mr. Raider over any more; he simply did not come. Perhaps she wouldn't let him, or perhaps she didn't see him any more. We couldn't be sure she did, and there were signs, by her sad face, that she didn't. Perhaps his was a stratagem for getting rid of Osella, we simply did not know. And yet Osella pretended everything was normal between them. She went out on Thursdays and Sundays and sang in her choir and went to his club afterwards, or said she did. Did she, I wonder? New cars brought her home. But she still quoted him a lot: Raider say this, Raider say that, "Raider say if I give up church singin and take up jazz singin I got a future as a entertainer. But I don know, I'm a churchgoin woman, and them entertainers ain't always types you would want to mess with, as a type of person, excep Raider. I knows what John Henry would have said. Well, he's dead, though, and he was a old-fashioned man some ways. But he's a livin presence to my heart, too, and that's how it should be. Raider say a widow should respeck her husband's memory long as she lives, but that don't mean she can't remarry. Well, John Henry was a lot older than me, and we always knowed I'd live his widow. Raider say . . ."

I suppose if I think about it until I die I'll never sort out Osella's lies from her truth, for she must have been mad all along.

If I could meet someone, anyone I wanted, I think I would meet Mr. Spinner and get him to show me his tool. Then I'd ask him if all those things are true. But would he tell me? What a lot of lies the world is.

"Mr. Spinner, tell me very frankly, did you ever by any chance expose yourself to Mrs. Barnes when she was in your employ?"

"I beg your pardon, Madam?"

I must think about Big Raider. Perhaps he is still very much involved in all this. I have no theories about Big Raider at all, and that kind of worries me.

6 From fear to joy. What is the pattern of human life? Tonight the angel of optimism is ascendant. Though mistrust of life still seems like a reasonable stance, now I feel ashamed of mistrust, the way you do when someone gives you a present when you thought they had forgotten you. Decide upon joy. I feel strong in knowing that all will be well in my life—if ever it can be well—by, let's say, next Wednesday. Well, I can wait that long, and defend and be strong that long. Easy.

In a way the wild excitement I feel when I think of it is more like the wild terror of other recent moments than it is like the middle moments between terror and joy, say, like this afternoon when nothing was happening at all. Fed on fresh persecutions, I have worked up a desire for the life of excitement, I guess, and now am driven mad when things are quiet and blank like this afternoon, with the children gone and Ev better, reading comfortably on the sofa and watching television, and us locked in so cozily I could not bear the thought of going out to look for tires. It would have been a perfect time to work on my paper but I couldn't. The clock ticked, my mind raced around the room resenting the stillness, I wrote with limp fingers, limp words, while my real thoughts were peering into closets like a bored child, thinking why doesn't something happen? Why doesn't the sender of poison letters come face me? Where is he now?

Then in a single moment the aspect of the world changed again, with a magnificent flourish, with a great flinging wide of doors. I think perhaps I caused it myself, by creating a blank space in my life and heart where my resentments about Andrew had been, by letting myself weep and rail, thereby clearing a little light space in the middle of the gloomy patch of things into which joy could now come rushing. Maybe our sufferings, however unlikely and of our own making, maybe even the petulant fear of loneliness, are the means by which you earn the right to great happiness.

I mean that Andrew called after these weeks of silence, and it is as if something is healed and repaired in the world, and restored to rightness. I feel whole and tightly stoppered like a bottle of something fragrant. I know the Famous Inspector would be amazed by this; I am myself, and yet I'm not, for I really did in my secret heart believe in love and think it would prevail.

I was sitting there and the telephone rang; I felt no special leap of heart. The phantom phone-caller bores me, Osella bores me, and otherwise it would just be a friend, or somebody selling me something. Then this stunning event, a silence and a faraway voice, distant and familiar, "Hello, N., this is Andrew," as if perhaps I wouldn't recognize him after all this time.

I can hardly describe how I felt or what I said. I felt like an unthawing brook, with the great chunks of ice beginning to wash away down my veins, hopes starting up with a rush, with a gush, my life beginning to trickle and flow. My joy flooded in just to hear his voice, before I knew why he had called, yet in a way I knew, of course. His voice was not happy, it contained a note of mournful fatigue, yet I lavishly, joyfully, tumbled all over the first few telephone words, gurgling, "Andrew, oh, Andrew."

"I'm calling about the letter. You got the letter?"

"Yes, yes . . ."

"I'm sorry. I didn't mean it of course. I *did* mean it, at the time, when I wrote it, of course, but I can't stand it. Without you, being without you."

"Oh, Andrew," I began, "if you knew how it made me feel, opening it. I cannot explain, the horror . . ." Thus my first words were reproaches, yet Andrew is someone I can tell how I feel, so I knew this was all right.

"If you knew how I felt when I wrote it, my frozen hand," he said. "I felt dead. I couldn't write any more words or explain, but I knew you would understand that."

"I didn't, I didn't understand anything, Andrew, no, I just felt furious, no shocked." My fury at Andrew now released itself, querulous words, and my heart pounding, "I couldn't understand how you could do such a thing to me—no, not to me, it wasn't that, I just thought you were doing wrong, going against your heart that way, thinking you could just go back to your other life as if nothing had happened. Things never can be as they were, don't you know anything? I couldn't believe you could think that Cookie could ever forgive you, you would just have to pay and pay . . ." and on and on I went, saying all the things I suppose I had been thinking all these weeks, but Andrew bore all this vituperation and complaint manfully and laughed at me, and at himself.

"I know, I know, my love, I know all this. I've left home again, that's what I'm calling to say."

The roar in my ears again. "You've left again?"

That is, he—Andrew—had left Cookie again. I should have been defended against joy of that nature at someone else's expense, but felt it all the same. Cookie is just a log lying across a beautiful forest path, a stone in my road, and I tried not to think of her sitting in her empty dream house puzzled and sad, having given the best years of her life to Andrew, etc. He had left Cookie that morning, clothes and belongings, too.

"I've checked into the Fairmont, as a temporary measure, and made myself cozy insofar as that's possible, and in fact am about to go catch a plane. I have to go to Chicago, that's how all this came about." His voice was excited, and mine was, so that we shouted all these words at each other.

"How, tell me, what's happened?"

Andrew considered. "You have to understand that the last two weeks have been the worst time in my life," he said. "But I've endured them in good faith. With Cookie, I mean. I've been civil and concerned—I've been *trying*. The household seems to be made up of pairs of eyes watching me—erratic creature, what will he do next? But me bent on doing my duty, oh, yes, and going to the office, and just making my mind up to a life of duty and doing my work, but anyway, I was packing my bag for this trip to Chicago. Had laid it out on the bed, was stuffing my socks into my shoes, and my thoughts went something like why are you taking an extra pair of shoes to Chicago, you'll only be there a couple of days; and this was followed by the thought, very clear, no, you're never coming back to this house; take your shoes."

Well, I could understand that; sometimes something

from the recesses of yourself speaks up very clearly announcing things. And Andrew was listening at last; that was something. He was hearing his inner self and paying attention. Relief was just seizing up my heart through all this, and love heating me up.

"That was it, the incontrovertible inner voice," Andrew was saying. "I packed the rest of my clothes and some other stuff in boxes—we've still got a lot of movers' boxes around—and made my announcement and came here. It was so easy. After all the agony the other time, and this time it was so easy.

"I don't suppose you could come along, to Chicago," Andrew suggested.

"Oh Andrew, how I want to."

"I have to meet with some lawyers tomorrow afternoon, then, depending on what happens, we go to court first thing Monday morning, and it should be all over that day or on Tuesday. I expect to be back Tuesday night. It's a simple matter."

"That isn't long. I could. Oh, you come here. I can't go with you, Ev lying sick here, and the kids coming back tomorrow, and school . . ."

"I know, darling, it doesn't matter. I want you so much. I feel like I've already done my time. I don't want to wait any more, to be with you, but we can stand two or three days, it's to be a lifetime, it's all right."

"You could get a flight directly here to Sacramento from Chicago."

"If I can't get a flight to Sacramento, I'll drive up from here as soon as I get back," Andrew said. "Tuesday night or Wednesday morning."

"I need comforting," I said, and after that our talk descended as it often does to the exchange of loving confidences, and then I told him about the troubles we were having here, about the photograph, and the tires and the savaged door—all of it. Andrew was concerned about this.

He said he would call somebody he knew on the police force here, and that I must keep all the doors locked, that sort of thing. Like me, he could not guess who it might most likely be.

He would come to me soon, he said, as soon as he could, and he loved me and would always love me, he said.

"I can't live without you, that's what I've discovered," he said, one of those histrionic things you say and really mean, and yet of course it isn't literally true. But I felt it, too. "My life is changed forever. You can't do things and then undo them," Andrew said. "Our love is the fact."

I don't know what we said, at the last, or how I pried myself away from the phone when we were done. I know I just sat there a long time holding on to the phone, this lifeline to Andrew, and thinking about the pattern of human love.

And yet, after all, it feels two ways to be a winner. I was excited, chilled and shaking—it was hard to breathe —with happiness. But part of me doesn't like that feeling of being a winner. If life is a combat, then you may win but lose another time when your form is off. I could see too clearly poor Cookie sitting there like a soap-opera wife in her pretty house. I know what it is to be dismissed by Andrew, too, after all. Cookie knows a lot about him I don't know, I suppose. I know some things she doesn't know. I don't think people should play tug of war. I would have turned my back and gone on my way, I would have; it isn't my fault that Andrew has come back to me now. It has to do with the truth and integrity of love. Love turns out to be true and we all ought to be glad of that. You'll be glad someday, I could tell Cookie, though maybe she won't. Anyway it isn't up to me to say. I can imagine Andrew's hard eyes looking at her: I'm going for good, they would be saying, and I can imagine all the things she would be thinking: how can this happen? How does love die?

What would Cookie be thinking, actually, and what should I think? Both Cookie and I must have read the same column in the morning's *Chronicle*. I read such things ashamedly with beating heart, feeling they are spelling out fate for me. I bet Cookie reads them, too:

DEAR DR. CARRUTHERS:

    We are in our mid-forties and have a wonderful marriage, but suddenly I learned that my husband was seen with another woman. It seemed so silly I just couldn't take it seriously, but now I learn they are having an affair. I don't know whether to discuss it with him or ignore it. I don't want a divorce, our years together have been so happy. And our sex life has been good, or at least I thought so, and it has not changed recently. I had been planning a visit to our daughter in Arizona, but perhaps I should postpone this? MRS. P. M.

DEAR MRS. M.:

    If the visit isn't urgent, I'd put it off. If your husband is typical, his foolish behavior isn't going to last very long. He may simply be panicked about approaching middle age.

    Women aren't the only ones to experience the menopause, you know. Men, as they grow older and face the prospect of diminished sexual powers, are apt to experience an urgent prompting to catch up on experiences that they may have denied themselves. The men who feel this most acutely are usually successful, active men, often completely faithful to their wives until this time. But the urgent need to demonstrate sexual vigor, along with restless discontentedness and a feeling that life has passed them by, can be the symptoms of psychic menopause.

    A victim of this syndrome cannot be entirely blamed. It is likely that your husband's love for you is basically undiminished. Therefore, it is likely that his affair will not be a serious or long one.

Honesty, I feel, is the best policy in a marriage. But in this case, I believe it might be wiser not to say anything about his behavior at present. When this crisis passes, it will be easier for him to resume his normal life if there have been no violent upheavals. Of course, if matters persist, or threaten to become permanently damaging to your marriage, you will have to act. Meantime be understanding and patient.

There are, of course, things a wife can do to help her husband through this difficult period. She can take care to make herself as physically attractive to her husband as possible. In our culture, men are much more apt to have kept themselves physically and mentally young because of their professional lives, while women sometimes "let themselves go." A husband feels as young as the woman in his life looks—that's a good rule to remember.

You might also consider a vacation, getting away together. A change of pace and locale can be stimulating and relaxing. At home, you should try to find some new project or hobby that the two of you can share. Most husbands, *all things being equal,* would rather, much rather, stay home.

Words of wisdom in this morning's paper for Cookie and for me.

I didn't tell Andrew about my pregnancy. It didn't seem appropriate; it would seem like a trick, or it would scare him. I can tell him another time. I should have asked where he was staying in Chicago, then I could call him up this minute. Andrew is *there,* corporeal, existing for me. I can flood my mind with thoughts of him, or weave chains of flowers for him, or whatever I want.

I felt, besides exquisite happiness, proud of Andrew, the way I feel proud of the children when they do brave and grown-up things. He had addressed himself to life in a brave way, done things that had been hard for him. I felt like a witch in a cave, alluring and blandishing, and now my victim had come, the victim of my view of life.

Mostly I just danced and floated around, and Ev, who had heard me talking, beamed happily with relief for me.

"Don't worry about no man," she had said once. "Do to suit yourself." But now she smiled and said, "You surely like him, don't you?" and oh, I surely do, I surely do.

7 It was Saturday night and we were happy; this is the way Saturday nights ought to be, snug, the world in order, Ev and I got our lives and spirits in order; we put the lights all on and had music and didn't think of the murderer beyond locking the door.

Unexpectedly Clyde came, about eight-thirty, with brother Beverly in tow, Clyde carrying the perennial little brown-paper sack wrapped around a bottle.

"None of that for Ev," I said in a bossy voice.

"Oh, no, we wouldn't have nothing to drink in the house here, Miss N., don't worry," he said.

"Ev's still in bed but she's awake, she's watching television."

"My, she's gone to bed early. I figured to catch her before she'd went out," he said with some bitterness in his melancholy voice.

"She's been quite sick," I said. His face changed; he was truly surprised by this, he hadn't known.

"Is she bad?"

"Well, someone attacked her in the laundry room on Thursday night and she's been bad ever since, throwing up a lot. I think it's her old trouble, but getting hit brought it on." I was sure from his face he hadn't known about this.

"Well, that's bad, very bad," he said. "Ev taken bad," he said to Beverly as though Beverly had not been standing there. Beverly nodded his somber corroboration.

"What that man want?" Ev called crossly from the bedroom. Clyde sought an encouraging glance from Beverly and approached Ev's door.

"Hello, honey baby," he said mildly, "I hear you sick." She was sitting up watching television. Clyde and Beverly approached with a reverent, hospital-like demeanor. I hovered in back like a nurse. Over Clyde's shoulder I caught from Ev a glance that seemed to say that she was up to dealing with this, so I retreated and settled down, blissful about Andrew's phone call, just treating myself by thinking about it over and over and not thinking about any of the bad things that had been going on. It's funny how your mind can make bad things not matter.

"Why you comin round here, Clyde?" I could hear her say to him.

"Well, Ev, I guess you know why that is, I wish you'd listen to me. I've said I'm sorry and—"

"And I done told you . . ." Ev's voice rising and sharp. Beverly came back out of the bedroom, shutting the door behind him, and gave me an uneasy smile.

"That is one determined woman, I have told Clyde," he said.

"I never have been sure what they fight about," I said.

"Plain truth is, she hasn't no forgiveness. You rouse up a nice quiet woman like Evalin and she ain't never gonna simmer down. I done told Clyde that."

With all of us living in this little place, there's no use me pretending I don't know what goes on in Ev's private life, but I do pretend around A. J. Not around Clyde.

"I'm afraid she just doesn't love him," I said, love seeming to me at that moment sufficient explanation for any vagary of anybody's behavior. Ev loves A. J. I could even accept that, such was the benignity I now regarded as the essential attitude of fate toward humans, however much it may try you and torment you at first. "I'm afraid she loves A. J. She's certainly been with him a long time."

"A. J. ain't no good and never will be," Beverly said. "Evalin know that, too. But on the other hand Clyde done a lot for her, bringin her up from Texas and more. She shouldn't have married him if she gonna treat him like this."

"Clyde isn't very settled down, that's what Ev says. Ev would like a place of her own," I explained.

"A. J. Harper gonna buy her a country mansion no doubt." Beverly laughed and lapsed into silence; perhaps by his sorrowful but resigned expression he was contemplating some domestic disappointment of his own, and turning his cap around in his hands like someone playing an obsequious role in a movie. In Ev's room we could hear their raised voices, and presently Clyde came out, eyes wet and hands trembling. He and Beverly took their leave. Ev crept to the bedroom door and looked after them.

"Ain't that a shame," she said. "I hate a man that cries." Then she ran to the bathroom and threw up, the first time all day. I guess she had found the whole thing that unsettling.

"I wish he'd quit me. You see how he don't do me no good," she said when she came out again and sat gingerly down on the sofa, in a little pain. Then she seemed to feel better. "Maybe we seen the last of him at that if he got it through his head at last. That brother of his wasn't ever a good influence, but he keep him up alongside like he was his mama."

"Beverly? He seems pretty respectable."

"Seems so, don't he. Well, he ain't. Clyde would keep a job if it wasn't for Beverly. Beverly takes him out to the races. I ain't ever been sure just where Beverly gets his cash hisself, either. Clyde ain't ever been up to anything bad without Beverly started it."

"I guess you never can tell," I said, feeling disappointed in Beverly, indeed in the gentle Clyde.

"Clyde went to jail once for Beverly," Ev said, and then, as if remembering this was no longer her problem, she sniffed and smiled and curled her feet up more comfortably.

"You know," she said, "I don't think I'm ever gonna have no man to be what I thought to have when I was a kid. You have a different idea of it when you is a kid."

"I didn't think about men at all, not at all, until after I found myself married," I said. Then it's too late, or almost.

"I never would fool around with no boy," Ev said. "The boys back home would want to fool around—you know—and some girls done, but I had to have a man. Go on and come back when you is a man, I'd say. But I sure don't know what I thought a man was."

"I know *who* I think is a man," I said, ravished by my thoughts of my Andrew, intelligent, handsome, virile, tender personification of manhood; it was all too beautiful to be true, and too lucky—imagine out of all those fakes to have come upon the one real one.

"You take someone like Clyde, he look all right, but he ain't, always cryin and goin on. That's the way, there's a lot who look all right."

"I don't know how you tell. It's a matter of luck, I think."

"You take A. J., he don't look as good as some—well, he ain't as good as some. That's what I mean. You give up your notions then you feel a lot better. It's a matter of what suits you, and A. J. suits and Clyde don't. I don't know if you got to have reasons more than that."

"I don't trust reasons anyway."

"That's why I figure to get a little place with A. J. and we can do all right, and I just feel good about that."

"Well, I hope you aren't sorry," I said, a sourpuss thing to say since I had every reason to believe in love again. But it was A. J. I didn't believe in. Ev wasn't mad, she just laughed.

"You got to follow your own heart," she said, laughing. "Follow Your Own Heart" is a TV program she likes. But it's not a bad phrase, I guess.

Anyway the king of her heart turned up about ten, right after this, wearing a purple suit, some kind of shiny rayon. Oh, well.

"You comin out?" he asked Ev, looking puzzled at her bathrobe—why was she sitting around in that?

"I don't think so. I ain't too good," Ev said. "I been sick, A. J.," and she nodded a warning tiny nod at me, I guess meaning not to say anything more than that. I wondered if she suspected A. J. about the laundry room.

"You come out and have a little fun, do you good," A. J. said, winking at me with his yellow bloodshot hating eye. I could imagine A. J. pummeling Ev, waiting in the dark and doing it, and winking at me now about it, as if I knew.

"You comin?" As Ev had continued to sit there.

"I can't, I really ain't been good," she said.

"She's been horribly sick," I said, "hasn't kept anything down in two days, she couldn't possibly go out." What do you know, his stare said, what do you know about our stomachs?

"Well, that's a terrible shame," he said, sitting down on the sofa next to her. "Want to come outside for a little ride is all? Tell you what, I'll take you for a ride in your car, just ride around a little wouldn't hurt you." Ev shook her head. He looked at me, hating to talk around me, deciding I wasn't going to go away.

"I could take you round to have a look at the place I

rented," he said. "Gave the man the bread today, got the key." Ev looked at him in wild surprise.

"You got our place?" He nodded.

"Hey, A. J., that's great." Her smile grew and grew. Even A. J.'s single-minded misanthropy seemed to melt, and in his smile I could see a faint trace of what he must be like when he is nice, and when he isn't around me. A. J.'s smile had a nice quality for a moment. They both began to laugh.

"Tell me about it," she said, patting his arm. It seemed like a private, special time for her, so I went into my room feeling that despite poor Clyde's disappointment our household had suddenly found favor with the household gods.

I just wanted to be by myself to think reveling thoughts. It was cold in my room, so I got undressed and got under the covers, and then I was struck down right away by the weariest exhausted feeling I have ever felt, so that I couldn't think any thoughts at all but just lay there sinking away. Well, sure—it drifted through my head—it makes sense. I'd been prowling around in the nights, sleeping on the sofa, waking at every noise, worried, half awake for the past four nights, watching and frightened; of course I would be tired, and sleep could come on now; with the children safe at their grandmother's and Ev on the mend happy with A. J., and, the chief miracle, with Andrew nearby, my lover again, exhaustion and relief overwhelmed.

I remember thinking that this must be what it feels like to bleed to death, and that thought reminded me of course of our murderer again, but all I could summon up was oh, well, if he comes tonight he'll just find us, that's all.

Sometime later, I don't know what time, I struggled awake a little and dimly heard Ev's and A. J.'s low voices in the living room with perhaps some scuffling and Ev laughing, saying, "Get away, go along," not angrily, and then rummaging in her bureau, which stands on the other side of the wall of my bedroom, so I can hear the drawers slide. Keys rattling, A. J. leaving—it even got through to me that A. J. was taking Ev's car—yet I could not rouse myself to object but just thought, well, please God he won't wreck it, he's never had an accident yet; and Ev's footsteps in her room were the last thing I heard.

Sunday, January 5

1 My first waking thoughts started up where the last ones had dwindled off, with remembering that Andrew had called, hoping that A. J. hadn't crashed Ev's car and feeling grateful that the marauder hadn't interrupted our night. I lay in my bed warmly happy, reviewing these wonders. Today for work, and then tomorrow, Monday, school would begin again for the children and for me, and the world would take up its accustomed business, and it was a new year. The internal contraceptive device had as yet made no difference to my internal state on the one hand, but on the other we had no further symptoms of botulism. I ought to have known, of course, that radiant happiness lying in warm bedclothes is not a prudent state of mind.

After a while I got up quietly to avoid waking Ev. I was enjoying the silence of the empty house, and made coffee and got back into my bed with my books. I was refreshed, my mind felt so strong it felt able to work at

three times normal to make up for all the timorous moon-
ing time-wasting I had done and now had to make up for.
My brain became full of furious linguistic speculation,
clever little paradigms bubbled forth, hand dashed out
words and arrows, pages and pages full, until about ten-
thirty, when, as if it had been dropped from a great height,
the wrongness of the silence shattered over me.

Coldly I pushed the books aside and went for some
reason to the unusual length of putting on my shoes and
bathrobe. I stood for a minute shivering outside Ev's closed
door asking for her, and then when she didn't answer I
opened her door.

As if asleep, just as in the common phrase, with her
eyes closed, her head resting it seemed comfortably on
the pillow, mouth open a little, but heaviness and silence,
a tangible shroud—no, a color. She was the wrong color.
She had faded to a gray chalky color, like a dark cloth
which has been washed too often; her luster or her deep
force was gone, so I knew she was dead, though I had
never seen a dead person before. I am sorry I can only
put it in this hard, bitter way—she was lying in such-and-
such a position, she had turned the color of old bark—
but otherwise I weep. I seem to weep more now than when
it first happened. To keep away the tears when that is
necessary, I have to present it to my mind like a scene
from a movie, viewed by me from a distance, me in my old
bathrobe shivering at Ev's door, looking at Ev's long arms
lounging deadly, tucking up the bedclothes around her
belly because her stomach had hurt her.

I crept closer, too shocked to feel anything but chill
and hesitant curiosity, wanting to find out what I hated
and feared to know. Her lips were apart as though she
would speak, and she seemed warm, she seemed to exude
warmth although plainly dead. I had thought the dead
were cold. The thought passed through my mind that
perhaps the process of dying was one of having the warmth
taken out of you, that in the moments of death the room

around you would be heated by your escaping life. More blankets to keep the life in was my wild thought, and I reached up to pull the pink blanket around her shoulders, seeing only then that the warmth was because she had her heating pad lying across her belly beneath the covers, warming her poor belly; there was the cord still plugged in. I left it plugged in and stood back stupidly; I am such a failure and never do at terrible moments what I afterwards wish I had done. Then I ran away, and now I wish I had sat down with her awhile and arranged her covers and untied her headscarf and folded her hands. Instead I ran away, sparing myself the sight of my friend dead, just her shell left, and went into the living room where I stood for a long time with wet eyes but not crying or thinking, not doing anything. I stood just trying to get some sense of this terrible event, but I could get no sense of it at all. My heart had swollen up.

In a few minutes it came through to me that I had better do something, and this was a kind of relief; instead of stupefied inaction I was seized by resolution, order and effectiveness; I sank into a massive composure that carried me for quite a while. First I called Mr. Hoaglund, the manager, who came right over and pulled the bedspread over Ev's face and called the doctor.

Mrs. Hoaglund was with him, right at his elbow but keeping one eye on me the whole time she gawked at Ev, too, and back at me as if she feared I might do something distraught or odd: I was her department. She wore a sumptuous long red velvet robe, improbable and incongruous, as if she had been surprised out of a secret life to come attend to this bad thing. I just—I don't know—stood around.

"What happened?" she asked me and Mr. Hoaglund. "What caused it?"

"Overdose I would guess," Mr. Hoaglund said. "Was she a user of drugs?"

"Drugs?"

"Was she depressed?" Mrs. Hoaglund wondered anxiously. "Is she really gone? Sometimes you can't feel the heartbeat but they aren't gone. A mirror. They say . . ."

"Well, I've called the doctor, that's all we can do," Mr. Hoaglund said, and, after considering a moment as we stood staring at Ev's form with the bedspread covering her, reached over and pulled it back down, revealing her face again. It was the same, lying there as if asleep, ash gray.

"We ought to try to find out what it was she took," Mr. Hoaglund said, looking under the bed.

"She'd been sick!" I cried out. "She'd been sick for several days. But we thought she was better, she seemed a lot better last night."

"It gives you the creeps," Mrs. Hoaglund said, "a young woman like that. To think how sudden you can be carried off."

"Heart," Mr. Hoaglund said. "Could of been a strain on her heart."

"She got sick on Thursday night after what happened in the laundry room, remember? After that she began to throw up."

"Internal hemorrhage," Mrs. Hoaglund said. "That can happen." But Mr. Hoaglund shook his head to indicate that it could not.

Well, I didn't know why Ev was dead. I didn't understand it.

"Sometimes rheumatic fever as a child," Mrs. Hoaglund was saying. "My niece. Let's make you a cup of coffee, dear, and the doctor should be here, we'll find out what he says, there's nothing we can do for her, poor thing."

"We ought to be able to find out what it was she took, an empty bottle or something," Mr. Hoaglund was saying, going into the bathroom.

It occurred to me I had better call Gavvy's parents, to tell them what had happened, so they wouldn't bring the children home in the middle of all this. Or maybe Gavvy would bring them back, knowing I was alone now. This frightened me. I realized that I still felt afraid of Gavvy. That didn't make much sense, but I was, and in spite of his friendly, his impersonal smile. He would be glad that Ev was dead was my thought. But I had to tell, and so I called Gavvy's mother, and I could hear my thin little composed voice saying calmly, "I'm afraid that Ev has died here suddenly in bed in the night, and it would be better if the children maybe didn't come in the midst of all this. We have to have the doctor and her relatives and arrangements."

"Of course, how dreadful," Gavin's mother said in a disapproving way, finding in this a good example of the unsuitable environment I provide. "We'll keep them here until we hear from you."

Mr. Hoaglund came back with Mrs. Hoaglund and a couple of neighbors gathered on the way. I became conscious of a certain social strain on them arising from their uncertainty about Ev's and my relationship. I wasn't the bereaved, was I, so was not exactly deserving of sympathy; on the other hand I'd had a shock, and anyway I was the only person around who did deserve the sympathy which everyone wanted lavishly to give. How clearly I remember all this part, and yet at the time it went by in a formless timeless way as if we were all under water. People came in to sympathize with me because I was better than no one. Mrs. Hoaglund fed me coffee and toast and I ate. Some students next door, who had never spoken to me at all, came and had coffee and I think they wanted to view the body, but I didn't invite them to. It was as if someone had painted crossbones on our door, so that the people in our units and perhaps the whole world knew. Like vultures of death, like flies around sticky death, I could see them outside, kids and people pushing baby carts, looking covertly at our door.

A doctor came and went into the bedroom with Ev and listened to her dead chest in a ritual way with his stethoscope not tucked into his ears. Then he asked me a lot of questions, about her illness, about her previous illnesses, about what the symptoms were, when they had come on, how long her hospital stays had been in the past, had she had a big New Year's Eve? He wrote down the answers on a form, shook hands with us all and prepared to leave.

At some point, and I think at this point, the telephone rang. Mrs. Hoaglund answered it; answering the telephone is I guess one of the duties the bereaved is spared. The poor woman's face, as I watched, changed from brisk solicitude to one of amazed indignation.

"Hiss, hiss, hiss," the telephone was saying, Osella's husky sibilants audible across the room. Mrs. Hoaglund held the telephone away from her ear and boggled at it.

"White-trash whore," the voice said.

"Hang up, hang up, we've been getting these crank calls," I said, and Mrs. Hoaglund dropped the receiver as if it were a dead hand. I wondered if Osella was checking up on us, to see if I was home and what we were doing.

Mr. Hoaglund came up close to me and spoke under his voice, with a kindly touch on my shoulder: "What did you want done with the body?" He nodded toward the doctor, whom he had been consulting. I suppose I looked witless, without idea.

"I've talked to the office," the doctor said. "The coroner's office. They can take her away now and the next of kin can claim the body from there, from the morgue. The body belongs to the next of kin. I think we'll be having an autopsy. Shall I tell them to take her away now? Unless there is any special reason—religious observance—you might—?"

I didn't really understand. I think I had imagined they would take her picture and measure things, or that more people would come and more questions would be asked. I thought this was the beginning. It didn't seem possible that this was the end; they would take her away now, when it had been only, it seemed, an hour since I found her. I know it was longer in reality.

"Who *is* her next of kin?" Mr. Hogalund asked. "We ought to be calling them."

"Her husband, Clyde, I guess, or her parents." I didn't know how to get in touch with them. We would have to look in her address book.

"She has an address book," I said, and Mrs. Hoaglund seemed to understand what I meant, that I couldn't bring myself to root through Ev's stuff with Ev lying there.

"I'll have a look," she said. The doctor left. I just sat, and I remember that was the first I looked at the clock, and it was three in the afternoon.

I think if I had understood, had had my wits about me, I wouldn't have let them just take Ev away like that so soon; she ought to have had a place to lie so people could visit her a last time; I bitterly regret that. But the coroner's men came, men in white jackets over policeman pants, carrying a stretcher. They nodded discreetly, inquiringly. Mr. Hoaglund inclined his head delicately toward the bedroom. I should emphasize the tact and respect with which everyone behaved, even normally quite objectionable people like Mr. Hoaglund, even Mrs. Hoaglund, for I guess it was she who took the sheets off Ev's bed when they had taken Ev away, and folded the blankets on a chair the way it is done in hospitals when a bed is waiting for a new patient.

I didn't see them carry Ev off; I pretended to be a long time in the bathroom. I listened to them carry her off, silently with no remarks, only the shuffling dead-march sound of their feet. That was the end of Ev, I have never seen her again.

"A nasty shock for you, dear," Mrs. Hoaglund said for

the twentieth time when everybody was gone and Ev's room was tidied up and the striped bare mattress revealed. "I'd leave her things right where they are until her people can get them."

"Did you find her book?"

"No, she didn't have any addresses. I looked everywhere. She had a sort of diary but it didn't have any addresses. I wouldn't worry; her people are sure to call, aren't they?"

I wasn't sure they were. She had sent Clyde away with such finality, and she seldom heard from her parents, though she dutifully visited them. They were old and waited for her visits. I couldn't seem to think this problem out but instead blinked stupidly, I suppose, or shrugged, for Mr. Hoaglund said, as he and Mrs. Hoaglund prepared to leave, "It doesn't make too much difference how long. That is, they refrigerate them."

2 "You'll be all right, you're sure, dear?"
I'm sure, sure, yes, of course, so they all went away and the house was empty—even, it seemed, empty of me. It was as if I wasn't there, I might as well have been a table or a chair.

The house was bare of life. Where was Ev? And what shall I do next, I kept thinking, not desperately but like a bored child. What I did was get a can of Colt 45 Malt Liquor from Ev's closet, where she hid it, and sat drinking it at the kitchen table. With the drink or the solitude, what followed was a little like thawing after frostbite, the experience of pain at each extremity. Felt pain but still had no thoughts. There didn't seem to be anything to think *of*. Perhaps I could call Andrew, if I knew what hotel he was staying at. I tried to think of the names of Chicago hotels: Blackstone? Sheraton? Chicago Hilton? I suppose there are millions of hotels in Chicago. Resentful was how I felt, and angry for Ev's sake, just when things were working out; how can you follow your own heart when it stops beating without you knowing it in the night? If I should die before I wake. I tried to think of practical matters, of how I was going to tell her family, and how to find A. J. and Clyde; would A. J. bring her car back? Did she wake before she died, did she have a moment to realize she was going, would you want to or not? I don't know. I had a million thoughts suddenly, which I am still having, so I don't know which ones came then and which have come to me since.

The principal thing that came to me then, as I sat there, came like the touch of cold fingers at the back of the neck, disgusting and dread—came like the touch of a murderer. It was only then that I saw that all I have been saying, we are going to be murdered—boring my skeptical friends, dreaming and brooding of nothing else, fearing the killer approach in the night—all this had come true. That is, the murderer had struck just as we had feared and he had murdered Ev.

I had not thought of it just like this before. Ev's trouble, its natural course, had been in my thoughts, and thoughts about fate and justice and injustice, but I had not realized that this was in fact the feared thing, the justification of our fears. It was only that it hadn't happened exactly as I had imagined. It had sneaked up and now was gone by without me realizing that the murder was at hand. That happens a lot in life, I guess, that the thing you were dreading happens offstage, at the wrong time. Was that it? you say. Was that all?

3 After the thing you feared has happened, what you feel is a sense of anticlimax, impatience, even self-satisfaction. Congratulations, marvelous organism, to have come through this dreadful week of terror and apprehensions and still be sitting sturdily on a chair in your kitchen drinking beer at the end of it. This was apart from my grief for Ev, which was to grow worse later but was not my principal feeling now, for she had been taken off so softly and with such dispatch I could not realize it. Now only concern for the practical problems, and a bitter satisfaction to learn we had not misconstrued or underrated the malice of our enemy and his plans for us.

Mostly I had a feeling of the end, like the end of a play. The events are over; it now remains to pause and reflect. As at the end of a play, purged by pity and fear, you emerge with altered aspect, strengthened in spirit. You wrap yourself in your warm new purity and strength and step off briskly along the new street.

But sitting there I began to make out dimly where the new street led, slowly came to see it stretching off into a future built up on either side with a predictable landscape of police departments and courtrooms and detective laboratories and people, police and judges bustling along the street, too, and the Famous Inspector—that is, some actual counterpart who would now have to see to this murder. A murder is the ending only for the victim, but for everybody else it is a beginning. Some real inspector would come, I would have to talk to him, he would take notes. I am ashamed to say it was kind of a relief to realize I would be talking to him, when I had thought all along it would be Ev telling him how the murder had happened to me.

"Who do you imagine it was?" the new inspector will say. That is hard. I would have to think of the true answer to that now, and could not indulge my fancy and speculation. Who really? Clyde, A. J. or Osella. I couldn't imagine Gavin hurting Ev, for why should he? I forgot then about the time he had hurt her. I truly did not know who I thought it was.

I supposed I should call Gavin's mother to say something more to the children. Everyone would be wondering what was going on. I supposed I should look in Ev's drawers for her address, which had to be there somewhere; she couldn't just lie at the morgue for months until Clyde happened to come by here. But I couldn't think of any way to find him, or her parents, whose last name I couldn't remember. I wasn't sure when to expect the Famous Inspector. What would the doctor have told him? Perhaps he would wait for a report from the coroner.

Tomorrow morning I could go find A. J. at his car wash and tell him. But what if he was the murderer? Perhaps I shouldn't tip him off; unaware that Ev was dead, he could be tricked by the Inspector into saying, "Sheeyit, I didn't hit her hard enough to hurt her," or something like that. Perhaps I shouldn't meddle in this.

Perhaps Ev had not died from blows but from love. Perhaps A. J. had insisted on making love. "Git away," she had been saying, and "Stop that, you," but maybe he'd insisted, and her frail and disordered body unable to endure it had been precipitated into fatal agonies by his thrusting inside her.

A. J. was the last person to see her alive. Had she been alive when he left? Was I sure of that?

They should not have taken her away so quickly, they should have left her on the bed for us to sit by her and cry, and for her father and mother to come and see her, or we should have had candles.

Maybe now I can move out of this unit.

How can Ev be dead? Did she mind? Did it make any difference to her? Did she bring her death on by daring to be cheerful and plan to take driving lessons?

How I badly wanted Andrew, and I suppose if I had called him he would have come instantly, for Andrew has concern for distress, and practical good sense, too, but of course I couldn't call him, and in a way I wouldn't have wanted to give myself that comfort and joy. It didn't seem right. It would be disrespectful of Ev to use her death like that.

I sat and sat at my kitchen table, I suppose not moving, staring off into the falling dusk without putting the lights on, like an old discouraged person, trying to work this out. But the police never came. Soon I couldn't seem to stay awake, so I went to bed, though it must have been early. Perhaps I had been poisoned or given a sedative, I remember thinking that. I wondered if the doctor had given me some drug, or Mrs. Hoaglund had, or perhaps I had botulism and would die in my sleep like Ev, but I wasn't going to try to keep awake for that.

Monday, January 6

1 I awoke before morning, imprisoned in a dream which, knowing myself to be awake, I nonetheless could not shake off or climb out of; my head was stuck in it; across my inner eyes the dream event repeated and repeated itself. We were trying to get Ev into her coffin, a small square packing crate of slats into which she couldn't fit. So we had sawed off her legs. Evidently she was frozen, for these legs were bloodless and solid, leaned up against a wall, flat and smooth where they had been severed, like sawed logs.

Yet this dream was less terrible, I knew, than the things I would have to remember when I became fully awake, so I hung between sleep and waking but finally my mind opened up despite me to admit my real room, a dark box with streetlight creeping in at one window around the blind, and I remembered on the other side of my thin wall Ev's empty room with her striped mattress, and Ev herself was where? In a morgue. "They refrigerate them."

And once I had promised her to see her into a good coffin. This was now my most vivid thought, and it brought me the rest of the way awake, to think I had made her an important promise which I wasn't going to keep.

The coffin business came up once when she was writing in her book, an autobiography she was writing which caused her to think about her childhood, things that had happened to her.

"If I died," she had looked up and said, "I'd like to make sure they put me in the coffin right away and bury me quick. I've always had a fear about that, after some-thing that happened when I was little. My granpa died, he was an old man—I remember him—and they done laid him out and done everything proper. This was in the sum-mer. My granpa, my daddy's daddy, this was. They was gonna bury him on the place, round in back of the woods. We had the funeral, the minister come, and a lot of people, for he was old and knowed a lot of people. They had·put the coffin on a wagon to carry it around to the place, and we was walkin along followin the coffin when suddenly the lid of the coffin rose up and a hand retch out, every-body screamed and run, the horses run, I run, too, and didn't see no more till we had crept back, and my daddy was cryin. See, the corpse had swole up inside the coffin, and as we was going along it bust open the coffin. That was the only time I ever see my daddy cry, how he done loved *his* daddy and now he ain't even buried him right. I seen my granpa's belly swole up twice the size, it was his belly done split open the lid of the coffin, and I thought then and there, I have thought a lot of times since, I hope they puts me in quick in a strong one nailed down tight."

And then she had laughed at his morbid notion, and went back to her writing, and presently she said with a shiver—somebody passed over her grave right then—"You would see to it if I died?" and I had said, "Sure."

2 Well, I didn't want to lie there thinking in remorse, so I got up and dressed and made myself toast thinking meticulously about toast. The door to Ev's room was closed and so was the door to the children's room; they might have all been dead, and I was alone. I longed self-indulgently for my children, knowing I could have them, they were not dead, and I tried not to think of Ev. Or I tried not to think of her lying dead but as she was, alive and smiling. That is still the problem; my memory of her dead gray face blots out her smile.

I wished for a brisk competent chat with Andrew about what I must do now, what I must say. I tried to imagine what he would advise, and how he would think I was brave. I was thinking of myself. I saw Ev's shoes in the front closet, her good shoes she changes out of, very high heels and pointed toes. I looked at them expecting emotion, because I had heard someone say once that looking at a dead loved one's shoes is particularly sad, but it wasn't, not sadder than anything else. These were just shoes.

I thought therefore I must be composed enough to go in there and find her book but I wasn't. Her other things unloosed my tears—these were the first real tears I had shed, with pain like a knife in the throat—her lime-green negligee, old slippers, pincushion, hot comb, a letter in an envelope postmarked 1947, something she had kept for over twenty years, but I didn't read it. The force of your caring has no power over being dead; being dead rules everything out. I can't stand that.

I wept half an hour on her mattress until my head ached, and then pulled myself up and looked again at the heating pad, cord wound neatly around it by Mrs. Hoaglund, and the bare striped ticking and the absence, the inexplicable quality of emptiness and goneness. Dead *and* gone, I kept thinking, dead *and* gone, now seeing the distinction.

I found her book right in the nightstand drawer, and her parents' number, McCabe, no current number for A. J. or Clyde, just a long string of old numbers crossed out. Phone numbers for herself, neatly written, Evalin McCabe Wilson, a dozen numbers one after another crossed out and my number at the end.

So I had been up for hours and expressed my grief and had more coffee and it was still only eight o'clock Monday morning. This was the day the New Year was to have begun, me back to the university, the children back to school, a new week of a new year and a new life, but now look, and even thinking about Andrew was not enough to cheer me up except in theory. I knew I did have something to be happy about but it seemed wicked to think about happiness and love.

It seemed to me that if the police would hurry and come, I would plan to go to my Old English seminar at eleven, that this would be a particularly good thing to do, distracting and positive and future-facing. My professors would understand why I hadn't finished my term papers: a murder at home. I had never bothered to wonder about them before, but now I saw how it must be for other people who are involved in murders, too. You see them in the papers lit up by lights, overcoated people crowded all around them, the photographers speaking to them, gawkers pushing forward. But then, you realize, everyone goes away after the picture is over and leaves them in this same morose and desolate silence, so desperately lonely, and it is only eight o'clock in the morning with hours and hours and hours to go.

Too early to call her parents. I knew that perhaps I should go see them—you shouldn't telephone with bad news—but my tires were flat and anyway I had to stay here for the police. The morning dragged along and the police didn't come. I had the puzzled, wounded feeling of a person on a snipe hunt. I had missed or misunderstood something. Why did no one come?

About nine-thirty I called Ev's folks. "I'm afraid I have bad news," I said so they could set their minds. I wondered if I should have said, "Maybe you'd better sit down." I couldn't tell how her parents felt or what they thought. "I see," they said, and "Thank you very much," and that they would come for her things and go to the morgue to see her.

After that, in quick succession, Bess called, and Gavin's mother called to say she had sent Polly and Petey to school and kept Ivan and India with her, and when should she bring them home again? She has about a one-day tolerance of small children. Andrew didn't call, but he never calls during daytime hours. At ten-thirty I couldn't stand it any longer, just sitting there wondering what they were doing, so I called them, the police.

"It's Mrs. Hexam," I said. "I'm calling about the murder." A silence, expressive of puzzlement. Maybe people don't call them in the mornings about murder, or maybe murders don't happen in the morning.

"Yesterday, the murder of Evalin Wilson."

"Just a minute, please." Sound of shuffling paper, not an exasperated but a serious pause. It is a serious word, I thought, not one they take lightly. It was even pleasant, in a way, to wield that word; it was the only power I have had in so long.

"Wilson. A coroner's autopsy is scheduled today. I think you want to call the coroner's office," the voice said.

"No, I want the inspector, whoever will be investigating it."

"No investigation is planned, I don't think," the man said politely. "Do you have additional information on the matter?"

"Additional? Well, I haven't given any. No one has asked me anything. But I would appreciate it if we could do that part, because my children have to come home, I can't ask my mother-in-law to do any more, and—"

"Just a minute," the man said, and presently a new voice came on saying, "This is Inspector Dyce," in such a way that I knew I had to start my story all over.

"Inspector Dice," I liked that name, dice suggesting the tincture of chance which sullies justice.

I explained again, the increasing urgency of my voice, I could hear, alarming him and damaging the calm sanity of my words expressing my view that now the murder had been done we should get on with it, on with the particulars so that Ev could be put in her coffin and the children could come home and it could be all over with. I know how I must have sounded.

"Let me be sure I understand," said his smooth reassuring voice, used to dealing with nuts and hysterics. "The victim you think died as a result of being beaten in the laundry room of your building on Thursday evening. Was this incident reported?"

"No, I don't know, I don't think so," I said, striving for calm commanding tones. "It's unfortunately the kind of thing that happens frequently here." From my long words he would see I am not the kind of person who lives here, though I happen to live here. "The manager feels a little diffident about continuously bothering the police with things nothing can be done about." I hoped he wouldn't construe this as a criticism of the police; it wasn't, but only a criticism of things.

"It doesn't sound like much can be done about this," Inspector Dyce said. "An unprovoked unreported anonymous assault three days ago, four days ago, rather difficult to follow up on now. Of course it matters some in reporting the cause of death."

"Well, but maybe you can find out who did it. What if it was her personal enemy? Don't you want to know who her enemies were?" For I couldn't believe he could mean what it sounded like he meant, to dismiss the matter.

"There might still be clues, fingerprints," I said. "There are people who were after us, they—"

"I think we'd better come out and talk to you, Mrs. Hexam," the Inspector interrupted. "Meantime the autopsy will be done today or tomorrow, and much will depend on what the cause of death is determined to be."

But I could not understand that, either, because the cause of death was murder.

3 "My dear child, how awful for you," Bess said, enfolding me, which I do admit I found comforting. "You stayed here *alone* last night? Why on earth didn't you come to me last night, or let me come down here? Great heavens!"

And "Oh, the poor thing," looking into Ev's room as if to confirm that I was telling the truth, that Ev was really gone, or maybe even to discover that she had come back again. I had a crazy expectation, almost, of hearing her say, "Why, here's Ev sound asleep."

"I'll go get your kids from Ida and pick up Polly and Petey at school and take them all to my house, would you like that? Or do you want them home? I expect you want them home. I'll bring them here. Now you must give me a cup of coffee and tell me about it in detail."

Bess was still here when Mr. and Mrs. McCabe came, plump silent people with impassive expressions. They had gotten dressed up, Ev's father in a suit and tie, Ev's mother in a maroon knitted dress with a cameo. They sat quietly, hearing my account of it; then Bess consoled them in bright ladyish tones while I sat dumbly. It had come over me that I had been responsible for Ev and had let this happen, and that her mother and father must blame me a lot.

I tried to tell them that Ev had gone to bed happy. I

thought they would like to know that, but they didn't seem interested in details of that sort. Perhaps they were rightly above that kind of sentimental reflection, were inconsolable.

"I been tellin her a long time now she got to look out for herself better," Ev's father said, "and I been expectin somethin like this for a long time."

"Too much foolin around. Evalin been foolin around since she been ten very nearly. Always so fast and blind around men. I done told her, too," Ev's mother said with a tight mouth and emanating a quality of anger I thought proper, probably directed at Ev, who didn't love herself well enough to take care of herself, and at a world which did not love her at all. The world does not prize the likes of Ev, said Ev's mother's tight mouth.

"You'll be wantin us to get at her things and get them out of here," Ev's mother said, and we all stood up to go do practical things. Bess and I drove to the market in Bess's car to get some empty boxes for them to pack her clothes in. Her mother looked through the clothes, frowning and shaking out her nighties, seeing, I guess, whether or not Ev had minded her about decency. It doesn't seem fair to be subjected to judgment by your mother after you are dead, but you are. Anyway Ev's nighties are all good and decent. The sweater Ev had tried to knit we found in her bottom drawer. I had tried to teach her to knit, bought the wool and showed her how. She wasn't very fast at it. Then she said she'd left the knitting on the bus, and here it was in her bottom drawer.

After the clothes we got the lamps and dishes from the cupboard in the garage that she had been going to put in her new place, stored away since the last time, waiting for the great day.

None of this took long. Ev's parents, impassive, stowed it all in their car. They were grieving, I am sure, but they were also "behaving" and constrained by Bess and me, would not say much. I suppose they were thinking about their next errand, going to look at Ev wherever she lay. But they did sit down a minute when we were done.

"We sorry about this, Mrs. Hexam," Ev's mother said. I didn't understand for a second that she was apologizing for her bad daughter Ev. She meant she was sorry for causing me trouble, not that she was sorry about what had happened to Ev.

So then the thought came blurting out of me that I really had not let myself say but it had been lying on my heart. "We should have had the doctor on Friday," I said. "But I thought she was getting better on Friday. But I should have called for the doctor anyway." I should have called the doctor, and now that I have admitted this I know I will never be rid of the thought. So it was my fault. But she did seem to be getting better, and she dreaded the doctor. Oh, God.

"One thing about Evalin, she always caused a problem everything she did in her whole life, that was her nature," her mother said. "Some people just like that by nature."

"Mind you, we love Evalin, her bein our daughter," said her father, "yet it's true, she be like that."

"The other girls could get on right from the start, Ev she never could."

"Oh, please," I said, stupidly beginning to cry, which was the most unsettling cruel thing to do but I couldn't help it. "I'm not complaining, I'm apologizing, we should have had the doctor, we should, I, oh . . ." and Bess encircled me with a protective arm around my shoulders and the poor old parents, greatly distressed, tried to reassure me.

"Now don't take on," they said, and such things, "You done right, we are sure. You'd have called the doctor if Evalin had said, her a grown woman over forty years old, she had a mortal fear of doctors . . ."

"I should have insisted, I should have insisted," I

tried to stop saying, with Ev's poor old father beginning to cry, too.

"Ev went peaceful," he said. "That is something I never expected, and not in no hospital, that's a blessing, she had a mortal fear of hospitals."

"We just sorry it come on you so sudden," Ev's mother said, and her husband and I sat with tears streaming down our faces, but her little old face was bitter and hard. I could not guess what she felt.

"Ev would want you to have something to remember her by," she said, standing up as if to go. "If they was something you would care to have among her things?" Her tone was one of abrupt decision, as if she had been considering whether or not this was a proper gesture.

"Oh, no, that's all right," I began to protest, but then saw that it was wrong to say there was nothing I wanted among Ev's poor things. And I did want one thing; I wanted her diary, the record of her poor life. I had always wanted it, for I had always been afraid that although she thought it interesting enough to write about, she despised her life so much that she would lose that book or burn it when she had finished. Her parents evidently held her life cheaply, too, for they insisted I also take a box of new handkerchiefs they had found in her drawer.

"Oh, how sad," Bess said. "Poor old things, will they be able to manage everything? What pain for them, when they talk to the police and realize she didn't pass so peacefully at all."

"I'm not sure the police will say anything to them."

"Well, I'll be off for your children and see you later," Bess said, and mantled herself in her good woolen tweeds and got into her shiny green car.

The thing was, as we were saying goodbye, I partly noticed in my corner eye a figure — a man, I thought — but as I turned to look at him directly, he disappeared around the end garage. He had been watching us and now stepped out of sight, not wanting us to see him. But, in a feeble cast of winter sun, his shadow showed on the concrete, unmoving and waiting. Bess didn't see him and I didn't mention it, but when she had gone I stood and watched. The shadow stood, too.

I had the idea that I should bravely walk down to the end and look around the corner and confront this lurker, maybe our murderer rendered harmless by daylight, who would bluster excuses about being there, not knowing I know. "Well, hello, A. J.," I could imagine. "Back again, Gavvy?" Or it could have been Osella, just the impression of bigness and bulk sidling quickly, large and sly, and I didn't think she would assault me right out there in the open. "Jus come to see mah babies," Osella would say. "Just coming to continue our talk," Gavvy would say.

But the point is that now I had the idea, too, that if I confronted this quiet shadow, rounded the corner and our eyes would meet at last, there would be no one there. The sun under its cloud again, the still outline was not so clearly staining the cement; people come and go in these units, they dart and sidle from their natures, from their guilty hearts and it has nothing to do with me. If I bravely walked down and looked around the corner, then nobody would be there; he would vanish, it would prove to be a post or bush casting that shadow, and as long as I did not look at it, it was the murderer. I got tired of watching before the shadow did, so I still don't know if it existed or not.

I went into my unit and locked the door and for some reason changed my clothes into a respectable dress and put clean sheets on Ev's bed, and put the bedspread back on. The Famous Inspector came about twenty minutes later.

4 The Famous Inspector, Inspector Dyce, was younger than I expected, a large sandy-haired young
man with a mustache calculatedly dashing to dispel any
quality of severity, and wearing a blue pin-stripe suit,
pink shirt with matching pink handkerchief in his jacket
pocket. He was carrying a clipboard on which to write
down what I said, and on which he wrote from time to
time, though I never could discern the relation of my answers to the moments he chose to write upon his pad of
yellow paper. He cased our unit with his sure sociologist's
eye and I could tell he didn't think much of it. I liked him.
He was, of course, much more actual than the Famous
Inspector I had formed in my head from stories, and better-
looking than that inspector with the red hair; I suppose
that's why I liked him. He had qualities, a third dimension,
a smell—cigarettes, I think—and so on; this was diminish-
ing at the same time that, by reminding you of the complexity and surprising variations that any other brain
but your own slow one could think of, it was reassuring.
I mean, being real, he was bound to be cleverer than the
stupid Inspector in my mind. So I was glad to see him and
talk and cooperate and I felt much better.

"Perhaps," he said when we were sitting comfortably,
"perhaps you'd better begin at the beginning," so I told
him what had happened.

At first I didn't tell him everything, not exactly; I
didn't wish to tell him about my divorce and my lover, and
I couldn't see that it mattered. But I told him about Ev's
men, A. J. and Clyde, and about Osella. I explained that
she had been our maid, and that she was mad, with jealousy over the children, and might have hated Ev because
they were Ev's babies now. Then talking of Osella led me
into talking about our former life, with Gavvy and the other
house, and the Inspector had heard of Gavvy, which of
course he would have, so then I told the whole thing. Afterwards I tried to remember how he had got me to do this

without ever seeming to ask; he seemed to know how to count on people's overwrought garrulity.

"Gavin and I are divorced," I said. "I go to school, I'm getting a Master's degree, to 'fit myself for a future life,' which is how the judge put it—do you think people will need Master's degrees in the future life, Inspector? And then I . . ."

"And Mrs. Wilson had been helping you, minding the children and so on?" the Inspector would say, writing on his pad and keeping me to the subject. "Babbling," he would be writing of my monologue, "subject babbling."

"Ev baby-sat. With the children so young I need somebody . . . these things had gone on for over a week, I still haven't got my tires fixed, I don't even know if the insurance will pay for them. It had gotten so we didn't know what to expect next, and we didn't know for whom they were intended, I mean the vicious acts. There was nothing to do but be careful and watch out and wait."

"Why didn't you call us after Mrs. Wilson was attacked in the laundry room?"

"I don't know. I left it to Mr. Hoaglund. Although he said there wasn't any point, it happens so often around here and nothing is ever done. But also, at first, I didn't think it was related. I didn't think a person could mistake Ev for me. . ."

The Inspector smiled his composed, knowing and rather sunny smile. "So basically you've imagined these other threats were directed toward *you*, not Mrs. Wilson?"

"Yes. I suppose I still do. I suppose I feel that Ev's death is a mistake. She was frail, in spite of seeming strong. Such blows might not have killed someone else."

"A mistake. Just so. Misadventure. Well, much will depend on the cause of death," he said, and looked around the unit as if it would reveal something to him. "Have you received any more threats or nuisances since the, ah, since yesterday morning?"

"No, well, one phone call from Osella. Mrs. Hoaglund answered it, so she can testify. . ."

"That's all right," Inspector Dyce said. "You don't know the addresses or whereabouts of any of these people: Clyde Wilson, A. J. Harper or Osella Barnes, is that right?"

"That's right," I admitted. I might as well have made them up, these shadowy people existing for me alone.

The Famous Inspector shifted in his chair and, putting his clipboard to one side and folding his hands in his lap, addressed me with an attentive and, I thought, compassionate gaze. "A murder is a serious business, you know," he said, a remark whose banality was at the time obscured by his confidential manner. Still it was not a remark you need to reply to. He waited for my reply.

"I *know*," I said, eyes filling, for the thought had come to me again that this was a serious business for Ev, and that no one had asked her how it was for her, that it was a matter of utmost seriousness for Ev and yet, as she was dead, it was of no consequence to her either.

"Certain serious social consequences."

"Oh, yes!"

"There's the investigation, setting up a file which will likely never be closed, on an insoluble crime. Many crimes, you know, are insoluble. Most of those involving a person found dead in an alley, found beaten to death or stabbed outside a bar or in a parking lot—places of confrontation. We almost never get the killer in those cases. There is a killer of course, and we put these cases down as murder. Homicide. But we almost never catch the killer."

"*You* think they bring it on themselves, by going into bars and quarreling in parking lots, don't you? *You* think a murdered person deserves to be murdered. I knew you would think that," I said. He opened his eyes, apparently surprised, not feeling he deserved any such attack.

"What about his enemies?" I said. "Why don't you talk to the other people in the bar, and they would tell you who his enemies were, who he was quarreling with?"

"He always has an alibi, the guy he was quarreling with. The guy he was quarreling with was always home with his wife at quarter past eleven. Always. The only ones we get are the ones still standing by the bar with the knife in their hand, the others never."

"What about all the women that are murdered, sex murders or rape victims, you think they bring it on themselves, don't you? It is well known that the police think this, that just by being women, women invite—"

"My dear Mrs. Hexam . . ."

"People can't just go around assaulting people, they must be prevented!"

"Prevention is my concern here," said Inspector Dyce. "If a murder had already been committed, it would be a matter for punishment, and punishment is another department. I am prevention."

"How can you prevent a murder, for God's sake, which has already happened?"

"Well," he said, "well, perhaps. But it looks like an Insoluble, and that's where prevention comes in. I hesitate even to open a file on an Insoluble, I'll tell you why. Unsolved murders are very demoralizing to the public morale. The public good, the same thing. When the public morale is low, we get more murders, so you see it's a circular state of things. So what I mean is really the prevention of future murders uncommitted, by keeping the morale up, by keeping some of the Insolubles quiet." He laughed a little at this; intelligent, this Inspector, so he knew how bewildering he sounded.

"But you can't evade the fact of murder by calling it something else," I protested.

"But you can diminish the degree of social destruction it causes. If it seems to people that the world is a place full of violence and crime, and that murder is not followed by discovery and retribution, then they are encouraged to indulge their desperation by violence and murder. Perhaps they feel they should, to perpetuate a certain view of life . . ."

"I am familiar with those arguments," I said, "but I am not a believer in capital punishment."

He smiled. "If, on the other hand, the world presents its smoothest cheek, then people will not strike at it. They will hesitate to interrupt peace and order. Therefore, sometimes we don't call murder murder."

"What do you call it, gracious heaven!"

"We call it 'unknown causes.'"

This seemed to me the most terrible thing to call it. It was the most terrible thing I had ever heard. "Please, someone has killed poor Ev."

He looked at me pensively and suspiciously, too, as if while deceiving me with his strange remarks and jaunty mustache, his wise eyes looked into my inside workings to see if I was especially malicious or vengeful; was I some fanatic on murder and retribution? I saw from his face that this Famous Inspector was more sympathetic than I to murder. I had thought it would be I who understood all illicit impulses. Often I don't understand lawful impulses. I had thought the Famous Inspector would hate sin and harry murderers but now I saw this was not so, and I became afraid of him.

"Well, we'll question the husband and boyfriend if we can find them," he said, standing up. "Much will depend on the cause of death." Still looking at me, now to see whether I had some special hatred for A. J. and Clyde, was some kind of slum Salome out for the heads of these poor men. He looked angry at me as if he wanted to crush me under his clipboard.

"Inspector," I asked, "what if the persons *didn't* mean to kill Ev, meant to kill me, still do you believe that his are idle threats? Don't you think he's serious? He is a killer; now he has killed. Will he kill again?"

Suddenly the Inspector bent close, putting his face close to mine and asked, peering at me, "Just who do you think is trying to kill you, Mrs. Hexam?" and I blurted out "Gavvy" before I had time to consider, so I guess that is what I really thought at heart. The sudden question works like curing hiccups. Gavvy.

Of course I had to admit to the Inspector that Gavin had never threatened me or hurt me except for hitting me that time, which I didn't mention, because anyone might have hit anyone once; that didn't constitute a murderous impulse. After the Inspector left, I did remember, though, that Gavin had actually hurt Ev before, had abused and hit Ev. This recollection chilled me; it brought up a lot of things.

It was soon after we had moved to this unit, and I had gone away for my first weekend alone with Andrew, the first whole nights we had ever spent together. It had been hard for Andrew to get away before this, but now Cookie had taken the children somewhere, or Andrew had invented a business trip, I forget. We were almost sick with joy at the idea of all those hours, of spending whole nights together, with no sneaking in and out and waiting until the kids were asleep and trying to hush the sounding bedsprings.

We weren't even sure we would get along together for such a long stretch; perhaps like children we would bicker or be bored. It was an important adventure. Excited as children, we drove to one of those dingy nice old motels along the west shore of Tahoe on Friday afternoon, where we made love and feasted and walked and slept and made love again in a trance of happiness the rest of the night, the day, the night again. I can remember lying in Andrew's arms in an absolute exhausted stupor, Andrew making love to me for about the ninth time, greatly surprising and delighting himself with these splendid but heretofore unknown powers, and then sitting up and saying in a reverent, astonished and yet judicious way: "This is one of the great days in my life."

But in the midst of this happiness, back in our unit A. J. came over to confront Ev about something, and they had an awful fight—an argument was all, she said later, but it scared Petey, who called Gavvy, and Gavvy came over to find A. J. gone and the place pretty much a wreck, and he slapped Ev, and Ev called Andrew and me, sobbing, telling us to come home because she was quitting. So we had to drive home a day earlier than we had planned. Andrew was kind and supportive, but I could see it made him realize what my real life is like, full of kids and problems. I think it scared him a little.

I had thought at the time, and I remembered it now, that Gavvy had acted to Ev in a way he had never dared act to me. "He cussed me, too; now I don't need to take that from him," Ev had sobbed. "He talked very dirty and cruel," she said, but she never would tell me what he had said. "I'm glad you got rid of that man," was all she would say.

"Gavvy," I had said to the Inspector. He, continuing to gather up his notes and put his pen in his pocket, shook his head in a curt indifferent way to assure me that this, from his experience, was unlikely to be the case.

"I guess you want to see justice done, Mrs. Hexam; is that mainly it?" he asked as he left, in his voice, I thought, accusation and disapproval. "Justice, is that what you're after?"

5 Well I've been thinking about that. Is that it? Do I want to see justice done, and the answer is no. I don't think I trust justice. Oh, I approve of it in the abstract, but do I for instance want it to be meted out to me? No, I don't think so. Too risky. Justice is a pretty obnoxious concept when you think about it, and mercy is clearly the better quality.

But for mercy for Ev's killer? My heart hardens at that. It's a problem what attitude to take to things like murder and sin.

I guess it might be safe to favor a sort of divinely administered retributive justice and a civilly administered means of keeping order, just to prevent people from running around murdering, with mercy and amnesty for everything that has happened until this minute, when the plan is to go into effect and all these sins and crimes are behind us and don't count.

I have had to ask myself, if the murderer was Clyde or A. J. would I want them to go to the gas chamber, and I cannot say I would. What would be the point? Osella? No, certainly not. If it was Gavvy—my heart dances for a second with the idea of sanctimonious Gavvy in jail. But I would not wish that, either—disgrace, difficulties for the children, where would the child-support money come from? Do insurance policies pay off if the insured meets death by justice? Do I hate Gavvy more than he hates me?

Such questions do torment the confused mind, which is the only possible state of mind when murder and death surround you. If a murderer is someone you know, as Ev's murderer must be, then I cannot wish him dead. Yet I cannot wish him loose going around killing, and I cannot wish Ev unavenged. You kind of surrender your own wishes in the matter.

The Famous Inspector looked long into my heart for signs of malice or angry vanity, and left wearing a disapproving face, and I was alone again prey to the depredations of malice and angry vanity.

A bad thing happened once to Ev and me. We had gone with the children to visit my old uncle in his retirement village, where there is a swimming pool. I was inside, talking to him in his apartment, and Ev took the kids behind to the pool. It was summer, hazy and hot. Ev was, I remember, wearing blue shorts and a white shirt tied up to make her midriff bare. I remember her saying if it got much hotter she was going to dive in in these clothes.

Presently I went around to have a dip myself, but before I had come within sight of the pool I could hear a loud berating voice, in a sort of hick accent, somebody shouting, "You get your black ass out of here," and I went around the corner to see Ev, terrified, backing off, and a huge man, bald and red-faced, wearing coveralls—the caretaker, perhaps—carrying a length of pipe and threatening Ev with it.

Dumbstruck—without stopping to consider—suffused with instant fury—I advanced on this man, screeching haughty denunciations at him: we were here as guests, what did he mean using such language, waving that thing around—angrily I ran at this man. But he simply turned around, raised his pipe and readied to hit me, too, and I cowered, too, like Ev; I cringed and began to back away like a pitiful cowed animal. How can I describe, though, my suffocating rage?

How can I describe my suffocating rage, the disbelief, the shock I felt that this could happen. I had never in my life been physically threatened or insulted or told to get out, by anyone, of anywhere. Me! Dear me.

That must have happened to Ev often—or, no, she would avoid letting it happen; she would not go places where a man would shout obscenely and make her get out. She would know from long experience which places to avoid, and white retirement homes full of old Legionnaires, good-old-days bigots, would be one of them for sure, and I had led her into this humiliation.

What I'm getting at, it seems clear that a lot of my indignation then was for my own sake and not really for Ev. I couldn't accept that a person could threaten *me*, and be undaunted by my superior social station and my womanhood and God knows, all because I was associated with black Ev trying to swim in his swimming pool.

Ev and the children and I retreated to my uncle's apartment and there, grinding my teeth in a rage, I planned to call the police. I was coldly planning to accuse the man of attempted assault with that pipe, and if that wasn't a crime, then I'd accuse him of actual assault. I think I was quite willing to lie, to say he had hit me, to bring him to justice. And my anger and desire for retribution was much greater then than now for Ev's murder; why is that? Have I been beaten down in some way? Or grown up? Or is my self-regard really more important to me than Ev's life? That is a horrible question.

In the end I didn't call the police, because my uncle began to weep and to say that Mr. Chandler, the brute, had always been kind to him, and Mrs. Chandler brought things she had baked, and if we started making trouble for Mr. Chandler he, my uncle, would have to move. My old frail uncle. He was backed up by Ev, who plainly thought it was silly to make a fuss. But she was hurt. It was to have been a nice day and now was spoiled, a familiar sequence of events, as I've learned.

"It don't make no difference. I don't care what no ignorant man says," she kept telling me, in the voice of her mother: you don't care what no ignorant man says. "There's plenty ignorant whites like that in the world. You can't let them get to you." She was patient, but I, I, bitter and unable to bear my powerlessness, composed revenges, lying awake at night, against that man, composed speeches to make at his trial, thought of magic and spells to kill him.

I can't bear to be crossed, there's the truth; I'm a child unable to stand being crossed, and I do not will that Ev should be dead. I will she should not be dead yet she is dead. My blood steams like cold blood poured on hot rocks, my pewter heart melts and runs in steely rivulets in the heat of my rage. Yet she is dead. Am I not grand? What a

grand raging figure, yet Ev is dead, and everything everything goes against my wishes.

So I can understand why Osella would keep the need
of magic and the belief in it; what an antidote for powerlessness in a world where everybody else is white and thin
and preoccupied with their intellectual whims and sexual
hijinks, leaving her to clean up. Well, I don't know what
Gavvy was preoccupied with; perhaps he just wants love
and success, like everyone else.

I think it was probably Osella who attacked Ev in the
laundry room, though I wish it had not been. I wish it had
been Gavvy. It just conceivably could have been Gavvy;
I know now that he hangs around the Zanzibar. But it's
just wishful thinking. The thing is, if it had been Gavvy
I would know how to feel. It would be clear he should go
to the hospital. He is sick. It would be so simple. Perhaps
he would even go to the hospital himself if he realized to
what a state he had gotten, hiding in laundries, beating
women. Perhaps I should write him an anonymous note,
in case it was Gavvy, letting him know that Ev has died,
so he could see he has really gone too far now. Or perhaps
Gavvy's parents could do something. But they never will
do anything, because they feel he is so perfect. But I don't
truly feel it can have been Gavvy; I am only giving myself
airs to think he is still battering at the confines of my
world. He has I think quite another sphere now, and his
smile was trying to be clear and peaceable.

But you feel the need to do something. I choke on inaction, I have no patience. How am I to exist, supposing
I'll go on existing for another forty years—how can I do
this without patience?

That's how it was, I must say to myself, and get busy
with other things. But it's so unfair that Ev, who never
hurt Osella, should be lying dead because of—because of
what? Unknown causes is maybe the only way of de-
scribing it.

Of course I do see that it's just as well not to be pregnant, if I was pregnant. The wish to have a baby by Andrew is sentimental and I guess masochistic. I know it is a wish to keep a hold on him, however slight. The bonds of paternity are slight. Andrew would simply hate me if I had a baby.

Well, hate is a kind of relationship. So is fear. We were all bound together by these, before everybody wandered off leaving me here. Or perhaps it is that I am free, everyone else is still caught in the meshes of these passions. Gavvy and Osella flailing at the meshes, and Raider entangled now, too, by cupidity if nothing else. Maybe A. J. Harper will cut Clyde Wilson's throat one night, maybe not. Probably not, but then again, why should I denigrate A. J.'s passion by saying that? Maybe he will. Anyway I'll never hear about it, no one will put it in the papers. Unknown causes, they will say, looking down on Clyde's bleeding corpse in some alley.

6 When Inspector Dyce had gone and I was alone, I was again subject to restless and unsatisfied anxiety, and fits of tears, perhaps of self-pity. At three-thirty Bess came back with the children — Polly and Petey, whom she'd picked up at school, and Ivan and India, whom she'd collected from Gavvy's mother. Bess and I had a cup of tea and Bess took my mind off death by telling me Joe had been in San Francisco on a case and had stopped off Friday afternoon to see Andrew and Cookie Mason in their dream-house love nest with its original wooden drainboards.

"Joe says things were not exactly rosy around the Mason household," Bess said with her meaningful smile.

"Very, very strained, and Cookie has dyed her hair a horrid color red. And Joe said, 'Is everything all right?' Meaning, naturally, at the office, they never talk about their personal lives, having known each other, what, twenty years, I'll never understand men, but anyway Andrew gave him an anguished look and said things have never been worse, and Cookie apparently burst into tears and ran out of the room; well, poor girl, you have to sympathize to some extent . . ."

I could hardly conceal my glee. "This was on Friday? Well, Saturday Andrew called to say he'd moved out and left Cookie." I think Bess jumped a little, surprised by that. I told her about it.

"I'm not sure whether you're living right or living wrong," she said.

"I'm not sure myself."

"Well, take care," she said. "Andrew is nice, and very handsome, but kind of a prig, don't you think, and not easy to live with either, I imagine. Cookie has told me a lot of things over the years."

"Andrew is perfect," I said, and we laughed at that, the oldest and wryest of secret female jokes.

My heart was lit up with spiteful happiness over the scene between Andrew and Cookie. Then Bess left, taking with her the luster that for me surrounded someone who had talked to someone who had recently talked to Andrew, and the room darkened and my children came up to me, and Ivan said, as I had been dreading one of them would do, "Where's Ev?" Polly and Petey, who had been told about Ev, swung around alertly at me like weather vanes, wondering what I would say.

"Ev's gone away," I said miserably, this miserable lie shocking Polly and Petey more than the truth would, their mother lying. They glared fiercely at this liar their mother.

"Come into the kitchen, P. and P.," I said, and there

took them on my lap and, whispering, delivered an account of the tragedy, how Ev had died from her sickness, and her mother and father had come for her clothes. This particular sent them off into anguished, furtive tears. Through our tears we heard Ivan and India giggling over a new ring-toss game Bess had bought them. P. and P. could imagine themselves dead and me folding up their clothes with finality and putting them away in a drawer. They wept for themselves at this tragic notion, wept, wailed. I wept for them, for Ev and for me. So it is with tears, that they spread this way.

While we were wailing, a knock came at the door and it was Inspector Dyce again, nodded, smiled his debonair smile, stroked his mustache.

"The deceased had a long criminal record, you know," he said. A pause. I considered whether he was talking about her trips to jail or what he was talking about.

"She's been in jail," he said.

"Well, it's a problem in definitions again, isn't it? If being in jail makes you a criminal, then she has a record. Well, being in jail does make you a criminal, makes you into a criminal, doesn't it, that's exactly what a prison re-former would say. That's just the point I made at the jail about the absurdity of keeping a perfectly decent woman in jail; why expose her to the criminal element?"

"Three *times* in jail," the Inspector said. "Oh, just drunk and disorderly, basically, I know, but it's not every drunk who also gets assaulting a police officer, disorderly conduct, abusive language, disturbing the peace, assault with a—"

"Well, she is a quiet and orderly person, persecuted exceedingly; it really opened my eyes about the different ways white and black persons are treated. . ."

"Yeah, doubtless, I know. Why I'm checking back with you, are you sure the laundry-room story is true? Could she be mixed up in something else? Or could there have been some antecedent injury, someone she was trying to protect, someone with a motive, criminal associates, was she into drugs at all or know any drug users?"

"No, nothing, quiet and orderly. Nothing she told me about," I protested, but noticing the irony of this, I who had wanted to tell him about her enemies when he wouldn't listen and was now denying them, and lying, too, because she had in fact come home with that cut New Year's Day.

"She seems to have been a violent woman," the Inspector observed.

But that is one of the paradoxical things in Ev's behavior, I had never resolved it: her gentle nature compared with the trouble she got into sometimes. The two times I know about she was in jail, once overnight and once for three days, just getting loud with friends, maybe belligerent, and then some neighbor or the friend calls the police and the first thing I knew Ev was calling me, babbling with fear and chagrin—drunk, too, maybe.

"Where are you, Ev?"

"I'm at Phoebe Ashburton, that's the women's jail— can you come down and get me outta here? . . . Doin? I wasn't doin nothing, then that mothafuckin Isobel, that's my cousin, gets a bug up her ass we're gonna wreck up her place, or I don't know what she done thought, goddam it's horrible in here, can you bring me down the bail? But you gotta get here before nine or they can't do nothing until morning, and man I don't want to stay here till morning, it's lousy."

Well, once I had the fifty and the other time not and didn't know where to phone A. J. or Clyde, though they probably wouldn't have had it either; they're always hitting up Ev. But I couldn't get her out, it was Saturday, and then they wouldn't do anything till Monday morning, so that made three days in jail and she hadn't done anything except maybe resist arrest, and who wouldn't? But she was morose for days after that, silent and depressed and weepy.

"Violence breeds violence," said the Inspector, funny how he really had this sententious streak I had expected.

"Poverty and ignorance breed violence." I have it, too, and the Inspector laughed mockingly to have made me say such a thing. It's true, though, about black and white justice.

"Well, if you're sure this had nothing to do with her criminal life," Inspector Dyce said.

"We all have something of a criminal life, Inspector," I said.

"Well, I'm surprised to hear you say that, Mrs. Hexam, I'm surprised to hear you admit that," the Inspector said gravely, and departed I guess on his searches. "Goodbye, Inspector," I said.

So it seemed that was that. There we were in our same unit, kids and Mom and suppertime like always. Polly was sitting sobbing in the corner of the living room looking at me through the lattice of her fingers. India and Ivan paid no attention to her. A world in which at least someone is sobbing nearby seems like the ordinary world to them, a baby view in which sometimes your friend just decides to cry, nothing strange about that. Petey stood a long time in the doorway of Ev's room, I guess meditating her goneness. I had that on my mind, and the words of the Famous Inspector, and an idea that had presented itself quite unwanted but most tenaciously about my dear friend Bess. With all this I didn't get around to thinking about supper until after six and the store had closed. There was nothing whatever to eat, except bread and breakfast cereal and a few things in cans and some lemons in the refrigerator. I couldn't remember when I had eaten last, or shopped last.

We had nothing for supper and the tires on the car were still slashed; these realizations, in turn, provoked the final one, embittering and unavoidable, that life had in no way changed in its particulars, suppers had to be cooked, and all that had happened, tremendous and tragic for Ev, and for A. J. and Clyde and Ev's parents and for me and the children, none of it had the power to affect the world in any way. For me things had gotten worse, because I was alone now with no one to help against murderers. For A. J., since he still has Ev's car, things might be said to have got better in a material way; maybe he is too wretched to count that but I doubt it. To Clyde she was lost in any case, and for Ev everything is simply over so you can't make any calculation at all of the pluses and minuses of her condition.

What can you do about any of this? You might as well be tied to a chair. I have never even screamed in my whole life, I am too timid and inhibited. What can I do about any of this?

Old A. J. driving around happily in Ev's car not even knowing. "Whatever you say, sir," I say to the Famous Inspector like a limp hand acceding. The kids and I walked down to the McDonald's hamburgers, just like that, and had hamburgers on the night after Ev's murder, and that entirely symbolized the probable future course of things, ordinary, unchanged. I couldn't stand that. If you are going to be murdered, there ought to be some point you can make by it, some objection to life driven home.

When we got home, I read them stories, and tried to think of where Andrew might be. Was there a Palmer House? Statler? But just thinking about Andrew was some help. I stayed awake until about eleven, hoping he would call me, but then it was one o'clock Chicago time, so I just went to sleep exhausted. Nobody called us at all—not Osella, not the phantom phone-caller—and no one knocked at the windows or terrorized us. This raised the possibility that the murderer knew he had finished his work and was satisfied now.

Tuesday, January 7

1 Whoever the murderer was or is at first seemed important to know. I suppose that is an impulse that need not be explained. Everyone has it, it explains the power of Bluebeard's room. You *will* open the door, you *will* draw back the curtain, you *will* look behind the arras to see whom you've stabbed. You will look out from behind to see who it is has stabbed you, and he will be familiar and be laughing.

As they say: I knew what I had to do. It seemed clear to me on Tuesday morning, rising clear-eyed on an ordinary school day early in the New Year, that besides having the tires fixed and finding another baby-sitter and tracking A. J. down to get Ev's car back or else the $150 she owes Mr. Probst, because I can't spare it, and finishing my seminar papers—it seemed to me that among these things, in about third place after the tires and baby-sitter, for life must go forward and events in their proper sequence, I would have to find out for myself who killed Ev.

Also it became clear to me on Tuesday morning I would have to find out for myself who killed Ev because the Inspector rang first thing to say he wasn't going to.

"I thought I'd tell you the results of the autopsy," he said. "Acute pancreatitis, conceivably initiated by some blows—there were some bruises—and undoubtedly initiated by New Year's partying. There was a lot of liver disease as well. No evidence of the victim sustaining a blow which would have in itself been fatal, though she had a nasty bruise in the middle of her back. Under the circumstances, with her history and you say there wasn't any violent scene you know of, we'll go for natural death."

I didn't say anything.

"Is that all right with you?"

"Is it up to me?"

"We could have a cornoner's inquest, this would be the next step, at which a group of jurors would hear medical testimony, and your testimony about the incident in the laundry room, and other evidence, and then decide what to call it—natural death, unknown causes, misadventure or murder. There are a number of things you can call a death. But I'm bound to say I don't see the point of an inquest in this case."

"Oh," I said, and couldn't for the moment see any point in disagreeing but just seeing him as a force of darkness disguised as a force of reason, and anyway I didn't know how to disagree, so said all right and thanked him. "But then murder is murder," said my chilly voice. "You can't just call it by another name."

"You are such a goddamned self-righteous absolutist, like all women," said the Inspector in a voice that sounded blazing angry, which I thought was unfair as well as peculiar.

"Murder is murder," I said, "but I won't interfere."

2 But I am the only one who seems to care. Inspector Dyce you would think would have professional curiosity if nothing else; he doesn't seem to care at all, or maybe he knows already. It wouldn't do to raise the issue of murder to Ev's old parents. Bess shrugs. Andrew—would Andrew shrug? I don't know, probably. God knows he has learned something about the shabby human heart, nothing should surprise him now.

Also you can't help but wonder whether people would care more, if there would be less shrugging, if Ev had been white. White or black, if she lived in these units I doubt people would care. So much of it around these days. But if she'd lived up on the hill where I used to live, then people would vigorously investigate, no stones would be left unturned, the whole world a rubble of stones, from looking for her murderer. Of course if she'd been white living up on the hill, she would have fewer reasons for drinking her insides away so she would die at a blow. It's hard to assign causes and effects. I had started by saying there is much I understand now, which I mostly would rather not have known, but there is much that can never be known, too.

For instance about Bess. Once you get onto this track of knowing, of suspicion, once you get this low idea of the human heart, you can't stop even if you want to. Like speed reading, you rocket along turning pages faster and faster noticing mostly the dirty parts.

For instance about dear Bess as she picked up the children for me and minded them and brought them home for me on Monday and was telling me the latest detail about Andrew and Cookie, and what their new house was like, everything—right in the middle of my feeling of love and gratitude to Bess came a flash of understanding of her. The riddle of her goodness began to be unlocked, one more bolt slid back allowing a big door to open everything to me, admitting also a chill wind. I could see right behind Bess's eyes as she was talking.

She was sitting on the sofa wearing a plaid wool skirt, sweater and her good pearls—her uniform, as she calls it—her good pearls a present from her kind indulgent husband, her long good legs in stockings and rather big feet in loafers. I just looked at her as she was talking and realized that behind her genuine affection for me, gleaming a little garishly in her bright eyes behind her ladyish spectacles, lay Bess's pleasure in my misfortunes.

People's misfortunes, it came to me, are what she takes pleasure and interest in. I could even imagine her talking to her other friends, though Bess is discretion itself as had been proved a dozen times, but I could hear her deep laconic voice speaking of her "poor little friend, the one that lives in the housing development with her maid—yes, really—well, the maid was an awful drunk and always in jail, much more trouble than trouble is worth, frankly, though an angel compared to the last one, a woman three hundred pounds who burnt her in effigy and became mentally disturbed. Just as my poor little friend's marriage was breaking up—to Gavin Hexam, the attorney. *Four* little kids, and now she's gotten mixed up with—well—a prominant figure—married man of course—and she thinks she's pregnant, and the most depressing things happen to her in that slum she has to live in, she's always having her tires slashed—I don't know how she hangs on. But now, the latest thing . . ."

Maybe she talks this way in her endless psychotherapeutic groups. Some of her groups have been going on so long they must have run out of things about themselves to talk about. She and Joe go to encounter groups, sensitivity training groups, psychodrama groups, and no doubt others. I disapprove of them rather, so she doesn't talk about them much to me. But she appears to enjoy those companions in misfortune.

Bess's misfortune is of course Lynnie's being retarded. To have waited all that time for the treasured child and then to have her turn out to be not anything hopeless and grotesque that would have to be put away somewhere but dull, slow, in need of special schools and extra funds and patient attentive hours and hours from these two highly intelligent mature adults her parents, just to assure that she learns as much as she ever can learn. Poor horrible Lynnie with her dull eyes and wet hanging mouth and petulant whine—for she has an unlovely character, too, demanding and selfish. Bess and Joe can't bring themselves to deny her anything; they must always be making up to her for her misfortune. I have thought of telling Bess, on one of those many occasions she has insisted that I "ventilate," which is what she calls it, that if Lynnie were mine I would teach her to be quiet and to sew. Actually I wouldn't tell Bess this; I have never ventilated my feelings about Lynnie because they would hurt Bess's feelings.

I don't understand Bess's theory of the emotions really, which represents yourself as a being whose inner mysteries you are estranged from. It seems to me that my worst thoughts are the ones that plague me most. Bess sees human relationships as a kind of race to reproach your friends with the hostile thoughts they engender in you before they can tell you theirs. This is self-expression, or rudeness, depending on what you call it.

Well, poor Bess, it isn't pleasant; it's hateful, it's another loss. Everyone is lost. I am so sick and despairing, with everything taken away from me. I should have called the doctor for Ev and now it's too late. I should have gone with Andrew or called him at some delicate moment, some crucial moment, and I didn't and now it's too late. I should not have thought these thoughts about Bess or happened to see inside her purse and now it's too late. Here I am a person almost thirty and everything is too late already. What shall I do? How can I be trusted to go on managing when I have shown myself to be so incapable, so stupid, so wickedly criminally negligent on every point?

Why sully even Bess with my anger and bitterness?

Of the worst I can never be sure, and at the least what does it matter if she finds all my experiences interesting; there is little enough interesting in life. I must find these tribulations interesting myself, in a way, or I wouldn't let them happen. If you are going to have lovers and a life of freedom and intellect, you have to expect unwed pregnancies and divorces and malice and mistakes. There is a safe way to conduct your life and then there is the other way, reckless and riddled with mistakes but I don't care.

But I don't feel like a reckless person, I feel the epitome of mousy precaution. A reckless person has, I think, a streak of wild joy running through him; I am always peeping, shivering, timorous. The life of the reckless person is ruled by bold laughter. I haven't laughed in weeks. I must stink of gloom, but how can you laugh at murder? I can laugh at the irony of being, now, a murderer myself, in a way.

3 If you can't be absolutely right, you can be absolutely sure, like an inspector, like a minion of the law, and that was my plan.

But first I tried calling the Fairmont for Andrew, in case he was back. I hadn't really thought he could be back yet, but it made me feel better to have tried. I was uneasy about Andrew; it had come back over me like a wash but I didn't give in to it. Andrew had said on Saturday night that everything would be all right now, and this was only Tuesday morning; two full days, that's no time at all. Two days elapse all the time between lovers, it was only that these two days had been so full for me. Andrew busy in Chicago. And Andrew would never tell a lie; it was a long time before Andrew had said I love you until he was sure it was so, because he would not use such an expression idly, or any phrase idly, and now he had said we would be together. "I cannot live without you."

My class in Structural Linguistics is Tuesdays and Thursdays, and I thought I'd better go, get right back to studying as if nothing were happening. Besides, linguistics is soothing because it has nothing to do with the real world. I asked Mrs. Hoaglund, with whom I now felt a certain intimacy, if she would watch Ivan and India. I knew this was exploiting Mrs. Hoaglund's solicitude and I didn't care; somewhere deep within, the voice of survival said Mrs. Hoaglund will probably sit still for this exploitation until about the middle of next week at least. I figured that's about how long sympathy for the murdered and the memory of it all will last.

I found I got a certain amount done at school, away from all associations of home and Ev. I explained to my professors about the lateness of my seminar papers, was commiserated with, and worked in the library until about noon. Life had reconstructed itself along the same old lines exactly, except that Ev lay dead, now in the undertaker's parlor to which she was to have been removed after the autopsy.

The first thing I did when I got home was to call the Automobile Club about my tires. They said the thing was to buy new ones, and then they would come and put them on as an emergency road service, on a low-priority basis. Then I called the insurance company, who said I would have to buy the tires with my own money, then submit a bill to them and they would reimburse. This meant I would have to buy the tires at Sears, where they have not taken my credit card away, and with any luck the insurance company would pay before the Sears bill came due.

Next I ate some peanut-butter crackers and tea, and then I went to have another look in the laundry room, to inspect it for clues. I don't know what I thought I would see, after all that time, and I'd already looked at it with Mr. Hoaglund and Inspector Dyce. Maybe I thought I'd see a vision or a name written on the wall. But the point is, you can't just put such things as murder out of your mind. You know you have to attend to them before they become an obsession, so attentively, obediently, I stepped into the laundry room.

It was the same old laundry room, smelling faintly of urine, or perhaps generations of Clorox. It contains only the washer, the dryer, the machine on the wall, long since out of order, which should dispense soap packets, a wooden bench you can sit on and a ledge above it running the length of the window on which rested several old magazines, an overflowing ashtray, and a wastebasket full of empty detergent boxes, candy wrappers, balls of wet lint, old cigarette packs. All was exactly as it had been on Thursday night when Ev was struck. Again I saw where the assailant must have stood, and how Ev would have hit her head on that machine.

Yet I felt certain — patiently, serenely certain — that if I didn't let myself be discouraged and walk dispiritedly away, and if I looked long enough fixedly with an utterly receptive mind at this room, all would become clear to me. I wanted a mystical experience perhaps, and although no ghosts materialized, my heightened concentration, my fixity of purpose, or something else, did enable me to see something new. Oh, it wasn't new at all, and was eminently seeable, had no doubt been there all the time for anyone to see; there was even a chance it had always been there, representing an odd coincidence. But it seemed to be a clue.

It was the ashtray. As I stood scanning the room with the blank fixed gaze of a medium, the ashtray came into focus sitting there as if it belonged, overflowing with cigarette butts and cellophane: a heavy glass ashtray with "Le Club Zanzibar" on the side.

"Of course," was my feeling, as though all had become clear, though nothing had become clear. I was as puzzled as to the exact meaning of this as I was satisfied with its presence. A clue with no meaning and yet a clue, a link to other people, maybe a weapon, for it was heavy and sharp. Feeling rather silly, I pulled a bit of torn sheet from the wastebasket and, using this the way a Famous Inspector uses his handkerchief to pick up objects on which there may be fingerprints, I picked up the ashtray, emptied it, and took it to Mr. Hoaglund to ask about it.

Mr. Hoaglund could say nothing one way or another about it. Mrs. Hoaglund remembered finding it outside the laundry room one morning recently and putting it back, but she could not remember whether or not it was the one that is always there.

"There's always an ashtray in there," she said. "Even so, they throw their cigarette butts on the floor."

The Hoaglunds assured me they themselves had never been, certainly had not been, to the Club Zanzibar. It seemed to me that all I would have to do now was go to the Club Zanzibar. You have only to stand in the right place and concentrate and all will become clear.

4 First, of course, tires. The car lying there in its limp rubber shreds unable to move. You can't do anything without a car, especially living out this far. So I called Bess to ask her to pick up Petey and Polly from school, and took Ivan to play with his friend Harry, another child in these units; and I saw I would have to take India with me, Mrs. Hoaglund had something else to do. I knew I could have left India with Bess—I knew it didn't make any sense to take a heavy three-year-old when we would have to be walking a long way, but I took her; I don't like her to go to

Bess's without the other children along, because I'm always afraid that Lynnie will push her into the swimming pool without Bess's noticing, and even if she did, and drowned her, Bess would somehow defend the action as permissible because it was spontaneous or sincere. I don't know. Lynnie does not deny, and is not prevented, her impulses.

By the time we set out, it was about three and already a darkish, cold and cloudy day. We had to walk about three-quarters of a mile, to Meadow Boulevard to the bus route. Not many buses come out this far. India walked slowly and complainingly, so I carried her as much as I could. India is a heavy little girl and I was tired, and it began to snow when we were about halfway along. I mention all this because it seemed fitting somehow, to toil along in the thick wet falling snow carrying a heavy burden in darkness; this seemed to mirror exactly my inner sense of burden and of struggle against difficulty, and the physical discomfort. I didn't even remark the oddness of snow, which rarely falls here. I guess I did realize dimly that I wasn't feeling right, but this seemed attributable to the snow and the burden.

The Sears is in a big shopping center off of El Camino. Tires and other auto things are in an annex around to the side of the main store where people can drive their cars in for service. India always wants to ride on the escalator, so we had to go to the main store first and ride on the escalator up and down, up and down, up and down until she would consent to come away. It was funny but I too liked riding up and down on the escalator: effortless and certain of destination, and no metaphorical threat either, because even if you go down you can go up just as easily. You don't say to yourself of it that it is like life, treadmill unending, treadmill unending.

Then we went to the auto section and found a salesman. He was pretty happy at the prospect of selling a whole set of four tires at once. "Two, maybe, is what most people get," he said. That limits the imaginative possibilities for the tire salesman, because a customer buying two must bear in mind the type of tire his car is already wearing. I wasn't sure what brought on in me this patience, this lassitude. I would not ordinarily talk to a tire salesman; I'd point, I'll take this and that, and leave. Now we looked at endless tires with different designs engraved on them, our salesman explaining at great length the usefulness of each sort in varying weather conditions—for instance snow or rain—cautioning me against the cheapest sort, which lack grip, and, equally, reassuring me that I didn't need the most expensive set, the kind he would recommend if I drove a lot at high speeds on the freeway. For some reason none of this made us impatient. Even India listened. I liked the earnest instruction, the idea that someone cared about what sort of tires my car had, and, most of all, I liked the idea that there were things like blowouts or skidding which were within human power to prevent or mitigate, unlike other things like death and hatred which were not.

Also I got scared and anxious thinking of my previous reckless indifference to tires, and how I had endangered the lives of my children, and I was determined to amend my former careless ways by choosing responsible tires now. Since there were a lot to choose from, and our salesman was so garrulous, this took a long time. India, bored at last, wandered off to play among the bumper guards.

Excuse me, I said to the salesman and chased off after her, stepping around a life-size cardboard cutout of a gas-station attendant and there caught sight of A. J. Harper browsing among the small accessories. I saw him, he saw me see him, and he came toward me carrying a headlight, I suppose for Ev's car.

Not knowing where they had gone to, I had consigned both Clyde and A. J. to the category of people that might blow in at will, like leaves, without volition, or whom I might never see again. Now here was A. J. stepping toward me with a mock courteous nod of greeting.

I think I would have hidden away, and so would A. J., if we hadn't seen each other see each other, eyes meeting so there couldn't be any mistake. I didn't feel ready for A. J., for telling about Ev, for talking about Ev's car, for accusing him of murder if it came to that. It was a question whether to tell him about Ev right here in the store or whether to ask him to step outside, or whether he knew already, or whether he was her murderer.

"Well, Mrs. Hexam, Ev got you out lookin for me? I've just been buyin her some brights." He waved a box. "I'm fixin to bring them over later on."

"Hello, A. J., I haven't seen you in some time," I said, I suppose sounding reproachful.

"I been sick the first part of the week. How's Ev?"

"Ev's dead," I said; it slipped out that way like a taunt while I was trying to frame some other way of saying it: I've got some bad news I'm afraid. Ev's dead. Maybe you'd better sit down.

That arrogant cool-cat smartass smile of his I hated faded off his face; he didn't gasp or ask me to repeat my words, he just stared, his eyes took on a frightened look, his smugness ran off him the way the melting snow was running off of me.

"You makin that up," he said after a second. I saw how thin he is; something shivered his thin body in its turtleneck sweater and dirty tight pants. Suddenly his face galvanized with fury and he leapt toward me and grabbed my arm. He glared into my face. I shrank, twisting my arm away. Our real hate and mistrust showed, I suppose, and frightened our salesman, who had followed me, and now was shouting, "See here, see here!" Interracial violence in the West Sacramento Sears. A. J. dropped my arm. "You makin that up. You better say."

"I'm sorry, oh, I'm sorry, I didn't mean to just hit you like that," I said, seeing him shiver and stare.

"What do you mean? Are you tellin me? Don't tell me no lies."

"I'm sorry. Ev died Sunday morning, or in the night Saturday night; she was dead in the morning when I got up." A. J. just shook his head to get the pain and confusion out, as if he were trying to get water out of his ears. The salesman watched us from behind the cardboard man like watching from behind a bush spying. A. J. sat down on the fake grass next to a lawnmower and put his face in his hands a minute.

"I—it's only Tuesday now," he said.

"I know, it's terrible."

"I saw her Saturday. I was goin on over there today. I got us this place, I would have gone sooner, but I was sick on Sunday—yesterday, too, didn't even go to work." Drunk, I suppose he meant, from Saturday night on. He was still shaking his head.

"She ain't been buried yet?" he asked.

"Lady, have you decided what tires you want?" the salesman interrupted. A. J. turned a baleful look on him, interfering honky, but then it seemed he welcomed this new thing to think about.

"You out shoppin, are you, just like that, with Ev lyin dead?"

"No, it isn't that, somebody slashed my tires, I have to buy four new tires. I think the insurance will pay but first I have to buy them."

"What you shown her?" he asked the salesman. "Let me see," and he went off behind the salesman, who looked relieved to have a man to deal with. India and I scuttled alongside.

"She don't need radials," A. J. said, "her car ain't gonna last that long," and after making some other distinctions he indicated which ones I should buy. I noticed how easily I relinquished my intention to learn about tires as soon as some man—even if, as here, a man I neither liked nor trusted—offered to pick them out.

Anyway, now I had four new tires, which the salesman and A. J. went behind the counter to fetch, and rolled out and piled before me in a neat tower, delivery Thursday or Saturday if I wanted them delivered. I hadn't actually thought about how I was going to get them home. It was hard to think about those damn tires with Ev's story to be told. But then A. J. said, "I'll take her home, help me out to the curb with them."

I accepted this offer; my ordinary mistrust of A. J. seemed suspended. Also his, perhaps, of me. The salesman helped us roll the tires outside where we piled them in the deepening snow. It had turned colder, or it was that I was wet, I was suddenly shivering and chattering with cold as we stood there. India, warmly dressed and happy, was trying to climb the tire tower. A. J., his hands in his pockets, watched into the Sears parking lot not seeing, not moving to go get his car.

"What did she die of?" he asked.

"Her old sickness, pancreatitis, they said. They said it could have been brought on by the blows, when someone hit her. Did she tell you about that, how someone was waiting in the laundry room last Thursday and beat her when she went to wash some clothes?" He did not look surprised at this, but he didn't look guilty, either. Getting hit was just something that happened. Then his face twisted up again.

"That fucker Clyde Wilson. Didn't want her going off with me. I'm gonna kill that fucker."

"The police don't think it was anybody. Nobody's fault. They aren't going to look for the person. But I don't think it was Clyde. It was just somebody, some brutal vandal."

"But who? They done it on purpose."

"Well, I don't know. There are a lot of violent people in those units. I don't think they meant to hurt Ev more than anyone else who might have gone in there." This was a lie. I wondered what he would have done if I had said that I suspected Gavin Hexam. He was still staring off across the parking lot and his eyes had a runny look with tears standing in them, but he wasn't crying. In the neon light of the Sears Auto Annex we both looked violet, purplish, and the falling snow seemed pink. A. J. scratched his head and blinked at his tears, his face drawn with remembrances.

"What else?" he asked. "Did the doctor come? Who came for her after she passed? Where is she now?"

Not a metaphysical but a practical question. I told him what I could, that there had been an autopsy, and that she was in the funeral home now, and the funeral probably Thursday. I didn't tell him about the police, or my belief in a murderer, but he believed in a murderer without me, someone who killed on purpose.

"Someone was out after her, that's plain," he said, and presently, "I had just got a place for her and me. I been with Evalin a long time now."

I shivered and stamped in the wet snow. I was feeling a little funny. You never know, I thought, when these symptoms of shock and sorrow would overtake you, days after; maybe they could be brought on forever, just by thinking certain thoughts, to make you queasy and wan just for thinking them, or speaking of them as we were doing now. My head swam oddly. India was drawing in the snow with a stick, patterns in the wet slush.

"I've did Ev wrong plenty of times. Ev was pretty dumb lots of ways. But I had made my mind up on Ev. She had sand once in a while. I guess she never did show no sand around you, though."

I just shrugged. I was thinking about sand running out.

"I had made my mind up that we was really going to do the middle-class trip. Shit, I can keep a job if it's worth keepin. It's these car-wash jobs that lay you off, you can't work when it's rainin, that's what'll start you drinking. Shit, yes. But it's no rule about it. I can get it together."

"She just should have cared more," I cried out reproachfully to her.

"Well," A. J. said, his expression now impassive, "I'll go get the car, and you stay here with the tires." He slouched off into the parking lot.

I felt funny still, and walked a little way to the bench by the door of the Auto Annex. When I looked back to call India, who was still drawing her lines in the snow, I saw that I had left a trail of blood, black blood in the purple neon on the pink snow. Surprised, I sat down on the bench. Blood trickled down my legs; I didn't know why I couldn't feel it, but I couldn't, I could only see it, really lots of blood filling my shoes. I could feel it around my toes, or maybe that was wet snow. Really a lot of blood and it frightened me; it was as if the blood were pouring out of my brain, leaving me unable to think what to do except to call to India to tell her to stay right where she was.

A. J. pulled up to the curb in Ev's Pontiac and got out. I watched him put the tires in the trunk. A.J. could take me home or perhaps to the hospital. Was I bleeding so much I needed to go to the hospital? I didn't know. You can't tell how much you are bleeding, it soaks your stockings. Even when you bleed a little, a cut finger, it gets all over.

Now it seemed that all the wetness all the way through me was blood-soaked wetness, freezing blood. It wasn't of course, but I am trying to explain my idea. I had put my hand over my eyes for a minute, I guess, for when I raised my head there was A. J. standing in front of me looking at the widening pool of blood in the snow at my feet. I only had to glance at his expression of horrified fear, of panic.

"Oh, Jesus," he said, and threw his arms out, half choked, then turned and ran to the car and drove away.

Well, I knew what he would think, why he would panic, and I didn't blame him. A black man doesn't want to mess with a white woman pouring blood, not even around here. He may even have thought I had been stabbed while he was away—by Ev's murderer, maybe. Maybe I would point a dying finger at him. I didn't blame him, but I wondered what to do next. People were coming in and out of the Auto Annex, I would just have to ask one of them for help. That is what I did, raised up my head and called to a passing woman and asked her to go in and get help.

Presently other people came and, supporting me on both sides, walked me off to a little clean room, evidently some sort of first-aid room in the Sears center. Someone came after us leading India by the hand. In fact I already felt better, perhaps was not even bleeding now, was not going to bleed to death. Mostly my feeling was of embarrassment to be the sort of person that leaves big squalid bodily messes in public places.

There was a nurse who pulled off my wet clothes and made me lie down on top of a towel, and presently she remarked that the hemorrhage was subsiding. As I remember, I didn't really care that this should be so. There is something rather peaceful about profuse bleeding; you think perhaps you would not mind if your life bled away. A person might watch himself bleed to death with some interest, the widening stain, the warm and flowing sensation, none of this is bad after the first fright. I just lay warm and relaxed thinking how a woman has only to lie on her back, to be made love to or to give birth or to let her life stream out. You can just lie there.

But you can't just lie there. The nurse took India away for ice cream, which reassured me, because it meant she thought I wasn't going to die while she was gone, and coming back she brought me up from my thoughts of A. J. and Ev with questions about my doctor and phone number, and who to call and the rest. I told her to call Bess. We didn't need to go to the hospital, the nurse thought, just home, so she rinsed out my pants and stockings and put them in a plastic bag for me, and called us a taxi.

5 Bess had come back to our unit with the older children and they were all waiting excitedly to see me as if I'd been off on a dangerous thrilling expedition and now they welcomed me triumphantly home. But it was just me feeling stupid and carrying my stockings and pants in the plastic bag, and India chirruping about ice cream. I sat on the sofa like a visitor and Mrs. Hoaglund came in carrying a pound of Canadian bacon and a cabbage.

"She didn't have a thing in the fridge," she said meaningfully to Bess, meaning that I had passed over the bounds of competence and was more unfit to cope than they had thought, and could I be trusted with my children? Nothing in the fridge! It was true I hadn't done any marketing, but there were some things in cans. I felt petulant and insulted at Mrs. Hoaglund's interference but slyly kept this feeling to myself since I would be asking her to baby-sit again. I went into the bathroom and hung up my stockings and pants, and then put on my old nightgown and got into bed as instructed. The pains in my back were mostly gone but I felt blue, unquestionably, and glad of an excuse to keep to myself.

"My darling N.," Bess said, leaning in the bedroom door like a mother, "you might have known this would happen." Her expression revealed her benevolent affection for me and the other unfit of this world. "I plan to stay here tonight, so don't worry," she said. "I'll stay in Ev's room." I was truly grateful for that. It seemed to me that another person lying in Ev's bed would exorcise its memories of Ev, would restore that room to a neutral and unowned condition no longer controlled by a dead person. You can't have these ghosts around forever.

I think I fell asleep a little, thinking of poor A. J., and when I woke up I felt stronger and got out of bed again. It was quiet—Bess had evidently gotten the children to bed—and she was sitting in the living room reading a *Saturday Review* she had brought. She looked up and smiled. It was nice to have her there. I thought of asking whether she thought I had stronger dependency needs than was normal or nice. That's the sort of thing she would have an opinion on.

"Bess, would you mind calling Andrew for me?"

Bess looked interested. Why would I not call him myself, her gaze seemed to say. It was too much to bear, all this, without Andrew, and yet I knew why I didn't want to call him myself. I didn't think he would be there, and his call to me had been a dream. See what a grudging cold unbelieving heart I have, for I had with my own ears heard Andrew's loving reassurances. But who dares put love to the test—not me, that's for sure.

"Telephone the Fairmont and see if he's back from Chicago. He was supposed to be back yesterday, or this morning." Maybe he was on his way to me—could that be it?—speeding here in a car from the airport.

"Would you mind?" Bess would dare; it isn't her love she'll be putting to the test, anyway. Bess looked sympathetic and said she wouldn't mind at all. I hid in the bathroom and tried to wash my legs better, and tried not to hear her talking to someone on the phone. When I came out of the bathroom, she said, "He checked out of the Fairmont last night."

"Why don't you call his old number, his family home," I said, how bitter even to think or say it. "Ask if he's expected." Then I went back to bed as if I didn't really care, and tried not to hear.

"All right, thanks very much," Bess said after a while to someone on the phone. "You too, dear.

"He's not there, he and Mommie have gone out to dinner, they should be back about eleven. It was Maureen I talked to." Her voice contained a note of mockery of Maureen's girl's voice, or maybe the mockery was of me, or of human expectations, and also mockery of faithless men, or of Andrew, who could not wrest himself from old red-haired crying Cookie and her TV programs and her unspeakable smell of Shalimar.

I nodded and shrugged at Bess; she watched me with a sly eye. I guess she was curious to see what I would say, or whether I would cry. I couldn't bear to be watched by Bess from the vantage of her safe life, so I closed my eyes and pretended to go to sleep again unsurprised.

After all, it was just what I had thought. I hadn't believed it ever. For things to have been otherwise, happy, would have violated too strangely the grain of life, of life here in these units, of life anywhere at all. The direction things run is toward misery—mine, Andrew's, A. J., Clyde, Bess—we must all wash around miserable, that's just the nature of it. But I hate coming to terms with that.

The units are quiet, it is the hour before the parties and fights get started in these units. The students in the next unit are playing one of their three classical records, Brahms's Fourth. Their others are Tschaikovsky's Sixth and *Scheherazade*. It's kind of sweet. Andrew and I have made love in here to that *Scheherazade* more than once, have failed to make it through, or extended on beyond, but have never come out even with it. I feel for Andrew a kind of exhausted desire and am struck with the grotesqueness of this, the unsuitability, a life extinguished in me and drained out and yet my feeling is this one of languorous concupiscence.

Or maybe that's nature, already prompting me to start another life up. It is a life feeling, and better that than the feeling of despair I try to shake off. That is like being cut off from earthly life and made to watch it; it is like being in a wheelchair, maybe, with shrunken wizened little limbs, being made to watch in front of you the embraces of great warm-blooded and beautiful animal people in ecstatic conjunctions. Or it is as if Andrew, not I, were dead, and I alive, battering at him in a frenzy of desire and panic, just trying to get the tiniest flicker of a smile to cross his face. Oh, now I can understand Osella battering the ground above John Henry's coffin, I understand that perfectly, just trying to get a smile to cross his face, or a word or a sign. Well, think of it, if I saw Andrew now, on the street or a bus, he would turn away his face. I could rush into the offices of Briggs, Harvill & Mason and he would turn away his face. That would be from cowardice. He would not like to see a person he had injured. These life and death thoughts tore my mind apart while my shell just lay there.

6 Then the next shocking recognition, right on the heels of Andrew's perfidy. You get used to this, I told myself, it's like being brought up out of a well. I was lying there in sham sleep but groggy, inattentive with self-pity and thoughts, when something prompted me to open my eyes and there was Bess standing at the side of the bed, unusually close like the bending figure of the solicitous over the dying.

I jumped a little, startled by the guilty expression just clearing off her face, something inside her head she erased from her face when she realized I had seen her. It moved across her mouth. Her eyes I couldn't see because light reflected, making mirrors of her glasses. Guiltily she stepped backward, pulling her beads with one hand. It had been some unacceptable emotion, of greed and malice perhaps, with which she had been about to pick the pennies off my eyes. I tried to see whether it was greed or malice or what, and it was malice. It was hate. I wasn't exactly surprised just then; you get used to this.

More hate. Eyes of blazing hate. I suppose it's a compliment to find that you arouse any emotions at all in other people. I am always surprised. But this was strange in my dear friend. Yet I felt that instant touch of chilly fear along the spine that always warns you.

It was, I think, this physical sensation more than anything that made me alert and believing. My mind left alone would, I suppose, have scoffed that I had anything to fear from my dear friend Bess, but there's no mistaking that chill. And I remembered all her lucid civilized references to the rages, the tigers of her mind she kept at bay with her psychotherapists and encounter groups. Maybe she had meant real savage tigers with knife teeth.

Baring her teeth, she said, "You know, you are a very lucky woman. You don't seem to understand how lucky you are."

I sat up in bed. "What?" I said.

"It makes me angry the way you don't seem to realize it. You take things for granted."

"What are you talking about?" I asked her, sitting up in bed, seeing I must attend to this, we were having a discussion.

"You can learn to do without love. Everybody does," she said.

"No, I never will do that, I hope," I said. Though I

had been thinking that is just what I will have to do. Without love forever. Bess paced around the edge of the bedroom rug, stepping on the perimeter only, around and around the little rug, her mouth working with torrents of words which apparently sprang there and were put down.

"You're young and pretty, you have nice, normal children, you're free, you'll have a profession, independence . . ." Around the rug, around the rug.

"That's true."

"But you're too stupid to grasp, to grasp . . ."

"Well, what?"

"Too stupid to grasp anything. You have the inner life of a cow or a child. Lynnie is more sensitive than you. You're so simple-minded. You have no sympathy for others, you're just hard and cold."

I suppose I didn't say anything, but watched and wondered if this was all true, her voice held much bitter conviction, and Bess is an intelligent woman, after all, well-informed on psychology. If you were too simple-minded, you wouldn't know if she was right or wrong—and there I was. And, I don't know, I didn't feel up to this, it was like having your tires slashed. I knew it was hate on her face.

"I might as well tell you my feelings, let them out, it's wrong to keep them bottled up," Bess said. Walking around the rug. "You take, you are a taker," she said. "You do nothing but take. Your normal children, having a maid, love affairs, not even appreciating how it is for most women or how you have reason to be grateful. You wouldn't work, you expect to have your own way." Still she paced, apparently determined now to say everything she'd ever thought, my dear friend. Well, you have to pay attention when someone sets out to tell you truths about yourself.

"And cold, you don't care what I'm saying now—well, you miss out on a lot in life, shielding yourself off from reality, from human emotion; I don't suppose you even know what I'm talking about."

I do, I thought, I'm not as stupid as she thinks. But later I changed my mind about that. I think I am.

"Here you've lost your lover, lost your baby, you just lie there napping. What did you do about poor Ev? What did you really feel? I hate you sometimes, I really hate you. I bet you never knew that; well, that's an index of how stupid you are, right there, about people, that you could never see that."

"I don't see why it should bother you, Bess, if my emotional life is low key." That was all I could reply. Is it low key? How can I know what hers, what the lives of others are like?

"A person could go mad trying to get through to you. You represent something to me and I think that's why I hate you." She had stopped, and now looked so menacing, so strangely transported with rage I was a little afraid she would batter me with her tight fists, and I got up out of bed to prevent this and went to the living room as if looking for something. Bess stayed in the bedroom.

It was then in the living room I saw something which made me realize that all she said was true; I'm too simple-minded ever ever to understand, people, Bess, anybody. How can I expect to get along in life so unimaginative that I could never ever for one second have imagined anything as peculiar and sinister as this, as inexplicable and un-expected? That's if it's true. It could be coincidence, could be, indeed, an excess of imagination which made me catch my breath. But the thing was, Bess's purse was open on the table, a soft gathered bag, wide jaws open revealing contents, the usual cigarettes, sunglasses, keys—and the unmistakable handle of a folding hunting knife, a heavy long strong knife, not one like you would carry in your purse to cut parcel string, but one that you might slash tires with, or doors.

Reverently, humbly I thought well, sure, come to think of it, it made a sort of sense. I mean it was possible. I saw how it could be. It didn't make sense but I could see Bess fitting into this and even how she might have done things. She could have gotten sick bags from the hospital where she volunteers and smeared the contents on my door and windshield, for instance. Could she strangle a cat? Anything was possible.

My thoughts were, more or less, of danger. Maybe this is it, I was thinking, the danger is at hand; I've been dreading and watching all week and now have let the danger in here with a smile. What I didn't waste time thinking were thoughts like "Bess? Impossible!" I believed in her like a shot and grabbed that knife and stuffed it under the sofa cushion just as she came in the room.

"I'm sorry," she said. "I'm as overwrought as you are. These days have been a strain on your well-wishers as well as on you." Her voice was like stiff paper.

"It's all right," I said, falsely smiling, wary.

"How are you feeling? Are you feeling better?" Smooth, smiling Bess face.

"Yes, fine, I'm not even bleeding now," I said.

"That's good." She held her limp hands out sidewise, showing me they weren't fists any more. "You know, I think you're insensitive sometimes, but that doesn't mean . . ."

"I am, I'm sure. Insensitive. I'm sorry."

"Yes," Bess said. "I'm sorry, too." We paused. "Well, I guess we should be going to bed. Where are the sheets?"

"The bed's made, I put clean sheets on yesterday," I said, I think sounding calm, in spite of panic rising higher at this idea she was going to stay the night. Well, she was right, I am, in the very company of my murderer, too inhibited to be rude and turn her out at midnight after all her kindness.

"Well, good night, old dear," she said with a deep deep

sigh, and went into Ev's room, shutting the door after her. I went into mine. These doors don't have locks so they couldn't be locked. When I heard Bess come out and go into the bathroom and water running, I crept out in the living room and took the knife from under the sofa cushion and carried it back to bed with me.

7 Sleep I thought would be unwise. I would have to listen all night for her; what if she came in here? What if she tried to go into the children's room in the night? Well, I had speculation enough to keep me awake anyway. I might as well have been an unsleeping object, a straight-backed chair sitting in my room, say.

I wanted to call Inspector Dyce with my speculations. Listen to this one, what do you think of this one: Bess is trying to kill me because she is in love with Andrew. Or else she is the loyal friend of Cookie Mason and wants revenge for Cookie in the name of good wives, or she is Cookie's spy and hireling. Or I think it is that Bess is mad like Gavvy and Osella, and all the world is mad but me and thee, Inspector. Oh, wait a minute, Mrs. Hexam; sometimes I wonder about you, Mrs. Hexam.

All right, but maybe Bess is in love with me? Or maybe she is driven by jealousy, of my love for Andrew maybe, or of my children. Would she try to hurt my children? I didn't think so but my ears listened in case she should step, should sigh. Why did Bess have that long knife in her purse, Inspector?

Maybe it was Bess who murdered Ev. Maybe Andrew was still at the Fairmont or on his way here and she lied and hadn't called his house at all. Maybe it was Bess hiding in the laundry with her ashtray from the Zanzibar; there is no end to speculations like this and the mind reels crazily on through the night. Maybe Bess is just a klepto, steals knives from hardware stores, steals towels from hotels, steals ashtrays from nightclubs.

Thus the mind reeling through the night, eyes staring awake. No sounds but the sounds from the distant free-way, screeches, engine noises dully humming in these units, people far away, faint voices, airplanes overhead and once the telephone. No sound from Ev's room. Per-haps Bess was awake in there waiting her chance as soon as I'd fallen asleep. I could feel her open eyes watching me through the wall as she sat like a straight-backed chair rigidly awake waiting.

About midnight I could hear her begin surreptitiously to pace; I could hear the almost silent scuff of her feet on the cold floor walking back and forth or else around and around, I suppose fighting the tigers of her mind, or else organizing them.

I am not making this up or dreaming it, I kept remind-ing myself. It is the middle of the night and now to top all else I have become afraid of my friend Bess, that's how fear seeps in and muddies your mind. But all the dead cats and mutilated doors have happened and Ev is dead, and it is really Bess in there walking around and my hand is on her long knife concealed under my pillow. Yet I could not believe it. I have a slow mind for distinguishing the actual from the unbelievable: is that really Gavvy on Osella's lap? Has he struck me? What do I feel? Is the future to stretch on forever without the real voice of Andrew or the urgent tenderness of his embraces; is that madness in Osella's eyes or is she only pretending? Maybe Bess is only pretending in there and this whole thing is got up to scare me. I know I will meet my death through my slowness to grasp these matters. It is my lack of imagination.

Once a pounding came on the wall and Bess was hissing through at me: "You were very stupid to imagine Andrew Mason would leave his wife for you. He never leaves her. He never has yet. These philanderers, they never leave their wives."

Only once did this whisper come through the wall but it was like shooting through the wall all right. What did she mean, he never leaves her? Philanderer? Is this cruelty or lies? Has Andrew lied to me—but I can never believe that. And I can't ever ask Bess to explain, either. I mean I never will, and so I must live with uncertainty, too. I never would answer back at Bess's hating voice through the wall.

She spoke once more: "I tried to warn you many times. Then I became fascinated by your blind fatuity, foolish credulity, willingness to be used. Oh, I don't defend Andrew, but you are so blind. . ."

Oh, shut up, shut up, shut up, I thought but didn't say.

Be sensible now. She's in there pacing around working herself up maybe. How could I keep her out if she tried to come in here, or tried maybe to go into the children's room? But think of all the chances she's had to push them into her pool, but then she wasn't worked up like this. It was dumb, I felt, really dumb but got up after a little while and crept into the hall and balanced my tin button box on the doorknob of the children's room so it would fall if she turned the handle. Traps against Bess, I can't believe I'm doing this, I was thinking as I lay on my bed again. From time to time a step imagined or real in Ev's room brought me awake. Bess in there.

Although I didn't sleep, I sank into that half-awake state in which one can think about things most clearly without on the one hand escaping from them and without on the other hand facing the lucid facts of things as they probably will be. Disembodied, the mind slips away be-

hind the façade with its severe columns and porticoes into
the shadows where the inner eye, adjusting to the darkness, spies all kinds of previously invisible things. It came
to me in my drowsy floating state, for instance, that I was
a monster of egotism to think that any of this, any of it,
had anything to do with me. The night was not peopled
with intent malign spirits circling around. All the people
I feared were probably asleep by now, not thinking of me
at all; why should they? A. J. sitting somewhere in Ev's
car shivering in his thin jacket drinking from his brown-
paper-wrapped bottle of gin, not of course thinking of me,
maybe not even thinking of Ev; same with Clyde. Or maybe
they do think of Ev, I don't know. Poor Ev lying dead,
not thinking of me or anything.

Bess began to speak again, hateful taunts only half
audible through the wall; then her voice stopped. Perhaps
she thought I was asleep. Perhaps was pausing to think up
new cruelties. I was silent. We stared awake at each other
through the wall but she didn't speak after this.

Gavvy asleep somewhere, Osella too, Andrew too.
Oh, what a damned long night, and me battling the whole
time to keep off thoughts of Andrew.

I don't know. I suppose Andrew will think of me,
his lost love, from time to time, sincere man that he is.
I suppose I'll get to be a reproachful memory, like something in an attic inducing little stabs of worry and regret,
a pale copy, unreal, shaken out from time to time to look
at. Cookie is real, with her golf-brown leather face and
Texas voice and her familiar place in the habits of their
friends, same old foursomes at golf, annual garden party.

I kept myself awake imagining him sleeping quite
soundly, having made love earlier to Cookie, thinking well,
this is a tolerable substitute, I can get used to this again,
it's kind of like a practice match, and if this were the real
game think of the performance of the true me.

Well, it's nice Andrew will have that to cheer him up.

Rage can keep you awake, all right, easier than danger. Half of what I feel is rage but half is unchanged love. That's funny, isn't it, the way you go on loving and I suppose I will be exalting Andrew over the years, exaggerating the passionate love, the perfect companionable happiness I think we felt.

I can see myself when I've become a withered old women always talking about how I was once beloved by the handsomest most successful man of his day, Andrew X, the Supreme Court Justice, of how in love we were, of how it was not to be. I wish I could not so clearly envision this anecdotal forlorn old crone.

Lying there, heart broken, body dissolving, even then a little dispassionate voice keeps on speaking in its mannered, cold clear childlike ever-vigilant never-sleeping mocking way—my own voice, wherever it comes from. There isn't any way to express despair. My voice keeps drowning out the incoherent voice of despair which tries to make itself heard. Like an ugly virus, despair crawling through the blood attacks the heart, attacks the pit of the stomach, makes the skin creep and yet can't make itself heard, is always repelled by the power of the cold little voice, combating, combating. Why won't it shut up and let me sleep the comfortable sleep of someone who is safe and not in despair?

Maybe you are the fortunate one: you *are* the fortunate one, the little voice says. Especially now there's no baby, that's a damn lucky thing, a little love child is not what you needed now, though it would be in form, just like you, to produce one; well, you can't be sorry about this little bit of blood, it's not as if it is a real child, maybe it never was, how can you know, and you never will know so put it out of your mind. What's to keep me back, assuming I survive this night? I must get some sleep. Well, at least I haven't got a black skin or sick liver or retarded child or joyless tedium of a bad marriage. Yet I don't trust anything. Never trust a man, as they say. That's how men are, etc. Well, get a good night's sleep one of these nights, *sola, perduta, abbandonata*—you could be smothered by all the ghosts of all the women this has happened to, if you let them in here.

No, you'd better not sleep tonight, stay awake. Imagine, imagine if you cannot believe. There she is pacing again, her slow heavy tiptoe sound, she is tiptoeing in a frenzied circle, how strange, how can you tiptoe in a frenzy; maybe she can't sleep is all. Doesn't want to disturb me, is tiptoeing worrying that she's hurt my feelings. But I think I hear her low laugh—yes, a laugh—and now surely there is a flicker of a shadow outside my window. I could imagine my room a cave now, myself a cave dweller forever made to look at the shadows of the real and I would never recognize the real when I saw it; now here was a real shadow, on the window shade, a figure between the streetlight and my window, near enough to cast a shadow, big enough to fill the window: but the reality was someone was outside that window.

You cannot just lie in bed, stupidly lie there. The safest place to stand breathing fiercely in the dark is flat against the wall next to the window, so if they can see in they won't see me, though they can hear the catches in my breath, I can hardly breathe. At least it isn't Bess, because I can hear her steps. What if she goes to the front door and slips the chain? She is waiting for the someone outside and they have planned this. But why?

Nothing, nothing, me breathing in the dark but then about three o'clock the telephone, the phantom phonecaller's hour, and quickly I darted for it, fear had taken me over.

"Help," I whispered into the phone, "help, there's someone trying to kill me here, help, there is someone outside. Please help. This isn't a joke. I can't talk any more. The murderer is in the house, please, please, please."

The silence. Was this part of it, more trickery and danger? Then I heard the phantom sharply draw in his or her breath, perhaps in fear or skepticism, and sharply replace the receiver, cutting me off.

Wednesday, January 8

1 It gets to be morning in spite of you, you sleep in spite of yourself; I woke only when a crash and the sound of scattering buttons woke me. But nothing followed, no stealthy hand turning the knob — the tin on the doorknob had just come unbalanced, maybe an airplane went over. I don't hear them any more. It was seven and I had slept lying on the floor against the wall under the window, and I was quite safe, though stiff.

I went to the kitchen and made coffee, trying to be quiet, and waited until the children and Bess would awaken and we would begin the business of yet another day. Sitting in the bright dawn in the kitchen I felt foolish. I had, I thought, as usual overdramatized and overreacted. All I had really seen, momentarily illuminated, had been as quickly clouded over, leaving doubt. Do you actually know what you think you know? Other people in the world seem to be masked figures wandering dreamily around who will for a flash pull away their masks, wink atrociously at you, grimace, then everyone is muffled up again wearing ordinary smiles.

Bess came out wearing her ordinary smile.

What had I seen? What had I really seen? A fleeting look of hate, a knife handle. Dozens of possible explanations for that. A heavy ashtray with "Le Club Zanzibar" written on it on my closet shelf, a look of fear on A. J.'s face at the sight of my blood. Gavvy once on Osella's lap. Had I really seen that? A parrot on a tree outside my window. Seen the last of Andrew.

All the true glimpses are so fleeting. Can you trust your senses, you wonder. No, you really can't. Good morning, dear Bess, I will probably say, how did you sleep? She slept well, she would say. Me, too, I would say. Yes, I'm feeling much better, no more blood, heart not bleeding either.

Will Bess and I go along as before, I wonder. Will she expect that? No, impossible, here is the long knife. What can she have had it for? I know I didn't mistake her look of hate. Bess got up, I heard her in the bathroom, and then she came out. The children woke up next so there was breakfast to get for us all, and it was true, Bess had arranged her face as lovers do after a quarrel and we chatted, and she said she would take Polly and Petey to school. Once she leaned over the breakfast table and touched my wrist. "I think it's better that some of these things are out between us," she said. "It's never any good keeping things inside us," and I thought, turning my face away, that always and forever I am going to keep my feelings locked bottled inside me. But I said, "I know, Bess."

And then it was true, she said she would take Polly and Petey to school, and, my bones freezing with terror, I let her. My fear was that now that the hate was out between us she would do something to them, but I sent them off just like that because in another way I couldn't bring myself to believe in hate and murder even when it touches my cold wrist or draws its thin knife across my throat. Here is the bright new day, it has nothing to do with yesterday; I can't even remember yesterday, we've got a new day going here. If only I get them back safely, I will close my life to Bess, I will. At nine when the bell would have rung, I called their school and asked and they had gotten there safely. Of course the children are here, Mrs. Hexam, didn't you see them off with your friend, that woman with the green Oldsmobile? She brought them as usual. All is a dream.

It was a bright morning, and whatever of snow had lasted the night now was melting onto the brown grass in front of our units, so Ivan and India had to stay in out of the wet. I let them watch "Romper Room" on television while I proceeded with my detective activities, for this was the day I would find out, if I did not know already, who had murdered Ev. I would settle my mind on it, I mean. Ev's mother called to tell me that Ev was to be buried tomorrow, Thursday; that is this afternoon but I won't go. Or perhaps I will, for it mustn't seem to anyone that I didn't love her, I did love her so.

I wasn't sure how to proceed with detective work but because I had read so many detective stories against boredom and housework, I did know a few things. I knew about fingerprints and intuition. I put my clues, the ashtray and the knife, out on the kitchen table and thought well, now what do I do with them? I considered calling Inspector Dyce about them, but no, he had forfeited his claim to this, I would fathom them first and tell him later. I was playing, I knew, and hiding, and wasting time, but play is the symbol and shadow, isn't it, of something real? "I know you and I know what you've done" went confrontations in my mind; "beware, because I have found you out."

About ten-thirty someone knocked on the door and it was A. J. Harper. He smelt of beer and was smiling. "I brought your tires," he said.

I was surprised. "Oh, thanks, A. J."

"I guess you thought I wouldn't bring them," he said. That's a real do-you-still-beat-your-wife question, and he was grinning in his old way, tense, angry and insouciant.

"Oh, I didn't think about it, I guess. I didn't feel too well."

"You apparently feeling better now?"

"Yes, thanks."

"You want me to put the tires on for you?"

"Well, sure. Yes, thanks, that'd be a great help."

"I'm not going to work until noon. The jack in the car?"

"Yes, wait, I'll get you the keys." It would be good to get the car fixed, and you couldn't always tell when the AAA would come. With tires I could go off after the murderer, but I didn't make that observation to A. J. He took the keys and went out to the garage.

I could hear him clanking around, and then in a while he came back with the keys again and said he'd finished, and I vigorously thanked him. He sort of hung around a moment or two more. I wanted to mention Ev's car, but didn't know how to bring it up. He looked strained, as if on the verge of saying something, but I didn't know what.

Finally he said, "Did Ev say anything about me at the end?"

"Oh. No, I didn't see her after you did, the night—that night. But before you came, around dinnertime, she talked again about the place you were going to get for her. I guess she thought everything was taking a turn for the better."

"Yeah. Well. Ain't it the way?" A. J. said in a bitter tone. It is the way all right. The question of Ev's car still hung between us. Finally A. J. said, "Well, that car of Ev's ain't too bad, how much she owe on it?"

"One-fifty."

"Tell you what, you don't need no second car, let me hold on to it and I'll pay you the one-fifty when I get it.

I should be gettin some bread from a guy that owes me. Anyhow I'm workin steady."

His bright anxious eyes. "Well . . ." Feeling that I wasn't managing this competently, "Well . . ."

"Couple of months I'll pay it off, you were just gonna sell it anyway."

"I suppose."

"Yeah. It's a pretty good car. I figure Ev would want it that way, she'd want me to have it, she wouldn't want it to go to Clyde Wilson."

"I know she would want you to have it, but I really need the one-fifty," I said.

"Sure, no problem," A. J. said, slapping his pocket, reminding me by the jingling of keys in it that in any case it was he, not I, who had them, and the car, too.

"Well . . ." I said. Then—it must have been a kind of an afterthought or habit, worth a try—looking kind of ashamed, A. J. said, "You gonna give me a couple of dollars for my time on them tires?" And I said sure and gave him two dollars, and thanked him besides.

"Sure. Well, I'll see you," A. J. said, walking jauntily off, and that was the last, I suppose, that I will see of him. Oh, poor A. J. It just came over me then that A. J. was so sad, smirking and trying to get along and live swank, and had been to junior college, and had no hope at all of anything. Everything was just a mess for him, and now Ev was dead, he didn't even have Ev's love and her admiring laugh to buoy him up in his manliness. Oh, poor A. J., poor Ev, poor Bess.

See, I am the fortunate one, I am the lucky escaped one, I knew, but went inside, hid in the bathroom and cried, sitting on the floor with my head on my knees and tears streaming down my legs.

253

2 In the afternoon while India and Ivan had naps, I continued my detective game, transforming myself into an inspector. I looked again at my clues, neatly laid out on the kitchen table. Knife and ashtray. Carefully I inspected the ashtray. No nicks or cracks suggestive of its use as an instrument of death. The knife had no shreds of door or tire, no bloodstains, nothing. It came from Abercrombie & Fitch in San Francisco and is just the sort of knife Joe Harvill would have, or Bess. I know this is the sort of thing inspectors think of.

One searches for fingerprints. I had read all those detective stories, every one at the Elmwood Branch Library, but I still didn't know exactly how you did this; ideally you should have a junior detective set, but lacking one you improvise. I experimented with glasses and various powders; I thought of calling Inspector Dyce. I discovered finally that face powder works. Lightly lightly you dust face powder with a bit of cotton over the surface of something. Then you blow it off. Fingerprints remain. The ashtray was of course full of fingerprints, hundreds of fingerprints it looked like. I could imagine they would turn out to be Mrs. Hoaglund's, those of people who had handled it in the intervening period, and perhaps, if this was the murder weapon, then those of the murderer, too, for plainly it had not been wiped or washed. But it would have to go to some crime laboratory, after all. I put it away carefully on my closet shelf again, uncertain what to do. The knife had fingerprints, too—mine, no doubt, and Bess's.

I knew it was fruitless and a nuisance to him, but late in the afternoon I called Inspector Dyce, hoping, I suppose, that he would have changed his mind and decided to track down Ev's murderer himself.

"Oh, hello, Mrs. Hexam, do you have some further information?" he said in a courteous, perhaps amused voice.

"Not yet. But I do have two clues, and if you don't mean to do anything, then I thought I would. But I thought I'd ask you first."

"The case can be reopened if you have important evidence, certainly," he said.

"I have an ashtray I found in the laundry room. It must have been there all the time. It comes from the Zanzibar Club, and that's the club where Big Raider, the boyfriend of the former maid Osella I told you about, sings, and I just don't see how that could be a coincidence. Anyway it's covered with fingerprints."

"We'd never get a doctor to say she'd been killed with an ashtray, for God's sake, she died of pancreatitis," the Inspector said.

"You said yourself she had a bruise; it must have come from a heavy object."

"My dear, that is simply not a hanging conclusion you're drawing there. Why can't you let it alone? I'm perfectly satisfied from everything you've told me, and I guess you've told me everything, that justice, in this case, is best served by Natural Causes."

"Well, look, I don't want anyone to hang—go to the gas chamber, I mean—it isn't that. But I don't want to seem to acquiesce in Ev's murder and accept it. Somebody has to protest."

"Are you a screamer and a protester, Mrs. Hexam?"

"You bet, oh, yes. You have to protest, otherwise life just—life just . . ." Though I am not a protester, or not any more.

"I suppose society must be grateful to its protesters, no question about that, but in this case, who are you protesting for, for what? What can be done that isn't worse than what has been done already, if anything has been done?"

"I should object in Ev's behalf; Ev would never object in her own behalf, shouldn't I see to it something is done?

Do I just shrug my shoulders, oh, well, Ev's dead, it can't matter to her now? Draw up my white skirts, step daintily over the mess saying that's how these people are? It seems only fair to Ev to take her murder seriously."

The Inspector sighed as if he knew he had a most difficult case on his hands, difficult and yet he was a patient man, not inclined to snarl or hang up; he waited.

"Well, I know that vengefulness is wrong; I don't say this from vengefulness. Perhaps it's from a love of truth and accuracy. I just think the truth should be known."

"Doubtless," said the Famous Inspector, sighing again. "Yet I think you give yourself airs. Love of truth and accuracy—you'd be the first person."

"Curiosity, then. But here's something Osella told me, about a cousin of hers with a vicious temper—Samuel, who cut the man's head off. Samuel cut a man's head off at a picnic, with his pocket knife—such was his rage and perseverance. Samuel was the mayor's gardener so the mayor stood him bail and the judge suspended sentence, and Samuel just went on taking his ritual turns around the mayor's rose garden with the mayor's lady inspecting the roses, and no one was anxious for a moment that Samuel would raise a hand against *her;* what he did at Negro picnics was not their concern."

The Inspector laughed.

"'But, Osie,' I asked her, 'what about the man who died? What about his family? Weren't they disgusted that no one would punish the murderer?' And Osella just shrugged and said, 'That's how them people are. That's the South, now, you got to remember. Anyhow everybody knowed Clarence Thompson been cheatin Samuel all along.'"

"Well, what would you have done with Samuel?" the Inspector asked, still laughing. "How do you expect others, Osella for example, to be full of clear moral vision when you aren't yourself, or are you?"

"How does anybody develop a moral faculty, Osella or Samuel or anybody, if no one expects them to make moral judgments, or to refrain from killing people? Ev's murderer . . ."

"Yeah, that's a problem. Well, Mrs. Hexam, let me know who it is and how you find out. I'm kind of curious," the Inspector said.

"I will let you know. I'm going to the Zanzibar Club tonight," I said portentously, as if all mysteries would there be solved.

3 Ivan and India woke up just before it was time to go for Polly and Petey. We drove to the school early and parked in front to wait. I was thinking Bess might come for them, too. She wouldn't know my tires were fixed. But I didn't see her, only them, coming out thank God with handfuls of drawings and papers, and Polly happy because she'd been put in a new reader. There's been a new death, I wished to tell them, Bess is dead to you; Bess and Ev and Osella and Daddy, that's the toll now. It is as if we were on a boat pulling out, the dark sea widening between us and people we know on shore. This is what has happened to the old people we saw in the park; it is why they do not talk to each other but stare off to sea. But Polly and Petey and Ivan and India are too little and should not have to make this lonesome voyage yet. But we have each other, we said in the park, where we went instead of going back to our unit. I'm just going to stay away from there. The children played on the cold metal bars of the climbing structure. They laughed and clanked their little hard shoes against the pipes; their cheeks reddened in the brisk air. Charming golden-haired little tots, the old unspeaking people would be thinking. The mother with her short yellow curls just like a child herself; how pretty, how sweet they are, how innocent and happy. See how the mother attempts to compose her features into an expression of radiant cheer, of expectation. She is quite a young woman yet.

It was warmer than Tuesday, and no snow, but it was dark by five. Then we went home and ate Mrs. Hoaglund's cabbage and bacon.

"Bless this food to our use and us to thy service. We ask it for Christ's sake," Petey said suddenly and looked at me, laughing as if he had said something wicked and hoped I would be shocked or mad. He said, "That's what Leslie always says before juice."

"It's all right to be thankful, it isn't funny to be thankful, it's right," I said with a tremulous voice unfamiliar to them that made them look at me and turn quiet. How beadily they watch me for any changes, as if I were their pet.

"We have our peace and safety and this ham for instance," I said. They agreed with polite reserved voices. I suppose they know hypocrisy when they hear it, for although peace and safety and ham seem sufficient at times they are not sufficient for me.

"I have to go out later, in case you wake up and I'm not here."

"Who's going to be here?" Polly asked.

"Somebody. I don't know. I'll ask those people next door, the ones who came in when Ev . . . or I'll get Mrs. Hoaglund."

"Are you going out with Mr. Mason?" Since Andrew is the only person I ever go out with anywhere at night. "No." So they were uneasy, too, all this strangeness: no Ev, no Mr. Mason. After his bath, Ivan threw things around giggling shrilly, and India banged her head against her crib and cried, and it seemed hours before they went to sleep.

The people next door, the students, had the rock on loud and a sort of burnt spaghetti smell from the kitchen, and papers and stuff around, and their seedy German shepherd who growled at me.

"I wonder if I could ask you a favor," I said.

"Sure, come in." That sisterly smile remembering I was the unfortunate in the next unit where the death was, formerly snooty and now made a comrade of. A couple of her friends said hello. Strong smell of cooped-up dog. Was this the next step down in some descent I was making, coming down in the world? Next would be getting some sort of big scary cur to keep me safe, some stringy-haired young man to keep me laid. This is Uncle Jeffrey, dears. I would, I suppose, have to do his wash. No Aid to Dependent Children welfare checks because of illicit cohabitation. Oh, my face flared up with dread, I hoped she couldn't tell why.

"Look, I have to go out awhile," I said, "and I couldn't get a baby-sitter. I mean, now that, I'll have to . . ."

"Sure, I don't mind, if you aren't gone long," she said, wiping her hands on the dishtowel she was carrying. And I would have to do the dishes, too, in my new life. "Will you be out very long? Because I have a psych test. It's not that I need to study, I need some sleep."

"Not long," I said. If I return at all, I should have said, for I am going out either to catch a murderer or to make my mind up. "Something to do with Ev's death. Loose ends, I guess you could say."

"That was really horrible," the girl said. "She was a nice woman. She used to think it was really bad if I went through the trash. I always look through the trash every week and she would, too, but she thought it was bad if I did, I could tell. I wanted to tell her, look, I have the same attitude to what society rejects as you do. But I never really got to discuss it with her."

"The kids are asleep," I said, smiling good night at her friends. "I won't be very long, I hope. It's important or I wouldn't bother you."

"It's no trouble, honestly, I feel good about it," the girl said.

I didn't go right to the Zanzibar, I just rode around in my car. I liked it—doors locked, windows locked, rolling around on my new tires. I can understand the expression "getting wheels." I know what they mean; it's a forward, rolling feeling. I know what I have to do all right, but first I'll just roll around a bit, looking at the world and how it's cleared up. Everybody's gone back to his old place, all the old mice to their holes. I'm a new cat now with my new wheels. Well, I can understand how a man might feel that way about an old blue Pontiac; it could take him places.

I'm going to move out of those units.

I'm going to get straight what I think about killing and death. What if it's Gavvy, and he says, averting his eyes, I may have been in the laundry room that night, but how can you prove it? What if Osella looks me in the eye and says sure, I knocked that nigger slut up the side of the head, and I'd do it over, too. Well, what will I do? Nothing.

"Oh, nothing, Bess," I can imagine myself saying. I can't bring the children over today, no, sorry, busy. We are going away. No, there's nothing to do about Bess either; we will always smile at each other but I'm going to keep out of her way, who knows when her bolted brain will slip. If, if, if.

If you don't let yourself think about other people in their madness or if you grant it to them, either one, and you don't let yourself think about chance, then you can get back on your feet.

Ev's in there, a storefront funeral parlor. If I went closer, I maybe could see her through the window. But the window is hung with a little lace half-curtain like a restaurant, like an oyster bar. I don't want to see the coffin anyway. Anyway it's dark on this street, and women don't get out of cars here at night. I just drive by, doors and windows locked, but I know she's there. Bess in her house or at her encounter group or her awareness session

or something. Osella is somewhere. We are all locked inside our heads. Our thoughts are rolling on like wheels.
The average female in a lifetime thinks enough thoughts
to stretch seven or nine times around the world. I myself
don't think that far. I wish I could keep my thoughts from
venturing out at all, I'm through the venturing. But I do
have to venture to the Zanzibar.

It's funny that people will go indoors, with gin and
odors and noise and laughing; it is so quiet along the river,
even this time of year. You'd think people would just keep
to themselves and watch the river. But at last I went, like
other revelers, to the Zanzibar where everything was to be
made clear.

4 The Zanzibar is the only semi-respectable place in
a rough part of town near the jail, full of old bars
and old bums and pinball-machine arcades, a pawnshop
with guitars and trumpets. Musicians I guess have to pawn
things often. A Salvation Army thrift store at the corner,
all the clichés of Skid Row, which is what it is. I parked my
car under a streetlight about two blocks away and was
already wondering if you should come to places like this
by yourself.

A certain atmosphere of excitement radiated from the
brightly lit display window, the flashing neon of the sign
overhead, the busily opening doors of the Zanzibar with
music leaking out into the street. There was something
going on in there, you saw. Soon I would be going in. I had
to build my confidence up, sort of. I am the Famous In-
pector, I told myself, I am going to find out.

I don't know, I guess I thought I would go in there and
the guilty person would just step forward, something in

the force of my gaze would compel this. For this trick I use a vacant mind, a photographic-plate mind, a Geiger-counter heart. I was scared but I think mostly just scared of being down here about to go into this dumpy nightclub, a woman alone. Well, you have to get used to that, a woman alone.

There was a poster outside, which I could see as I came close enough, it is specially lit. I stopped, struck dumb by it, unable to believe in it. My heart pounded with disbelief, with glee. Sex an ingredient in this, how could I have doubted it? Inside the Zanzibar, murder, whiskey and sex. What is the connection between sex and murder? Go in and all that will become clear to you. All will be made clear. The naked Osella makes everything clear.

Little old men stand staring at the extraordinary poster. No wonder they stare. The little old men are wearing dirty old overcoats of black and gray with torn buttons. They wear caps. They don't dare go in the Zanzibar. The poster reveals such heart-stopping wonders that they know they don't dare, their old hearts might stop. They wouldn't want to anyway; they are horrified, puritanical little old men. They are happy to have been discarded by society if this is what society has begun to demand for its entertainments. Society is disgusting and they are right to withdraw from it and rely on drink and tall tales. Puritanical little old derelicts wandering off remembering their mothers and sisters.

I didn't blame them. I was not so much disgusted, not so much staggered as excited by the idea, suggested by the poster, that the wonders and revelations inside would exceed even what I had imagined. Murder fell into perspective. I dropped back a bit, not to be seen staring.

Frankly I didn't like to be seen staring too long at such a thing. A woman alone, goggling at breasts, that's very peculiar. Other people walking by are also dumbstruck, astonished and embarrassed by turns. A little boy hides his face in his mother's coat while she gapes and grabs him. They step resolutely off. Two young men stagger off in fits of convulsive laughter. What did it in fact mean? The poster being stared at grinned back but did not reveal its meaning. A breakthrough, maybe that grin meant. "You nigger-haters tryin to keep me back, now I done broke through," Osella had said over the phone and the poster said this, too. "Ain't that something, all the time I never knowed you was nigger-haters, you comin on so sweet, now don think you gonna hold me back."

There was no one walking by who didn't stop short as if smashed up against an invisible wall and then wander dreamlike, with entranced eyes, closer to the poster. Then they laughed or shuddered. The little boy hid his face. Apparently it was impossible to walk by without being jolted to a halt, and that's power, I guess. It commands respect, I guess. As Inspector of all this, I tried to understand.

Potentiality is what that strange sight must represent, I thought, human potentiality, and this is rather inspiring as well as terrifying. Terrifying as well as inspiring, I suppose, and of course a horrifying reproof for the old and failed.

Reproved is mostly what I felt. The question of murder momentarily receded before my immediate sense of shame and inadequacy. Murder and other enormous acts seemed right in scale. Still, murder was what I was there to detect with my however puny personal force and I had better get on with it.

I went in. I was the Inspector. Mercilessly and clearly my eye would search the Zanzibar; my heart beat with the excitement that goes with catching murderers. In the mirror of the foyer I saw myself, cheeks bright with—it might have been fever but it was a kind of reckless haste toward resolution, truth and justice. What a relief.

Inside the door a curtain of old velvet I didn't remember from before had been hung to keep you from seeing the stage, so that you wonder and are drawn in, pushing it aside like the door of a tent to stumble into the dark, strong-smelling tent with folds of cloth falling softly behind you so you are entrapped. At first I hesitated, hearing behind the curtain the sounds within, the important clash of a musical ending, the sliding of chairs, voices and laughter subdued in the dark, rising. Did women come in here alone? Did white women? Could I be seen if I just stole in like a shadow and huddled at the back? I heard Big Raider's voice now, talking from the stage.

There was Raider on the little raised box stage with lights on him, looking out blindly at nothing, wearing a welcoming smile, light shining on his bald head, a big man out of scale in the small room seeming to be trying to compress himself, as if were he to expand to his full size and power, all the people would be shoved up against the walls and smothered except those who escaped gasping into the bathrooms. But he kept himself in. His eyes trying to see through the light had a wary studying look as they watched the audience.

As my own eyes got used to the dark, I could see the place was crowded, jammed; I had taken the last place in the room, in a draft by the door. The audience was not drinkers but was like the audience at an opera, dressed up and connoisseurs, arranged in rings around the stage. I didn't think I could be seen in the crowd, and I was wearing a headscarf, not like a prostitute or a woman any man would want to pick up.

"You done heard," Big Raider started out, and a roar began already from the laughing audience. "You done heard," putting up his arms against the roar, "of the Seven Wonders of the World." Yeah. "Now you done come to see the eighth." Yeah. He was laughing himself, and then adopted his ordinary cultivated city voice. "First, ladies and gentlemen, we have another little treat for you. I say 'little' advisedly. A little forecast of wonders to come, a tiny piece you might say. A mighty nice piece, gonna dance for us—Miss Lucy Brown! Little Lucy! Come on, dear."

Out came Lucy, a pale narrow-faced little blonde with a big bosom and wiggly body in a red satin jump suit, plenty of energy and a cut above the Zanzibar. She nodded, smiling, but then instead of launching into anything she seemed to be waiting for a cue. The audience sat waiting patiently, too. This was the first I realized that something was being filmed or recorded. My eyes getting used to the dark made me aware of a more sophisticated element than usually frequents the Zanzibar, or at least a different element, youngish, people in bright clothes and sheepskins sitting here and there among the tables with transformers and microphones and cords. A high camera pointed toward the stage from one wall.

Somebody gave Lucy the nod and a drumroll and she went into her act, taking off her clothes. It was Lucy's message to send sex into the air, I guess, to get everybody ready. Her naked biggish breasts jiggled and pointed at the audience and she rolled her ass around and around, and made squeaks and groans.

The funny thing was, I minded this, and tears came into my eyes, hot, stinging and sudden. I was thinking of my love for Andrew. It was that I understood what this dance was getting at. I could feel it, I could feel the fires inside myself, burning, burning unfueled, would just burn along futile and bitter forever. What a waste, I could not help but feel, with tears springing to my eyes, what a waste to nurse a holy flame of passion inside me without anyone to warm by it; I suppose it will just burn me out inside like a dugout canoe.

What ideas to be fanned by the feeble exertions of little Lucy. I suppose I am a bundle of dry twigs. Oh, that damned Andrew has taken everything away from me.

Little Lucy put her hand between her legs, bumped a

final bump, grind, screamed and bowed to enthusiastic applause. Now Big came onto the stage, clapping, and said, "This is a good audience here, I see the audience is with her." Laughs. "And now you folks gonna see something that's gonna bring joy to millions of hearts, but you gonna see it first here, and you gonna see it all." Clap, clap, the applause for Lucy swelled into applause for the next attraction. The stage lights went up brighter and hotter, and a low drum made noises like excited hearts. Technical men dragging cords and holding microphones made sudden dashes like a football team after the ball is snapped, and they, like the audience, generated a heat, a thrill to be at the heart of power where a star was being born if that is what was happening; whatever it was, it was compelling. A burnt electronic smell arose in the room from the amplifiers and other humming black boxes set about here and there in the audience. Big came on again and moved a microphone a few feet, glancing at the rear where a curtain fluttering suggested the Presence was near. I was excited now in a new way, participating with the audience in the sense of discovery, or privilege, to be in at the early incarnation of this wonder. Big Raider, grinning, came back and distributed some coils on the stage, directed by a waving man in front, and then looked ready to say something, and the drums came up louder, and Big, giving them a look conveying his notion that any ballyhoo would be inadequate understatement, said only, "Osella, Osella," in a hushed, thrilled voice.

The rear curtain now moved aside and a vision like a golden tent appeared in the opening. You saw that it was a black woman wearing a floor-length satin cape, but its dimensions and brilliance prevented her features from being distinct. The crowd applauded lightly but with restraint, waiting. Osella with her slow walk, folds of satin flowing immensely, waddled to the microphone and standing beside it looked down at them, grinning in delight at

their numbers and upturned white faces. Her own face was
all painted, which was horrible; her really not bad smile
and nice brown eyes were now framed by purple lips and
green circles. She wore heavy black false eyelashes. It did
give her a glamour, in a way.

"Hello, you-all," she said in her regular thin voice,
and glanced away to the side where Big Raider stood. He
nodded his head as if signaling her to move on to the next
thing.

With a swoop Osella reached out from under her cape;
her great fat arm came out and she unhooked her cape at
the neck. It fell disregarded to the floor behind her. Everything in the world would be disregarded in that moment
beside the riveting sight which emerged from the shining
folds, the naked Osella, a sight at first so horrifying and
then so immensely fascinating that the people watching
all drew in their breath, as if at someone about to do a
death leap from a high wire. But Osella did nothing at all,
merely radiantly stood, which was enough, with the light
gleaming down on the folds of her body, on her tremendous
breasts. She seemed to have been oiled, for she shone so;
one saw nothing but the gleaming immense breasts lying
across her huge belly, breasts astoundingly full and firm
like zeppelins overhead.

She wore little trunks of purple satin and nothing else
but a gold armlet around the expanse of her upper arm — a
brilliant stroke, a rather Egyptian, goddess-like adornment
calling to mind one of those frightening and horrifying fer-
tility goddesses with swollen bodies and timeless eyes and
the same engulfing infinitely absorbing quality Osella
radiated now. She seemed the embodiment of a principle,
passive and patient, frightening to men, I guess, absorbing
them into her immense proportions. She seemed a sort of
superfemale needing only the puny seed of men and she
would grow and grow and keep on growing. That is what
before our eyes she now seemed to do; she seemed to ex-

pand above the astonished audience. I, all women, would feel abashed with our little limbs and small bellies, at the trembling of Osella's superbreasts which she now shook ever so slightly at the gasping people. She grew almost double her size. She seemed to be breathing up all the air in the room.

Music had arisen, some rock song, not too demanding for Osella to sing in her awful voice; it didn't matter. In a way the lightness of her voice helped the overall effect; the mere human voice, the mere transient human impulses it was expressing ("Love me, Daddy, all night long") were pointless beside the female principle of which her body, grotesque and huge, was somehow the epitome and supreme incarnation.

But I shook off this spell: poor old Osella, looking younger, oiled, under the lights, her sagging fat—"a whole lot of meat" fattened up for old John Henry and now money in the pocket of the smirking Big Raider lounging proudly at the side of the stage, watching his treasure, with another man, a white man wearing a hat, like a circus promoter, both of them nodding with satisfaction. I wonder if John Henry was looking down and saw.

Now my eye searching the faces of the audience came upon another extraordinary remarkable sight; I had been right to come here, there was Gavvy at a front-row table at the side where I could see him plainly. He was with a young woman; that was interesting. She was looking astonished at Osella and laughing, but Gavvy was staring with the fixed rapt hypnotized stare of a slave, or maybe I exaggerated this fanatic slavish look, but his eyes never turned, his head never turned, he was transfixed. Well, most people were. But a couple of times the girl touched Gavvy's arm with a laughing remark but could not distract him from his devouring contemplation of Osella's cosmic breasts. He looked happy. Then Osella finished her song and was bowing queenly around and the crowd was cheering and screaming, and Gavvy, as if waked up, grabbed the carnation out of the vase on the table and tore at it, throwing the shreds of petals at Osella, and his girl laughed and laughed.

I could see Osella was happy, too. Like a gross baby, she loved the gasps, the bemused and stunned applause. She felt her power. "Ah has powers," she had always promised and now here they were. Perhaps she didn't even know where they lay, in the grotesque compelling proportions of her huge body. Anyway, what does it matter so long as you're a star? The ecstasy on her countenance. Osella the star. Maybe Osella the murderer.

"Why, Mrs. Hexam, I see we got all the Hexams here tonight," a voice said, and I turned to see Big Raider standing behind me smiling like a host, as black as a genie; here I was in his cave.

"Osella seems very pleased with herself," I said, my voice thank God coming out smooth and insinuating, self-possessed. I don't know where the self-possession, the confidence came from, but perhaps from the sensation that events were resolving, this was to decide all. Tonight's the night, unreal, important.

Inwardly I felt like a tricky Famous Inspector, speaking like one in rich insinuating tones, with watching eyes. "She's having quite a success."

"Marvelous for her after all these years, after all she's been through," he said, meaning, evidently, her difficult years with us. He smiled benignly.

"Her telephone calls are a nuisance," I said.

"I imagine so. I try to keep an eye on her, but you can't all the time," he said, not much concerned.

"My housekeeper Evalin, whom Osella attacked in one of her crazy rages, has died. Osella is a murderess," I said, not knowing, of course, whether this was true or not. Raider looked at me, taking his eyes off Osella for the first time. Osella was singing again.

"Last Thursday night about eight," I said. He did not smile. He was thinking back to see if that fit. Clearly it did.

"I have the ashtray, an ashtray exactly like this one, with 'Le Club Zanzibar' on it," I began, smooth voice, gaining confidence. "With Osella's fingerprints." I hadn't read all those stories for nothing, and Big Raider had not, I bet, read them at all. "With Osella's fingerprints, and it was found at the scene of the crime, the laundry room where the attack occurred," I said.

"Why are you telling me this?" Raider asked tensely.

"I haven't shown it to the police yet. It's in my safe-deposit box. I can always show it to them. I've left a letter explaining about it with friends, and an envelope for the police, in case anything happens to me."

Big Raider took my meaning. "I'll see she don't bother you. Anyway I'm taking her to Las Vegas in a few days, soon as she gets a little better adjusted to an audience situation, gets some more stage presence."

"Keep her away from me and my children, keep her away from the telephone. If anything happens, then the ashtray . . ."

"Would you really turn old Osella in like that? She been in your house, mother to your children all that time?"

"Well, Ev's dead, what about that?"

Raider thought about that. He looked at Osella again, rather respectfully now.

"Dead. My."

"Osella is crazy and a killer," I said, watching him to see if he believed this. Did I?

"That's a whole lot of woman, don't know her own strength, actually," Big Raider said.

"Keep her away from me," I said, "and I won't say anything to the police for now."

"She's got a good act," Raider said, "she's gonna make a pile."

"Keep her away from the telephone."

———

"Look at those tits," Raider said. "That's a brilliant woman."

"I have to go now," I said, suddenly feeling frightened by this risky game. I took a last look at Osella, transfixed with joy by the insane shrieks of her audience, smiling with stupid uncomprehending modest pleasure at their shouts, swaying a little, her horrible breasts like diving seals swaying, too, dipping and swaying. It was then, as she looked around for Raider, that she caught my eye, her eye lighted on me, narrowed, and then dismissed me. The poor little bitty woman no man would want, with a tiny special smile of contempt and pity, and her eye returned to her adorers roaring and her pink and brown toes with gold-painted toenails and gold sandals wide as hoofs covered with shreds of Gavvy's carnations of love.

"I'll see you out," Big Raider said and, taking my arm, led me into the foyer. I hoped he wouldn't come outside, because I was scared of him. Skid Row murder of mother of four.

But he didn't come any farther than the door. "Don't worry about a thing. Have no worries. Have no fears at all," Big Raider said. "Osella is a lot of woman but I can handle her."

"Yes, please do," I said with as much power and authority as I could summon, and walked off down the street to the sounds of Osella's triumph. Well, I guess her life will just be petals from now on.

5 Maybe my life will be just petals, too. You enter into a new state of mind like a new country. Maybe this is the heart of darkness, say I to myself; is that where we are? And if so, is it so bad? You learn to find your way in the dark, your eyes get used to it. It isn't what I would have expected living in North Sacramento, though. I feel better about things.

I wouldn't mind moving away from here, I was thinking, and thinking of Ev lying in her coffin in the storefront funeral parlor under a blue light, far far away. What had the place been like, in her mind, that she hoped to go to, with little starched curtains and a white satin bedspread? Life in Sacramento is not what I would have chosen if I had thought about it in time. I wonder how you do change your life. Osella was always talking about a Better Land she had in mind; I suppose everyone has one in mind. Andrew was to take me there, that's the truth.

Osella, her life will be just petals, I was thinking, and I was happy, and if she was the murderer of Ev, well, then nothing. Yes it is really only Andrew I'll miss, I was thinking in the dark to explain to myself my feeling of pain and tears when I was quite happy for Osella in fact. I here and now give up sorrow for Ev because it can't matter to her because she is dead, I will just mourn her to myself, but it is Andrew I will miss. I won't even miss useful Bess; on beyond hating and crouching in laundry rooms they are swept as by a wave. I felt weary in mind, like a student after a test who has remembered all, expressed all with exactness and now forgets all. Everything drains from the mind, leaving blankness and elation. But this same blankness accounts for the mistake I made.

Andrew and Cookie would be at home. I could picture them home. I know all the things in their house—Cookie's mama's Spode, Andrew's mama's Thomas Walton Sherwood secretary circa 1709. Before this I would never allow myself to think about how rich they are; now with all else I see I will be harrowed by their riches. What will Andrew and Cookie do all the rest of their evenings, I wonder?

Me driving through dark Sacramento streets. Them sitting among their beautiful objects, and Andrew reading briefs, and Cookie reading something dumb about the mind, *Modern Psychology Digest* or something about transcendental meditation. I expect she is trying to revitalize her psychic energies. It's too late to do much about her face. How easily I am led off into my hatred for Cookie. Maybe I should try to revitalize my psychic energy. I must try to make my mind into a pearl.

How nourishing my hate for Cookie is. Will hating Cookie Mason poison me? Maybe it will, maybe it will twist my life. Maybe I will years from now strangle their cat, maybe creep up on their lawn in darkness and savage Cookie's clothes hanging on the line, only they wouldn't use an outdoor clothesline — well, the dryer; hit, stab Cookie as she leans over her dryer. Tamper with the steering gear on her car. Will I? And will I feel this process of twisting and sickening to be anything out of the ordinary? Will a vigilant normal cell in my brain remain to say look, now, what you are doing is sick and wrong? Or will it just seem right at the time that I think of it; little by little the things I think of will seem right and natural one after another, buying this knife, tucking this bottle of blood into my purse. It already warms me with pleasure to think of tampering with the steering gear on Cookie's car even though I don't know what or where a steering gear is.

Love of course would prevent this poisoning and destruction of the cells. The transfer of energy and sweetness through the skin of two lovers lying side by side heals anything. My neighbors the students for example, although looking kind of grimy, I suppose transfer sweetness and healing which accounts for their kind of bloom, too, while I will just shrink and sour. None of us will have love tonight, not Osella, but she had a kind of love soaked up under lights from cheers, and not Ev. Maybe Gavvy will, and that new girl. What do Bess and Joe mutter lying in one another's arms, I wonder; the only cries of pleasure in the whole world were to have been my own in Andrew's arms and I'm silenced now. I hear no moans of pleasure in any street in Sacramento driving home, only see the pale blue lights of television sets and hear the baying of the German shepherds on their chains in the back yards all around as the thieves scuttle over the fences. Oh, but it's glorious Osella a sex goddess, that's one good thing, and imagining myself raving with hate tampering with Cookie's dryer, glorying with feelings of hate and astonishment, I drove back to our unit, put the car in the garage and got out.

Glorying in my feelings of rage and hate, stupid as Ev, like Ev dumb and trusting, I got out of my car not looking to right or left but full of thoughts in the darkness. With no warning an arm came around my neck, covering my mouth, gripping my shoulders, and someone caught my hands behind my back. My purse and car keys fell, I heard them, and felt hurting fingers on my wrists. I suppose I struggled some.

But here it is, said all my senses. All has been fool's gold distracting me with lurid glitter; I have been fishing in the wrong streams. What will happen to me? What will happen would always have been going to happen. Of course. Of course. Was this going to be my death now, the second stroke of the murderer who missed me in the dark the first time, and who, why? Who, who, who? There was no smell, no sound or feel that I could get to tell me.

These were thoughts of a split second as I was held against my assailant, then I began to move and struggle but could not scream with the arm across my mouth. Thinking also, just let me see who it is, and how stupid, stupid, stupid I am, I should have expected this. Please at least don't let me die without knowing who it is.

At the same time a man's voice whispered, "Don't struggle and you won't get hurt," and though you can't recognize whispers I didn't think a black man's voice, not A. J. or Clyde. But it's hard to be sure from whispers. Not Raider, because I had just seen him, or was it? Did he drive here fast, crazily on back streets to get here first, and he had a motive. Not Gavvy, I had just seen him.

Somebody just some stranger from these units, maybe not a murderer, maybe meaning it when he said don't struggle. I believed something in his whisper. But you should struggle. Here I was a tame victim, a lamb after all, standing with docility in the arms of my murderer. But my head was in such disorder after all that had happened, I couldn't produce thoughts, just a muddle of fright. I was held too tightly to struggle and I heard the door of my car being opened. This relieved me momentarily; a car thief, I thought, or someone looking for something, nothing to do with me. Or a place to stuff my body—oh, God.

Then the murderer, a very strong man, somehow lifted or pushed me into the car on the back seat despite my struggles. I mean I think I was struggling. Onto the back seat, on my back; well, that made things clearer, it's a position you understand. But the face of the murderer wasn't clear, in the darkness of the dark garage; then it was too close to be seen, and anyway I was kicking at his hands and struggling not to part my legs, I was crying out and gasping resistance while he was silent, was rather, I imagine, experienced and methodical, pushing my legs apart and pulling down my pants. As they say you so often do, I had the feeling this wasn't happening to me, yet I was wondering if he would strangle me afterward and they would discover me dead stuffed in my trunk, and I thought of my children. Your life goes through your mind like drowning and so you don't pay too much attention to what's happening to your bottom half. But it was happening all right. So wrapped up was I in my thoughts and my dread I may have, for all I know, moved rhythmically according to long habit with the deep purposeful thrusting inside me of the organ of this unknown man or maybe I lay there unresentfully. Was he unknown? Could I tell from the feel of him? Are men all the same in the dark? I can't remember, I just remember thinking well, this part won't take very long, and it didn't.

And that was all. There was no murder to follow.

Somehow I feel that it's finished now. I haven't even locked the door.

My assailant withdrew with, I think, a nod, of salutation perhaps, and I sat up dazed but not hurt in the back seat and watched him open the side door of the garage and steal out zipping his pants. But I couldn't see him; he could have been anybody. He could have been black or white. I used my skirt to wipe my thighs and hunted for my house key under the car. I was shaking with terror and amazement, and also with a strange elation. I stayed in the garage until I was calm. Then I went into our unit and my neighbor, waking sleepily from the sofa, told me a peaceful good night and noticed nothing wrong from my smiling face. My children as I looked in on them stirred contentedly.

I don't know. I felt happy. Anything bad can happen to the unwary, and when life sends you the *coup de grâce* you have a way of knowing. So I felt better then, thinking well, that was the *coup de grâce* and here I still am. There is a badness to things that satisfies your soul, confirming that you were right about what you thought was what. But I would like to know who that was in the dark. It seems important: is life fascinating or boring? Is everything clear and decided, or are there possibilities for wonder unbounded? The man could by his size have been Andrew, though that makes no sense, or A. J. or Clyde, though I think the voice was wrong, or Raider or Gavvy hurrying here through the night. Most likely it was some madman neighbor who has been lustfully watching us all along, unknown to us. It could even have been the Famous Inspector. It almost did seem to me as he passed out the door that the moon illumined the imperturbable and knowing features of the Famous Inspector. Perhaps it doesn't matter at all.

I feel better. You can change; a person can change. I feel myself different already and to have taken on the thinness and the lightness of a shadow, like a ghost slipping out from his corporeal self and stealing invisibly across the lawn while the body he has left behind meantime smiles stolidly as usual and nobody notices anything different. You can join the spiritually sly, I mean. Well, maybe I'm making too much of this. I mean your eyes get used to the dark, that's all, and also if nothing else you learn to look around you when you get out of your car in a dark garage.

PLUME **DUTTON**

Contemporary Fiction for Your Enjoyment

☐ **ABENG by Michelle Cliff.** This book is a kind of prequel to the author's highly acclaimed novel *No Telephone to Heaven* and is a small masterpiece in its own right. Here Clare Savage is twelve years old, the light-skinned daughter of a middle-class family, growing up in Jamaica among the complex contradictions of class versus color, blood versus history, harsh reality versus delusion. "The beauty and authority of her writing are coupled with profound insight."—Toni Morrison (274834—$11.95)

☐ **OXHERDING TALE by Charles Johnson.** One night in the antebellum South, a slaveowner and his African-American butler stay up to all hours drinking and playing cards. Finally, too besotted to face their respective wives, they drunkenly decide to switch places in each other's beds. The result is a hilarious imbroglio *and* an offspring. "Memorable . . . a daring, extravagant novel."—*The New Yorker* (275032—$11.95)

☐ **MIDDLE PASSAGE by Charles Johnson. Winner of the National Book Award.** "A story of slavery . . . a tale of travel and tragedy, yearning and history . . . brilliant, riveting."—*San Francisco Chronicle* (266386—$11.95)

☐ **COPPER CROWN by Lane von Herzen.** The story of two young women—one white, one black—sharing a friendship amidst the divisive and violent racism of rural 1913 Texas. "A fresh, poetically evocative and down-to-earth novel."—*The Washington Post* (269164—$10.95)

Prices slightly higher in Canada.

Visa and Mastercard holders can order Plume, Meridian, and Dutton books by calling
1-800-253-6476.
They are also available at your local bookstore. Allow 4-6 weeks for delivery.
This offer is subject to change without notice.

PL117